Daan Fousert's novel, v
into English by Helen Mc
heart-breaking story of Dut... concentration camps during World War II, as seen through the eyes of three members of a Dutch family. No one reading this book can avoid being chilled by the explicit portrayal of the mindless brutality that war releases. Equally compelling is the portrayal of the indomitable human will to survive, truly against all odds. Perhaps the most amazing aspect of this novel is the triumph of civility over brutality. Buoyed up by an enduring faith, the survivors of these camps offer a living testimony, in the words of Mahatma Gandhi, "that all through history the way of truth and love has always won."

The authors do a masterful job of telling this compelling story. It is a must-read.

*– David Giesbrecht, retired librarian, B.A., M.L.I.S.*
*Abbotsford, British Columbia, Canada*

Comparing it with my own experiences, I found *Against All Odds* to be very representative of the conditions that existed in the Japanese concentration camps in World War II. Jaan Willem and Johanna Mobach, with their youngest son Jan, tell the story of the Mobach family before, during, and after the experiences they endured under the Japanese occupation. Experiencing horrifying things and witnessing the brutality in these camps had a lasting effect on most survivors for the rest of their lives.

In 1986, a group was formed in White Rock, British Columbia, Canada. Called "The August 15, 1945 Foundation," it was named after our liberation date. It was in this group that I met Gerard, the second son of the Mobach family. Gerard and his wife Helen brought love and understanding to our group. Sometimes Gerard talked about life in his camps, and it was gruesome. How could we have survived these atrocities? We felt like brothers and sisters. Our spouses and children needed support too because just living with us was not easy.

We know about the Jewish holocaust in Europe during World War II. This book, *Against All Odds,* adds to our knowledge of the other holocaust during World War II in the Pacific.

The Mobach family receive all my gratitude for telling this story. A big thank you to Helen for the translation!

*– Maria Christina (Miriam) Zwaan-van Veen*
*Surrey, British Columbia, Canada*

# Against All Odds

## A fact-based story of a Dutch family in Japanese concentration camps in World War II Java

**By**
**Daan Fousert**
**and**
**Monique Melief**

**Translated by Helen Mobach**

**Mill Lake Books**

Published by
Mill Lake Books
Chilliwack, B.C., Canada
https://jamescoggins.wordpress.com/mill-lake-books/

Cover design: Daan Fousert with Dean Tjepkema

ISBN: 978-1-7771926-7-9

# Preface

When I, as a Canadian, married Gerard Mobach in Berkeley, California, I was determined to learn Dutch so I could communicate with his family. I am grateful to Daan Fousert for giving me permission to translate this book into English. I wanted to do this in memory of my husband and as a legacy for our children and grandchildren. Gerard always wished that people would know this story and understand how terrible war is.

I would like to thank Dianne Marty for her copyediting of *Against All Odds* and my daughter Aileen Vildort for her proofreading.

I also thank my brother-in-law Jan Mobach, now 93 years old, for sharing his detailed memoirs of the Japanese camps with Daan Fousert and Monique Melief, who originally wrote this very gripping story of the Mobach family in Dutch in *Het Geluk te Overleven*.

*– Helen Mobach*
*Abbotsford, B.C., Canada*

# Preface to
## *Het Geluk te Overleven*

When Jaan Willem Mobach (1894), his wife Johanna (1896), and their three sons, Piet, Gerard, and Jan, depart for Djokdjakarta in 1930 on the ship "Indrapoera," they have no idea what awaits them. The years leading up to 1942—during which time three daughters are born—pass by in relative peace. That changes on March 8, 1942, when the Dutch East Indies fall to the Japanese.

All Dutch, Indonesian Dutch, and Europeans end up in Japanese internment camps, as do many Moluccans and Chinese. In these "Japanese camps," an estimated 30,000 people die of hunger, exhaustion, and torture.

"We were lucky." These are the words of Jan Mobach when he describes what happened to his family in the Dutch East Indies during and immediately after the war years. He has recorded his memories in a document in which he recalls his adolescence during the Japanese occupation of Java. Father Jaan Willem, also, has recorded his memories in *Prisoners of Nippon*. These two documents form the basis of this book, fulfilling Jan's great wish.

Because this book involves a whole family that was separated in the war and—pure luck—of which all members are reunited after the war, the experiences of mother Johanna would make the picture more complete. That is why I asked author Monique Melief to tell the story of mother Johanna from her perspective, based on the facts.

With the capitulation of Japan on August 15, 1945, WWII ends in the Dutch East Indies. But two days later, Java (Indonesia) declares independence. The Netherlands did not see this coming. The period that follows—the "*Bersiap*"—during which time many become victims of torture, rape, and murder by Indonesian nationalists, is, if possible, even more violent.

During these extremely unsafe and uncertain circumstances, the family members trickle back to the Netherlands, father Jaan Willem as the last one in June 1946.

– Daan Fousert, May 2020

# Father Jaan Willem

*January 1930*

A colleague who had decided to move to the Dutch East Indies aroused Jaan Willem's interest in an advertisement for eight teachers needed in a Christian school in Djokdjakarta, in mid-Java. Jaan also wanted to do this, and it felt like a calling. He applied, not doubting for a moment that he would be accepted. And although his wife, Johanna, whom he had married in 1925, was consumed with homesickness for her family in Driebergen, while they lived in Bolsward, Jaan Willem was sure he could convince her that his decision was right.

He could not let this opportunity go by. His dream of doing something significant in a new environment and of helping in the development of Christian education and a godly congregation, albeit in a distant land, could come true. From childhood, he had felt a strong missionary calling. He had wanted to go to a theological college to become a minister, but his parents, lacking money, sent him to college to become a teacher. Still, it kept gnawing at him, and so he committed himself as elder and organist in the church.

In The Hague, they were happy with his application and he was warmly received. People with a dream and an ambition like that of Jaan W. Mobach fit the profile they had in mind. The interviews had gone well, and now there was the final conversation during which he would receive the results.

"Does your wife support your ambitions, and what does she think about moving to the Dutch East Indies?"

He had not anticipated that question, let alone discussed the matter with Johanna. Nevertheless, he did not hesitate to answer.

"My wife supports me in everything I do and looks forward to this wonderful opportunity for me and our family. We have been married for five years now and have always dreamt of such an opening."

"In that case, we have good news for you. You have been hired. Congratulations. At the beginning of the new school year in August, you can start. You may now begin preparing for this great journey. We will arrange for you to move in June this year."

Jaan Willem went home, sure of his new appointment. What remained was to tell his wife and to prepare her for this tremendous change in their lives.

*Monday, June 2, 1930*

At the quay of the Koninklijke Rotterdamse Lloyd in Rotterdam, the ship MS Indrapoera sounded its horn for the last time, indicating that its departure was imminent.

A few hours earlier, Jaan Willem and his wife Johanna had boarded the ship with their three children: Piet, four and a half years old, Gerard, just turned three, and Jan, almost two, to set out for the foreign Dutch East Indies. Also, Johanna was once again pregnant. That her family was not at all happy with her husband's decision was evident from the fact that it was conspicuously absent, while Jaan Willem's family, in copious numbers, stood on the wharf to wave farewell. Earlier, Jaan Willem's family had been permitted a peek around the impressive

2

passenger ship, their eyes popping at the dining room, on the decks, and in their cabin. Eventually they had to leave the ship, and although there were no weepers in Jaan Willem's family, a few tears were wiped away. Jaan Willem and his family remained waving on deck until they were completely out of sight.

# Mother

*June 2, 1930*

Why is no one from my family on the wharf? Even though nobody agrees with Jaan's decision to leave for the Indies, I had secretly counted on it. I allow them to show their displeasure—we are all outraged—but couldn't Father and Mother have come for my sake? How long will it be until I see them again? It is precisely from them that I learned that I must follow my husband, so what can I do about it?

Thus, no farewell for me. And almost his whole family showed up. Unfair, isn't it?

The first thing this morning was the tour of the ship. As if we were going on a vacation. Jaan, the children, his father, and all the others were wildly enthusiastic, except for me. I felt only cold. Until the very last moment, I searched—to the point of desperation—for arguments not to have to go along. It all went too fast. I could follow later, with the children. Is my pregnancy no excuse? The long sea voyage will definitely not be good for our new little one. And what about giving birth in the tropics? Darn it, I don't want to go to the horrible Indies at all.

And in the meantime, like a proud peacock showing off his feathers, Jaan showed off the cabin where we will be staying. A spacious cabin, one must admit. Two elegant steel couchettes attached to the wall, and beside them, a sofa and two washstands. A large wardrobe. An elegant carpet on the floor. As if I care. What a sham. Darn it, it's not a family outing. The guided tour took forever. The

4

engine room, the promenade deck, the dining room, the stairwell. Our boys went crazy, especially when they saw the pool, nothing more than an old moving box with a tarpaulin stretched over it. But I could strangle Jaan.

Not a word crosses my lips. Only a little while ago, I buried the hatchet. And yes, we expressed a renewed promise to each other and confirmed it. But if I am honest, I really have no choice. Where in heaven's name am I supposed to go?

I can't forget. First, Jaan took me to Friesland; that was hard to stomach. Moving from Driebergen to Bolsward was the first big shock. No consultation: it was no more than an announcement. My heart froze when he told me. Away from my family, away from my familiar surroundings. I didn't want to go, not even then. Finally, I accepted it. With the explicit agreement that in the future, in a timely fashion, Jaan would involve me in his decision-making. Yes, promised, really and truly. I can still see him standing, with his hand on his heart.

Until that day last March when Jaan walked in earlier than usual. I was just sitting at the table with a cup of tea. "Johanna," he began, sitting down.

I was immediately alert.

"I have something to tell you."

Another move was in the offing; I had already suspected that for a long time. In recent weeks, Jaan had been to The Hague a few times, and that had not escaped me, although Jaan thought I hadn't noticed anything. He wasn't sure how to begin; he was waffling. He didn't like his work in Bolsward; that was something I had to understand. I knew that he didn't get along with his director, although it wasn't clear to me why. And since I

5

hadn't heard anything about it for a while, I honestly thought that he had accepted it. Jaan was nervous, drawing circles with his feet. Then came the big news.

"I have been to The Hague a few times lately. I have mentioned that, haven't I?"

No, not really. I had deduced that, which is not the same. It was childish, I admit, but I didn't respond. A little satisfaction. It was perfectly clear where the conversation was going. We would move to The Hague.

Jaan continued to flounder—painful to watch—and I decided to help him out. A second move; it didn't matter anymore. To leave Bolsward didn't do much for me.

"Are we moving to The Hague, Jaan?"

Another cough, some fiddling with his jacket, and then out it came.

"Well no, not to The Hague. But to Djokdjakarta in the Dutch East Indies." He couldn't say it quickly enough. But wait, what did he say? Did I hear correctly? To the Dutch East Indies?

"Did I hear you correctly, Jaan? Where are we going?"

"Johanna," his tone was stronger, "we are going to the Indies."

The blood drained from my face. This couldn't be true. I didn't want to believe it.

"You don't mean it, do you, Jaan?" My voice cracked. "What do we want in the East Indies?"

"What do we want in the Dutch East Indies!?" Jaan shouted angrily, his nostrils flaring. "We are going to the Indies." As he stood there, snorting like a raging bull, I didn't know what was happening to me.

"I have a job as a teacher at the Christian school in Djokdjakarta. That is why I travelled to The Hague. And that's why we're leaving for the Indies." And that was the end of it.

Screaming and yelling, I rushed to the hall and grabbed my jacket from the coat rack, with only one thought: get out of here.

"Who do you think you are? Miserable fellow. Lousy guy." Piet and Gerard, who were building a block tower in the back room, began to cry in shock.

"So mean. So sneaky. How could you do this?" Tears rolled down my cheeks. "Have you forgotten what you promised me? First you take me from Driebergen, away from my family, away from my familiar surroundings. Do you, by any chance, remember your promise to discuss far-reaching decisions with me first? No, we are going to Djokja...what's its name, or whatever the lousy place is called. I'm not going, as long as you know."

Get away. I couldn't think of anything else. Flight was the only option. Into the woods, untraceable for Jaan. At my wits' end, I wandered around for hours, total chaos in my head, no idea where to, no clue for how long. Suddenly it was dark, and I became angry all over again.

"Dark outside, dark inside, did God come up with this?" Oops. I was not allowed to think like this. Panic. Where was I? Shivers ran down my spine. Cold sweat. Had I been going in circles? Should I turn around? How long I had walked like this, I don't remember, but at some point I recognized where I was and found my way back home.

And now I stand here like a puppet, waving at Jaan's family. It should feel like a fresh start with the family; at least, that's what I have told myself. To regain my confidence in Jaan. Help me please, I want to say. I want to be a good, obedient wife to you. But not a word comes out.

He hurt me deeply. In everything, I have to follow, but I don't want this.

After waving for a long time from the ship's rails, at dots they imagined were Jaan's family, they returned to their cabin to settle in for the long journey to Batavia that would take four weeks.

On the first evening in the hotel in Batavia, Jaan Willem, who was looking forward to the adventure, had to contend with a hysterical Johanna who blamed him for taking her away from her family. She was so upset and hysterical that she tore her dress. For Jaan Willem, she was inconsolable, and, in his ignorance and lack of understanding the reason for her anger, he told himself that this was a hysterical phase in her life and that she would eventually accept it. When she appeared unresponsive that evening, he decided to pay no further attention. "What you deny doesn't exist," and his method seemed to work. It was not mentioned again, and eventually Johanna accepted her fate.

After a lengthy train trip the following day through the Presanger, they arrived in Djokdjakarta, and the family was housed in the Mataram Hotel.

Once they had settled in, Jaan could report to the school board, where, to his surprise and also his annoyance, he was told that he had been assigned to a school in Wates, a somewhat quiet and remote place, twenty kilometers west of Djokja. There they were housed in a tiny house. Jaan Willem was a man of his word, and that's how he expected to be treated as well. Initially, he accepted the decision of the school board, while continuing to remind them of their agreement that he would be placed in Djokja. His tactic was successful, for after a relatively short period in Wates, he was appointed teacher at the Christian-Javanese School of the Bible in Koelon, one of the four districts of Djokja, where he would later also become head. They moved to #2 Bedokweg in Djokdjakarta, to everyone's great satisfaction. Even Johanna was happy with the house. Annie was born there in 1938.

It was a beautiful white house with an open front veranda including a rattan seat. Next to the veranda was a bedroom and behind it, the living room with another bedroom next to it. From the living room, a staircase led to the *emper*, a covered walkway by which you could reach the outbuildings. In these additional buildings were the *dapoer*—kitchen, a few *goedangs*—storage rooms, and the *mandikamer*—bathroom. The latter was totally unlike anything they were accustomed to. It was a dark gray cement room, where there were always a few *tokés*—a sort of gecko—on the ceiling. There was a deep cement reservoir full of water, with a *gajong*, a mini-colander with a handle used to rinse off the soap.

With much guidance and tact, they had to persuade little Jan to enter this room, that to him seemed wet and dirty. He screamed when he had to stand on the wet ground with his bare feet. The only way to goad him into this area was to have him go in with his mother, who then took a bath with him. Slowly Jan overcame his fear and became accustomed to the hollow sounds of the room and the staring eyes of the *tokés*. His fear of the scary space gave way to an adoration of his mother at whom he could stare while she was bathing, completely naked. At first she could smile about this, and his attention to her physical appearance seemed to benefit her. After a few years had passed, and he grew older, with an undiminished attention, she decided that Jaan Willem should take over this task. Little Jan seemed to yield to his fate until he had completely overcome his fear of the hut and could bathe alone.

Their life in the Dutch East Indies was now an indisputable fact and would probably have been successful had Japan not had its eye on the country's great oil wealth, a resource that it needed to wage its war in the Pacific.

After Japan's attack on Pearl Harbor, the Dutch government was the first to declare war on Japan on December 8, 1941. Japan's response was surprising, in that it indicated that Japan was not at war with the Netherlands. Japan was interested in the delivery of more oil and tried to achieve this through negotiation. Those negotiations failed, and when the Netherlands began to torpedo the Japanese merchant ships, Japan decided to take over the Dutch East Indies to obtain the necessary oil.

# Jan

*Monday, December 8, 1941*

With horror, they had listened to the radio reports the previous Sunday. Japan had treacherously attacked Pearl Harbor, killing and wounding many. Exact numbers had not been reported. The family had been staring at the radio. Regularly, Jan heard his father say, "My God," and saw that his mother was quietly crying.

"What does this mean for us, Jaan?" she asked Father.

His father, who was generally positive and tried to put everything in perspective, could repeat only, "to trust in God." For Jan, thirteen years old, many questions arose that he didn't dare ask, because he sensed that this was not the right moment. After the reports were finished, the house fell silent. At the supper table, Father remembered the dead and wounded in his prayer.

"Give them power and wisdom to bear this burden and to be restored again, Lord, and deliver us from the threat that hovers over this earth."

And during the rest of the meal, no one spoke with the exception of Annie, the youngest daughter who was three. She didn't understand what had happened and was seeking attention. But one piercing look from her father silenced her. Each family member was lost in thought and in that state of mind finally went to bed. Jan fell into a restless sleep.

The next morning, he went to school. He attended a university preparatory school. He was tired; nevertheless he was looking forward to geography class taught by his favorite teacher, Mr. Roders, a tall beanpole of a man with a serious face and bristly gray hair. A master storyteller, he was loved by many students, enthralled with his captivating stories. This Monday he failed. Tension reigned in the classroom. The attack on Pearl Harbor had made a deep impression on him. Initially, Mr. Roders just tried to teach. He didn't want to burden the students with alarming stories about the war. It was still far away for many of them. The buzz in the classroom could not be suppressed. The students whispered their opinions to each other. They didn't really know what was going on, albeit that it was very serious and that people had been killed in this attack. They had no knowledge of politics, let alone the potential effects that these world events could have on them. What they had heard from their parents, they repeated to each other.

Mr. Roders called them to order. From the gravity on his face, they could tell that this time he was not going to talk only about the lesson.

"Young people," he began slowly, "what happened yesterday created a deep wound in America and in the world. The attack on Pearl Harbor is not just an incident. It is a surprise attack by the Japanese navy under the command of General Isoroku Yamamoto. The attack is clearly intended to destroy most of the American fleet. This has succeeded. Japan now has control over the entire Pacific Ocean. According to the latest reports, more than two thousand Americans have been killed and over twelve hundred injured. This was totally unexpected, and therefore a great shock for the American people. This morning, America declared war on Japan."

Mr. Roders paused to process his own emotions.

Jan saw moisture in his eyes. Was Mr. Roders crying? Although he had stopped speaking, everyone knew that there was still more to come, and they all looked at him without a sound. Jan saw him swallow a few times. Mr. Roders wiped his eyes with a handkerchief, then put it back into his pocket. He seemed to have recovered. Yet his next words were halting:

"The whole world is now involved in this war."

The words, "The whole world is now involved in this war," echoed in Jan's head. Hesitantly, he raised his hand.

"Yes, Jan?"

"Is there no country then that is not at war?"

"Of course, there are still countries where no war is being waged, Jan, but what we will see is that more and more countries are drawn into this war. We are all connected to each other. In Europe, war is raging against the Germans. Japan will feel free to rule this region."

Another student raised his hand.

"Willem?"

"How long will it last, sir?"

A faint smile appeared on Mr. Roders' face. "If I knew that, Willem, then the world would hang on my every word. I don't know. It could take a long time because it is such a complex war that it can't be solved just like that."

He looked around the class, anticipating more questions. Each student absorbed his words, weighing them against his own thoughts and experiences. Then Mr. Roders said resignedly, "I expect that I'll soon be called up to serve as a reserve officer. You will probably have to do without me for a while."

As he spoke, he glanced at his watch and realized that class was over. He took out his briefcase and put his things into it. He closed it. Then he stopped and looked at each student, one by one. Jan caught his glance and returned the look for a few seconds, after which Mr. Roders turned his gaze to one of the others. Then he said, "All the best to you. I don't know if we'll ever see each other again."

Jan saw a sorrowful look in his eyes. Mr. Roders took a deep breath, walked out of the classroom without looking back. The students who remained quietly behind were so stunned that they dared not move. After a few moments, they looked at each other.

Jan stood up first and said, "Class is over."

*January 1942*

Whenever Jan heard the drone and rumbling roar of airplanes in the distance, he immediately ran outside, seeking the best position to get a better view of what was about to fly overhead. He had to see! He was in a phase of inconvenient curiosity. Since the attack on Pearl Harbor, stories about the Japanese buzzed more and more frequently through their home. The threat was discussed but not considered real. Jan wondered what Japan was planning for the Dutch East Indies.

He perked up his ears when his father made covert remarks to his mother or whispered quietly not to underestimate the danger posed by the Japanese. From that conversation, he learned that Japan had a solid reason to annex the Dutch East Indies:

"Not only because the Japanese have an interest in our oil, but even more because the native Javanese hate the white colonials, and the Japanese can help drive them out."

Jan wondered how that was possible. The Javanese were Dutch just as much as they were. He couldn't believe that the Javanese hated them. Wasn't his best friend Rahmat a native Javanese, and didn't his own parents have friends among the locals? He didn't dare to broach this topic with his father, because when he had done so a short time ago, his father had replied gruffly, "Jan, those are issues for adults. You don't understand them. We must leave these things to God."

He didn't get that either. Whenever there was something difficult, they were supposed to leave it to God. What good had that done so far? He trusted more in what he saw and heard.

Jan climbed up to a flat area between their house and the outbuildings, his favorite lookout. From there he had a good view. He stared at the impressive dark green monsters in the sky. The roar of the engines thundered between the whitewashed houses quietly basking in the sun. The sound was menacing and overwhelming, filling him with a fear he had never felt before. Mr. Roders' story suddenly became palpable, right before his eyes. Would his story and his parents' conversations, quietly overheard, now become reality?

By now, he knew enough about airplanes. Who, at his age, didn't dream about them? Staring at the sky, he recognized the American Liberator bomber. It flew over their house like a wounded bird. One of the four engines was ablaze. In addition, he saw many holes in the wing and in the fuselage, where the curled aluminum was clearly visible.

The airplane flew so low that he could distinguish the silhouette of a crew member in the cockpit. It was a flash observation that deeply affected him. Soon the airplane disappeared behind the trees and Jan realized that it was landing at the new military airfield Magoewo, ten kilometers east of Djokja. Later, he heard from one of his friends, who had also seen the plane, that on a mission to Makassar on Celebes, the airplane had been hit by Japanese anti-aircraft guns. That was irrefutable evidence of the Japanese advance on Java.

After seeing this airplane, he ran inside to grab his drawing supplies from his room. He was obsessed with everything related to flying, and tried to draw as many models of airplanes as possible, and to carve them out of wood. This morning's image had made a deep imprint, and he wanted to record it on paper. Later, he would look at the drawing, recognizing that for him, this is when the invasion had begun. He wrote the date below the drawing.

Regularly, he went with Rahmat to the *ketellah* plantation, a field of root vegetables, at the end of an airstrip. They knew they weren't allowed to go there, and that if discovered, there would be severe punishment. Their passion for airplanes overcame the threat of security guards. Using a secret path, they had made themselves a lookout in the field, well-hidden from the guards but close to the planes which flew so low that you could almost touch them. They got goosebumps every time an airplane thundered over. For them, airplanes were a powerful and trenchant symbol of supremacy. Together they expanded their knowledge of airplanes, and, more so than others, were capable of distinguishing one aircraft from another, whether it was a Glenn Martin bomber or the Curtiss Falcon scout. Their great love was a three-engine Fokker-FVII passenger plane. For just a few guilders, you could enjoy a sightseeing flight, but for them this was limited to a dream, which they sometimes fantasized about for hours.

As the air danger of the threat of war increased daily, the Djokdjakarta air protection service had instituted all kinds of new measures. At various points, there were tall iron masts on which sirens were mounted. They were huge loudspeakers which, when they began to blare, rotated so that everyone could hear. When that happened, his father and mother ran through the house to close all windows and doors and to obscure them with blue paper. Despite the tension that this generated, the solidarity within their neighborhood grew. All against one.

The danger drove people together and suddenly they began to speak and consult with each other, even those who otherwise barely spoke to each other. Mutual helpfulness increased and people showed compassion for each other. In Djokdjakarta, air-raid shelters and trenches had been built. Those who could afford it constructed their own air-raid shelters.

One day, his father had taken Jan and his brothers, Gerard and Piet, to the city center, near Fort Vredeburg, to view the air-raid shelter constructed there by the government, an underground cellar hidden under a meter-thick layer of earth. Inside there were numerous supporting beams and rough planks thickly coated with tar. At the entrance hung a thick curtain of sailcloth, to protect people from the possibility of penetrating mustard gas, feared for its dire consequences. And to make the whole picture even more grim, large placards depicting ominous images warned people of this invisible and chilling danger. After seeing these images, Jan had nightmares for many nights, feeling suffocated and then waking up screaming. It seemed so real because he had buried himself so deep under the covers that he barely got any fresh air. Crying, he fought his way out of the blankets to wake up gasping and panting for air, soaking wet with cold clammy sweat.

In the center of the air-raid shelter was a long, wide bench where people could sit back to back. For Jan it felt as if he would be buried alive there. Fortunately, they didn't need to use this shelter because their neighbor, who was quite rich but also their landlord, had his own shelter built in the garden next to theirs. He had told Jan's father, that in time of need, they could use his shelter.

For Jan it was a dark and frightening period. A serious threat for which he had no words hung in the air. The city was plunged into pitch-black darkness and the streets were deserted. The only sound they heard now and then was that of the block watch rapping on windows and shutters while making his rounds, urging the residents to cover or extinguish the light escaping from the house.

Every day, Jan lived in suspense, awaiting the call to go to the shelter. But as the days, weeks, and months went by without a call, his tension eased until a sudden and totally unexpected air raid was sounded. Fortunately, at that moment they were all at home, and Father ordered them to go quickly to the neighbor's air-raid shelter, and to take their evacuation bags. They each had such a bag, homemade, woven from reed, with a large "E" embroidered on it along with his or her name. In the bag were some clothes, a towel, and toiletries. Their father was always prepared for an evacuation.

Jan and his brothers and sisters, the twins in front, ran to the shelter, followed by Father and Mother. There they looked for a place to await the course of events.

Father and the neighbor guarded the entrance and Jan made sure to find a place close to them. "Now it's going to happen," he thought. In the distance he heard the drone of the airplanes. Could it be the Japanese? He felt conflicted. His fear made him hope the danger would soon pass, but his curiosity made him wish that this was now the real thing. War was a threatening and thrilling concept if you had never experienced it. While they were sitting there in the shelter, they suddenly heard dull droning in the distance. The neighbor and his father dared to go outside, and were not aware that Jan had joined them. They stared for a long time at the blue sky, where nothing could be seen. Suddenly, and completely unexpectedly, Jan saw six silvery white airplanes flying high above them and moving slowly in a westerly direction. Under the wings he saw the red circles. Silently and with a racing heart, he watched the Japanese bombers. "Will they come back?" was the anxious thought that came to his mind. When, after some time, the "all clear" signal sounded through the loudspeakers, everyone, relieved, crawled out of the shelter. Father and the neighbor provided information. They speculated on the purpose of the flight, pointing to the clouds of smoke in the east and listening for explosions in the distance. The war, they said, was now imminent. Excitedly, Jan told his brothers and sisters what he had seen.

Jan was gripped by the tension of this brief event. It had touched him deeply. Until now, there had only been talk about the war or listening to the reports about the war on the radio and the communiqués of the military forces. It always seemed far away, but today it had come very close. In Djokja, the enemy had shown himself above the city, and that fueled the discussion about what was still to come.

From that moment on, monitoring military movements, such as the marching columns of the KNIL— *Koninklijk Nederlands Indisch Leger*—Royal Netherlands East Indies Army—became a regular part of Jan's daily activities. In spite of the fact that he was already 47 years old, his father, like others, was drafted into the Landstorm, the corps of armed civilians. Some time later, his father was uniformed in the rank of sergeant, but to his relief, he was rejected in Bandung in February 1942. Even Jan's toys had a military tone, because he had built entire armies from lead figures which he cast and colored himself. He stole the lead from the roofs of houses that had been empty for some time. He also built wooden planes and even an entire cardboard fleet containing his masterpiece: the aircraft carrier Tromp.

Playing *Cops & Robbers* was a popular pastime for Jan and his friends, but this was quickly transformed into war games. Like his friends, he was surrounded by conversations about the war. War was the daily topic of conversation. There was speculation, and this gave rise to fear. Everyone had an opinion and tried to force it on the other. Some were convinced that it wouldn't go as far as war, but others were certain that the Dutch army would be too strong and would immediately defeat the Japanese. Still others were convinced that the Japanese invasion was imminent and would have dire consequences. Jan didn't know what to think. For the time being, he experienced everything with tension and excitement, and processed it in his war games with his homemade soldiers and a cardboard fleet, which he considered invincible. He also admired the pilots in their dark brown uniforms, leather leggings and aviator goggles. They were his heroes and he wished himself in their place.

*End of February 1942*

News of the battle in the Java Sea in which the fleet led by Rear Admiral Karel Doorman was lost, and the subsequent Japanese landings on the north coast of Java, followed by an increasing number of terrifying communiqués, reinforced the feeling of vulnerability and utter helplessnesss in the Mobach family. In his mealtime prayers, Jan's father humbly implored God for grace, and for the enemy to have insight into its hostile and inhuman actions. As Jan peeked at his father during prayer, he saw the disbelief and despair in his pleading face.

"Will God help us, Father?" his sister Aafke inquired after Father's prayer.

Father struggled with his answer, wanting, on one hand, to give hope, and on the other, not to lie. "God will never forsake us, my dear. You can always rely on that."
Still, his answer did not take away the omens of a punishment to be meted out to them. Women and children from the other islands were already being transferred to Java. Rumors of the impending invasion of Java by the Japanese army fueled the fear. Everything indicated that they were trapped like rats, and had nowhere to go.

In the evening, Jan sat on the stairs to listen to the conversations between his father and mother, who were convinced that the children were asleep.

"We should have left much sooner for the Netherlands!" shouted his mother desperately.

21

"In order to fall into the hands of the Krauts there? We wouldn't have a ghost of a chance in the Netherlands either."

"At least we would have been at home with our family, in familiar surroundings. That would have been better than to stay here waiting for them to slaughter us."

"We must trust in the grace of our Creator," he heard his father respond.

"So far, I have the feeling that He has deserted us. To what do we owe that?" His mother sounded distraught and sad. His father reacted angrily.
"Be quiet, Johanna! God never deserts His own. We must trust in His love!"

He didn't hear his mother respond to that. She was silent. Silence was her way of responding to his father's Christian convictions. In those moments, he always hoped that she would not stay silent and would simply say what she thought. Because Jan agreed with her. He'd sat on the stairs before and listened to their conversations. When she had expressed her homesickness and her longing for a life in the Netherlands rather than in the Dutch East Indies. In his heart, he agreed that God had surely abandoned them. His father kept repeating that they could trust Him. No shred of evidence supported that view. Rather the opposite. Moreover, he noticed that his father was not receptive to his mother's opinions or feelings.

The following Sunday, Jan, along with his mother, brothers, and sisters, sat at the back of their congregation in the church on Merbaboe Street in Djokdjakarta. His father sat on the organ bench as organist of the congregation. The church was full, and Jan listened to the sounds of the organ above the pulpit.

The service progressed as normally as possible despite the palpable tension in the congregation. The great turnout was evidence of fear and anxiety. People sought security in their faith.

In the middle of Reverend De Vries' sermon, the undisturbed attention of the churchgoers was shattered by the alarming whine of the air-raid siren. Devotion gave way to panic, which spread quickly. People looked around and stood up, prepared to leave, looked at each other again, then at the pastor. They hoped that he would speak the saving word. Children began to cry.

Suddenly came the hushed voice of the pastor: "Brothers and sisters! Stay calm; we are in the presence of our Creator. We will interrupt the service so that you have the opportunity to go to the air-raid shelters. Above all, be calm and dignified. Or, you may stay here in the church. We are all in God's hand."

Jan looked at his mother, who in turn looked up at his father, the latter indicating that she should remain seated. Around them, people began to stand up and shuffle hurriedly and nervously to the church exit. In the front of the church there was a commotion. A woman had gotten up and walked to his father to discuss something with him. When she stepped back down, she looked up briefly and nodded at his father.

He began to play soft and comforting music. With a clear, almost angelically pure voice, the woman began to sing with the soft and measured accompaniment of his father:

*A mighty fortress is our God.*
*A bulwark never failing;*
*Our helper He amid the flood*

*Of mortal ills prevailing.*
*And though this world, with devils filled,*
*should threaten to undo us,*
*The Prince of Darkness grim,*
*His craft and power are great,*
*And, armed with cruel hate,*
*His rage we can endure,*
*for lo, his doom is sure.*
*One little Word shall fell him."*

Jan had his doubts. "Imagine if we are bombed," he whispered to his brother Piet, who was sitting next to him. "Would God protect us then, and how would He do it?"

Piet responded seriously, "Maybe the bombs will fall beside the church or He might send the Americans."

Jan nodded. "One thing I'm sure of," and he looked around again, "the people in the air-raid shelters are much safer than we are. They were sensible."

Piet gave a scornful laugh. Jan had periodically noticed that sometimes Piet was indifferent. "Didn't the pastor say that we are in God's hand and that we don't have to be afraid? Why else would he be a pastor if he doesn't know that?"

Jan missed the cynical undertone and went on earnestly: "Then why did the others run away? Don't they trust in God? Does that mean they are unbelievers?"

Their mother gave them both a stern look, and they fell silent.

The music stopped. The people remaining behind looked around restlessly until finally, the liberating "all clear" signal sounded.

The paralyzing threat was over, and a sigh of relief broke the tense atmosphere in the church. The people from the air-raid shelters re-entered the church, and his father played the well-known and often-heard Psalm 23, "The Lord is my Shepherd." As the people took their places again, they joined in singing this psalm.

Reverend De Vries ended his interrupted sermon with the message that God had averted the danger, and that they could always rely on Him whenever they were sorely tested. And in his prayer, he entreated "God, the Lord, our Father," to give them mercy and protection, even when it seemed hopeless. The service ended, and people began leaving the church.

Jan shuffled out of the church behind his mother and looked around at the people who had returned from the bomb shelters, thinking, "They didn't trust in God, but we did," while he ignored the little voice inside that said, " If you had had the choice, you would have gone to the shelter too."

The wildest rumors were circulating about the landing of the Japanese at Rembang, rumors of the atrocities of their shock troops in Koedo and Poerwodadi and of the events a day earlier in Solo.

On December 8, 1941, the Dutch government had declared war on Japan, but since the Netherlands was already at war with Germany, it was unable to fight on two fronts. The invasion of Celebes took place in January 1942, the invasion of Sumatra between February 14 and March 28, 1942. The goal of the Japanese was to conquer Sumatra before Java, so that the western flank of the Allied defense line could be destroyed, and access could be gained to Java.

Anxiety about what was in store for Jaan and his family grew rapidly.

# Father Jaan Willem

Thursday, March 5,1942

It was oppressively quiet in Djokdjakarta's European quarter that day.

Jaan Willem was worried about the frightening rumors and asked God that they, as a family, would be spared.

The night before, the Dutch troops had left. No protection remained, and Jaan and his family were left to their own fate. A simple mistake by the citizens, an aggressive act by one individual, could be fatal for many. A few shots from Dutch people in the area resulted in widespread plundering of almost all European houses. During the course of the day, they learned that the governor of Djokja, earlier that day, together with the local commander and the police commissioner, in an open vehicle, waving a white flag, had gone to meet the Japanese shock troops. Djokja had been declared a so-called "open city," meaning there would be no more resistance. This "open city declaration" had prevented bloodshed and looting.

The houses in the neighborhood where he lived with his wife and children were surrounded by spacious gardens.

He had locked the windows and doors of his house and, for their safety, it seemed better for him and his family to wait together for events to unfold. That evening they went to bed earlier than usual. The next morning, their servants arrived at the usual time. From them they heard what the entry of the Japanese troops had been like. There had been huge crowds of native Javanese in the streets. They saw the Japanese as their liberators from the Dutch regime, and many had applauded them. Japanese paper flags and paper pennies and dimes with Dutch print had been scattered by the Japanese. Jaan looked at what their servants had picked up and brought to show him. They reported that many bystanders had shouted, "*Banzai Nippon*"—Long live Japan—but some had also shouted, "*Banzak Nippon,*" which means "Scoundrel Japan."

With some excitement in their voices, they reported to Jaan the fact that in the Dutch Society shop, the entire stock of liquor had been smashed by native Javanese rebels. The furniture had suffered the same fate, so that nothing was left intact. That morning, Jaan had already seen that nearby houses of Dutch families, had been looted. From a bystander, he had heard that fortunately, the families themselves had found shelter in time. The danger was coming closer each day. Although he was on the alert every day and anxiously awaited the reports, Jaan was relieved that insurgents stayed away from his home and family. He hoped and prayed that this was just an increase in intimidation, and that it would stop there. Fortunately, after this, life again became more or less normal. Jaan reassured his family, saying there was no longer any direct danger for them. However, leaving the house and appearing publicly on the street was no longer an option. Only behind the closed doors of their house could life continue fairly normally.

This was the most difficult for the children as they were used to roaming around freely and going on adventures. They did not recognize the danger until

Gerard, his second son, was held hostage by the Japanese for a whole afternoon in someone's yard. Then they quickly realized the seriousness of the situation.

Jaan urged everyone in his family, his wife and his six children, to be careful.

"It seems calm right now, and let's hope and pray that it stays that way. However, I forbid you to appear on the street in front of the house, and if you see anything worrisome, go straight into the house and lock everything."

# Jan

*Friday, March 6, 1942*

Jan was at school. Classes were relatively normal, and, as usual, the day had started with a brief assessment of the situation. Much to everyone's relief, the looting had stopped, and life had returned to a semblance of normalcy. The teacher was busy with his lesson when he was interrupted by the headmaster of the school. All heads turned to him. It was always urgent when he came to interrupt a class. He looked serious and distressed. All the students looked up at him intently, wondering why there was an interruption.

"Young people," he began earnestly, searching for words. Then he straightened his back and looked at them. "This morning we received a message that Mr. Roders has been killed. He was in an army vehicle with other soldiers, somewhere between Solo and Djokja. They were retreating and during that maneuver he was fatally hit by a Japanese bullet. Soon we will gather to remember him."
He paused to look at the class again, then turned and walked away.

As he left the classroom and closed the door behind him, Jan felt a chill he had never felt before. Out of the corner of his eye, he saw the headmaster walk past their classroom on his way to the next class, to make the same announcement.

The students looked at each other. Crushed, their teacher sat at his desk with tears in his eyes. Some of the students also began to cry. There was no point in continuing with the lesson. After he had recovered from the initial shock, the teacher turned to them. Jan saw that his eyes were still moist.

"Young folks, this message brings the war, which we perhaps have experienced from a distance, to our school and to your class. We've all known Mr. Roders, and I know he was popular with you. Probably, for many of you, he is the first victim of this war that you've known personally. How we will miss him and his stories. But his stories will also remind us of him!"

Then they were given permission to do something by themselves, or to talk to each other. After the assembly which took place at the end of the morning, everyone could go home, where Jan agitatedly told his mother the story.

Suddenly everything went very quickly for Jan. Until then, the war had been remote. Now events followed each other in rapid succession. Reports about the war came from various quarters. It began with the death of Mr. Roders.

A few days later, on March 8, 1942, the Dutch East Indies fell to Japan, and the Japanese gained control of the country. A day later, the students were dismissed from school because the Hogere Burgerschool—HBS—their school—had been commandeered to be set up as a prisoner-of-war camp. Their education came to a halt, and no one was able to say where the lessons would be continued. In the following weeks, a high barbed wire fence was hastily constructed around the beautiful white school building, so that no one could go in or out. The familiar building changed into a prison where hundreds of Dutch prisoners-of-war were locked up. Many men and fathers of his friends were locked up there. Since there was not much else to do, Jan regularly cycled with his friend Dirk, whose father, Dr. Zwaan, was imprisoned, to the building to deliver a parcel of food for him. Most often, they could drop off the parcel through the fence and have a brief chat with him.

He always said that he was doing well, and that Dirk should be kind to his mother, brother, and sister.

"And that goes for you too, Jan; be kind to your parents, your brothers, and sisters."

One day, it was completely different. In front of the fence surrounding the school, a large crowd had gathered. Native Javanese crowded in front of the fence. Jan and Dirk were stopped at the gate by a Japanese soldier who motioned for them to drop off the parcel at the guardhouse, an appropriated dwelling, across the street.

They leaned their bicycles against a tree and walked into the yard towards the house. Jan felt his knees buckling and would rather have turned around immediately and ridden back home. Still, he didn't want to abandon his friend, so they walked in together. They saw three Dutch men standing on the veranda of the house, and that gave them the courage to keep walking. As they approached, they were shocked to find that the men were tied together with chains and ropes. Their hands were tied behind their backs and they looked at the two boys with an empty and despondent expression. Their faces were ashen and tired, and their eyes blood-shot. A Japanese soldier stood near the veranda, guarding the three men. It was a frightening and threatening scene, certainly no herald of anything good. Anxiously, the boys looked around and handed their parcel for Dirk's father to a Japanese who barked at them, causing the boys to race back to the street. There they asked someone what was going on and were told that the men had been apprehended attempting to flee the prisoner-of-war camp.

"This afternoon, at four p.m., they will be executed on the sports field of the school. They have already had to dig their own graves there."

Jan and Dirk were shocked by this announcement. Their sports field a cemetery for people condemned to death? That was beyond their power of imagination and Jan was horrified at the thought. These men with whom they had just made eye contact were to be executed that afternoon. Unimaginable.

Still, their anxious curiosity won out over the shock and fear.

"I'm staying," said Dirk, who was usually a bit more courageous than Jan. "And you?"

"If you stay to watch, I'll stay too," said Jan, pretending to be tougher than he was. They propped their bikes against a tree and pushed their way into the crowd that had gathered to witness the execution.

There were already so many people crowded together that it was almost impossible to get through. With pushing and pulling, they reached the fence around their school's once-magnificent sports field. Jan had no chance to witness the execution because many indigenous young people obstructed his view. Later Jan heard that his brother Piet had indeed seen it. At home, Piet related what had happened.

"First they had to dig their own graves, and then they were bound to posts just before execution. The Japanese soldiers repeatedly stabbed their bodies with bayonets.

Then they were tossed into their pit and other prisoners-of-war were forced to fill up the graves. It was a warning of what happens when you try to flee."

Jan, who had not seen anything, did mention the tension and fear that he had felt. Outraged, he added: "Native Javanese were cheering while the men were executed."

All around him, Jan noticed that more and more men, including fathers, also from their own circle of acquaintances, were taken prisoner and locked up in the prisoner-of-war camp. The camp became so crowded that, over time, it was evacuated due to lack of space. All prisoners were transported by train to other camps in the country. From his friends, Jan had heard when the transport would take place. They agreed to take a look, even though their parents had forbidden that. On the day of the transport, Jan and some of the more daring of his friends were at the railway. For hours, they stood in the blazing sun near the railroad tracks. Finally the train arrived, pulled by a heavily chugging steam locomotive, struggling to haul the heavy freight. The boys climbed up the gravel bank next to the rails to get a good view. As the train passed them, they saw men in green uniforms sitting in front of the windows. Suddenly, among the people, Jan discovered Mr. Oldhoff, the principal of the Christian junior high school where his father was also employed. It seemed as if he recognized Jan as well. Long after that, in his mind's eye, Jan could still envision Mr. Oldhoff's sad face. At home, he didn't dare to talk about it because, in disobedience to his parents, he had gone to look at the train anyway. He did entrust his secret to his brother Gerard.

"I went to watch the prisoner transport. If you promise not to talk about it, I'll tell you everything."

Gerard's promise was enough for him to unburden himself of what he had seen.

"Did you see more acquaintances?"

"No, just Mr. Oldhoff. Would Father already know?"

"You would have to ask him yourself, but then you risk a thrashing because you were there. I would keep it to myself."

Jan followed Gerard's advice. Two days later at mealtime, their father said that he had heard that Mr. Oldhoff had been taken away. At the announcement, Gerard looked at Jan and winked at him as a sign that now their father knew it too.

"They ransacked Mrs. Vetter's house."

With this announcement, Jan's father came home upset and angry one morning. "Don't the native Javanese have any respect any more for the property of the Dutch? Have they forgotten what we have brought to this country?"

"Maybe we have brought too much and haven't appreciated their values."

His mother's reaction shocked Jan, and Father looked at her, astonished.

"How can you say that? If it weren't for us, they would still be living in the Middle Ages."

Jan saw his mother look at his father with resignation. He recognized the undertone of her questions and knew that his mother would rather never have gone to the Dutch East Indies. How often had he heard her sigh over this. Fortunately, his father left it at that, angry as he was about the looting of Mrs. Vetter's house.

35

Like everyone else, he knew that this plundering was the result of the utter chaos that had ensued after the Japanese invasion.

The native Javanese saw the Japanese as their liberators from the colonial Netherlands and thought that now they could strike back. The Javanese servants no longer showed up for work because they didn't want to and because they didn't dare to for fear of reprisals from the occupying forces that could be found everywhere. Civilian traffic in the streets had given way to military movement. Fear was rampant. What were the Japanese going to do? What measures would be taken?

Yet there was also hope. Rumors circulated that the Americans had landed on East Java and that a speedy liberation was imminent. They all appealed to each other for patience, and because people really wanted to believe in these rumors, they accepted them as fact.

"We must persevere. It will be all right. We can trust in God."

How many times had his father said that to his mother when doubts arose within her. In those moments, his mother often looked at Jan and he saw the tears and doubt in her eyes. He knew she no longer believed his father's soothing words. They were intended to reassure them, but they were usually counterproductive. Jan no longer believed it either, and neither did his brothers. If they knew themselves to be unobserved, they had regularly discussed this topic. Gerard was cynical and frustrated. Jan recognized that when Gerard made another comment about what you could still believe these days. Piet tried to ease the situation, not by reprimanding him as their father tended to do. Piet would say, "Everyone is angry with God and the church, because everyone feels abandoned. There is no point in saying that to Father. He just becomes angrier."

When Father came home with the news about the looting of Mrs. Vetter's house, Jan noticed that his father also had some doubts. Until the invasion, it had all seemed remote, and the rule of law still worked reasonably well. Now that the Netherlands had capitulated, everything collapsed like a house of cards. This allowed looters to enter homes with impunity, and haul away everything from the Europeans. Nothing was done about this, making the situation even more threatening. Danger could come from anywhere.

The *rampokkers*, as the indigenous looters were called, roamed around the city in large groups. When Jan dared to venture into the city, he saw overturned and burnt-out cars everywhere. In the distance he regularly heard the screams and shouts of the looters and it seemed to be coming closer all the time.

"We have to hide. Quick, everyone out to the backyard. They are very close by! They are already on our street!"

Never before had he seen his father, who usually worked calmly and deliberately, so panicked. He positioned his wife and children on the grass with their backs to the wall and gave everyone "weapons." His brothers had stone flower pots pressed into their hands, and he had an iron bar.

"If they force their way in, throw whatever you can find at them! Do you hear?!"

They heard the roar and cheering coming very close. They passed the neighbors' house and stopped in front of our house...for just a moment...

The tension was palpable. Everyone feared what might follow. What could they possibly do against such a mob? With dread in their hearts, they peered inside; the shouts were very loud now...and then it passed them by. The mob moved on, leaving their house untouched.

The family members looked at each other in confusion and Father actually began to giggle.

"How is it possible?" he murmured. "We have crawled through the eye of the needle!"

He folded his hands, nodded to them to follow his example, and said a short prayer of thanks: "We do not deserve to have been spared from the *rampokkers* today, dear Lord. It is your grace that always protects us. Thank you for so much love! Amen."

Still doubtful, they rose. The clamor was over but the silence was just as palpable.

"Will He continue to protect us?"

Jan heard the doubt in his mother's voice and was shocked by his father's harsh response: "If you doubt God, He may let you go, Johanna, and then there is no mercy for sinners!"

Jan saw the shock in her eyes, followed by tears, and she looked at him beseechingly. She seemed to seek his help, but he didn't dare to move. She turned and walked inside. Her body shook. She stayed in her bedroom for the rest of the day and didn't reappear until the next day. He saw that she had been crying, her eyes puffy and red. He walked toward her and took her hand.

"Don't be afraid, *Mama*; I'll always protect you!" he whispered. At that moment, she pulled his head to her bosom and kissed his hair.

"I know that, dear, I know that!"

Besides being organist, Jan's father was also an elder and clerk of the church. He was convinced that because of these roles, he had not yet been arrested and locked up in a prisoner-of-war camp. It also meant that he carried a lot of responsibility. Jan's mother had told him that his father had been rejected for military service because of his heart problems, but if Jan or any of the other children asked about it, Jaan denied it, saying that he was indispensable to the church.

"Jan, tomorrow we will take the train together to Solo." Jan looked up and asked why they were going there.

"Because that is where the looting has been the worst and we have to take things over there."

Indeed, to the amazement of his children, he had come home with two suitcases full of clothes, and now Jan understood that these were to be taken to Solo.

"You're going to help me with that, Jan. I can't carry the suitcases by myself."

The next day they went together to the Lempoejangan station of the Dutch East Indies Railways and boarded the omnibus train to Solo, some sixty kilometers east of Djokdjakarta. Jan was absolutely delighted at the prospect of his first train trip. As a family, they had never traveled by train in recent years. The train cars were crammed with native Javanese, who looked at them suspiciously. There were few Europeans in the train. Fortunately, Jan and his father were left alone, and when they arrived in Solo, his father breathed a sigh of relief.

"Fortunately, it is not very busy!"

Since there was no public transport, his father decided to walk to the governor's palace. Panting from the heat and soaked with sweat, they dragged the suitcases along, and arrived at the palace half an hour later. Many women and children had fled to the palace. The streets were empty, littered with paper, newspapers, documents, and administrative paperwork. Many houses were abandoned, windows smashed and doors demolished. Jan was dumbfounded. Of course, he had heard stories about the looting and destruction, but what he saw now was worse than all the stories put together.

"Did the *rampokkers* do all this, Father?"

"Yes, Jan, and no one was able to stop them. They took everything, right down to the nails. Take a look around you. Isn't it terrible?"

They shuffled through the papers, Jan kicking the pages away.

"It looks as if it has snowed," his father muttered. "Then everything is so white too, Jan, but then because of the snow."

He glanced briefly at his son. "Do you still remember the snow?"

"I can't recall, Father."

Silently they made their way through the paper and the garbage.

It felt scary to walk there, and Jan's father looked around nervously. Jan didn't feel safe and hoped nothing would happen to them.

"Father! Look!" Jan pointed to a dead dog lying among the papers. He had seen dead dogs before, but never a dog with a knife in its back.

"Brood of vipers!" hissed his father. "Couldn't they even leave an animal alone?"

At the governor's palace, there was a flurry of activity. On the front veranda and in the great hall, there were dozens of women and children but hardly any men. His father entered the big building while Jan waited outside. Many broken pieces of furniture, resembling wounded birds lying in the grass and between the shrubs, were strewn about the grounds. Jan overheard a conversation between two men a few meters away.

"A man had hidden money inside that wardrobe."

The man pointed at a smashed armoire lying in the grass a short distance away. "When he rediscovered his wardrobe, it seems his money was still in it, under a double plank in the bottom."

"What a lucky guy!" responded the other man.

Although Jan would really have liked to hear a little more, he saw his father headed in his direction, with a young woman accompanying him.

"I'm Mrs. Braber," she introduced herself politely. "And what is your name?"

"I'm Jan, ma'am."

His father took over. "Jan, Mrs. Braber is the wife of a BPM official.'"

"What is BPM, Father?"

"That is the Batavian Petroleum Company. Mr. Braber was arrested and placed in a prisoner-of-war camp. Mrs. Braber's house was ransacked yesterday and she managed to escape through the back door. Now everything is gone. She couldn't take anything with her, except for the clothes on her back and some money. Also, she has no children and is all alone. That's why she'll be coming with us and staying with us for a while. Then I can try to find out where her husband is imprisoned and find her another place to stay."

Jan stared at the woman and thought she was very beautiful. During the return trip, she talked a lot with him. He liked her very much and thought his father had made a good decision in taking her along.

Later that evening, when he was listening to his parents' conversation again, he heard his mother ask, "Did you have to take her with you now? Couldn't she go somewhere else?"

"She has no one and nothing anymore. It is our Christian duty to help her!"

"Why do you always have to do this? Does she really have no one else to go to?"

"She stays here until she finds something else. I have nothing further to say."

With the arrival of Jannie, which was how Mrs. Braber insisted on being addressed, tension in the house heightened. And not just because of the occupation. Jan noticed that his mother was quiet, glancing angrily at his father and Jannie. His father was very friendly, certainly to Jannie. The two got along very well. His father kept her well informed about his attempts to find out where her husband was imprisoned.

"I don't understand it. I have made inquiries at all possible locations, but don't receive correct answers. Don't they want to tell me, or don't they really know?"

"They know where they lock people up, don't they?" Jannie asked, a little panicked.

"Don't worry, Jannie. I'll find out. I'll see if the pastor can do something."

A few days later, he came home with the news that her husband was in the Benteng, as Fort Vredeburg was called, in Djokdjakarta.

"Some of his acquaintances are there too, so he is not alone. Those who have seen him say that he is doing well. Have faith, it will all be fine."

In contrast to his mother's initial protests at Jannie's arrival, which, according to Jan, were motivated mostly by her jealousy because his father got along well with Jannie, his mother was more welcoming to others who were also accommodated in their home. People were billeted regularly. Again and again people whose homes had been looted or confiscated, but also soldiers who had to be stationed. A Dutch soldier and his wife were also housed with them for a few months. After the capitulation of the Dutch army, another soldier, together with his wife and two children were placed with them. The soldier, Wout, was taken prisoner in Bandoeng shortly afterwards during a fight with the Japanese, and with a few other soldiers, was summarily executed. The news of his death hit them hard. To everyone present, Jan's father suggested that they remember Wout by praying for him. Everyone folded his hands. The room became very quiet, and then his father began to speak:

"Wout, I believe that God has not left you in the depths of hell. He has received you into the glory of heaven. In the tough battle of a lone soldier in the Dutch East Indies, you continually sought support from God and desired to serve Him. That is where your heart was, and as a variation on a Bible verse, we can say as a consolation: 'Where our heart is, there will our treasure be also.' We know now where you are, and that comforts those of us who remain behind."

Jan looked around the room at everyone who was there. Tears streamed down the cheeks of Wout's wife. Her children looked around dazed, barely aware of what had happened. Silence filled the room and was broken after a few moments by the solemn voice of his father:

"Let us pray the Lord's Prayer, the prayer that gives us comfort and hope...Our Father, who art in heaven..."

It was poignant; the horror of the war, and especially the death of people Jan knew, now came so close that he had nightmares about dying and being dead. He dreamt that he was dead and buried, and that earth was tossed onto his casket. Gasping for air and screaming in fear, he awoke. Because he was ashamed of this, he didn't dare to talk about it.

The freedom of Jan and his family members was becoming increasingly restricted. His father often complained about this because it mainly applied to the Dutch population and their children. The native Javanese were left alone. Soon after the occupation, everything had still been flexible. There had even been days when the Japanese played water polo matches with the Dutch young people. One day, when Jan and his friend Dirk wanted to go swimming, they were told gruffly to stay out. There were hundreds of Japanese thrashing about in the water, but there was no room for others. The Japanese became increasingly hostile towards the Dutch.

At mealtime, his father said that bank accounts were being blocked, and simply emptied. "On top of that, newer and much higher taxes must also be paid. I don't know how I will do that, because we are no longer receiving a salary."

Desperately, his mother asked, "How are we going to handle this?" Normally, they never discussed such topics at the table in the presence of their children, but Jan realized that his parents had abandoned that rule. This matter was that important.

"Don't worry, Johanna, we are still doing well," said his father at the table. "The church will help us, and thankfully, we withdrew all of our savings on time."

Jan had discovered that his father had hidden money in a small box in the wardrobe, safely behind the linens, in the hope that if there were ever a search, the Japanese wouldn't find it.

Due to the threat of house searches, his father had hidden the necessary valuables. He had left only the portrait of Queen Wilhelmina hanging. He had told Jan that if you didn't hide everything, the searches would be over quickly.

One day his mother and all the children stayed behind in the living room, when Father went outside in his tropical suit. He didn't get very far. Three Japanese soldiers with bayonets on their rifles stepped up to him. He bowed low, as this was now strictly prescribed, and called out, *"Tabeh toewan!"*—"Hello, sir!"

*"Pakean militer!?"*—"Military uniform!?"— one of them shrieked at him, as he felt increasingly apprehensive.

Father replied, *"Tidah toewan"*—"No, sir," to which the soldier repeated, *"Pakean militer?"* and Father responded again, *"Tidah toewan."*

They were satisfied with that, and Father hoped that they would soon go away. However, they headed for the house and he followed, fearing for the safety of his family. They stormed through the house, checking everything. In the bedroom, where the portrait of the Queen hung, the leader bellowed, *"Apa ini!?"*—Who is that?

His father replied, *"Ini nenek"*—old woman.

The man stopped and then burst out, *"Ini perempoen nommer satoe?"*—Is this woman number one? to which Pieter wittily agreed, *"Temtoe"*—Of course.

Despite the fear that the incident had caused, Jan reminded himself that it had also given them happiness. Later, they all had a good laugh because the Japanese had assumed that the woman in the portrait was his father's mother or his first wife. Disgusted, the officer had thrown the portrait to the floor. Then he pointed to a print of an Amsterdam orphan girl from an issue of the Haagsche Post and shouted again, *"Apa ini?"*

Father was rescued at that moment by Jan, who said, *"Ini gambar sembajang"*—That's an "In Memoriam" card. Then they paid no further attention. Arriving in the living room, the officer pointed to the portrait of Princess Juliana and Prince Bernhard and asked again, *"Apa ini?"*

This time it was his mother who quickly replied, *"Ini saudara dari saja"*—That's my sister with her boyfriend. "Sister" could stay on the wall.

A large photo of the Rotterdam Lloyd ship the Dempo was deemed suspicious and was taken away. Stomping their feet and shouting, they left the house, and Father heaved a sigh of relief, because they had not found a small money box containing sixteen hundred guilders, as well as eight hundred guilders scattered among a number of books in the bookcase. Had they found the money, his father would certainly have been taken for interrogation with all the resultant consequences.

"How did you come up with 'memorial card'?" Father looked at Jan in amazement.

"I saw one at Dirk's place. They are Roman Catholic, and if someone there dies, a memorial card is made to commemorate the dead. Dirk showed me the one for his grandma."

"You certainly fooled them!"

They laughed about this, at which point his mother said, "It's nice that they commemorate their dead in this way. That way they still remain with you somewhat. At least you won't forget them."

# Father Jaan Willem

*May 1942*

How often had he not walked past, but somehow today he paused to look at it: Fort Vredeburg, the old fortress in the heart of Djokdjakarta, built in 1765, and the palace of the governor before the occupation. Now it had been appropriated by the Japanese and used as a jail for prisoners of war. He watched the construction work around the main entrance. Heavy iron fences were being erected. The native Javanese builders were sweating in the full sun. The yellow bricks of the main walkway, which in the past had served as ballast for ships, lay peacefully in the sun. He wondered how long this peaceful scene would be preserved. He closed his eyes and pretended there were no other people. For a moment, he stepped back into colonial times. His heart ached because all of that was over now. It was one of the reasons why he had moved to the Dutch East Indies, to be part of that Dutch Glory. The Japanese had other plans for the fort. He thought about peace, and in his heart he prayed the prayer he had spoken daily since the day of the Japanese occupation:

"Lord God, creator of all people, including our enemies, restore their peace to their hearts, so that they will see their faults and let us go. But not my will be done, but Yours. Amen."

In the middle of June, the purpose of the fort became clear. In addition to a prisoner- of-war camp, it became a large relief camp. Notices were posted all over the city, calling on all men to report to the fort on June 30.

While they were sitting peacefully at the table, after Jaan Willem had just said grace, the plates were filled with food. His family, now back together as a family, began to eat. After taking a few bites, he put down his knife and fork and looked around the table.

"Next Thursday, all men must report to Fort Vredeburg for internment, which also applies to me."

As if in one movement, they all stopped eating. Frightened, they looked at him. They knew that this could happen. How many men had already gone before him. But as the days, weeks, and months passed after the capitulation, they had clung to the hope that internment of their husband and father would pass by. The blow hit hard and Johanna began to cry.

"That can't happen, can it?"

"There is no choice, my dear. Many have already preceded us, so there can be no further delay. Besides, it is for our own good, to protect us from the Javanese."

"What will happen to the children and to me? We will not survive this!"

"If we keep believing, we'll survive everything. You must be strong. You must all be strong. And it is only for a short time. The Americans are already in the Solomon Islands, behind New Guinea. By the next full moon, we can expect them, and then this will all be over. Let's enjoy the time we still have together."

Johanna looked at him with tears in her eyes and said softly, "You are always full of confidence, and able to give things, no matter how bad and sad, a twist of hope. Who says you are right?"

"We must keep up our hope and trust in our Creator. If we lose sight of that, we are all lost."

His words didn't take away her fear but only her appetite. She put her knife and fork on her plate and stared straight ahead.

*June 30, 1942*

On the day of his departure, they took him to Benteng, as Fort Vredeburg was called. Everyone carried some of his belongings that he was permitted to take with him. At the iron gate he said goodbye to Johanna and the children. He went through the gate and headed for the main entrance. At the end of the walkway, he turned and smiled. No one would ever see him cry or be sad. As the linchpin of the family, he felt that this was impossible. To his delight, he had noticed that Johanna had kept her composure at the farewell. That made him happy, even though he knew she was very distressed.

Fort Vredeburg was surrounded by a wide dry ditch filled with barbed wire. Escape was impossible.

The entrance gate consisted of a heavy iron railing with bars. Jaan reported at the gate and was admitted. He had to walk past a long table, behind which sat a number of Japanese who asked him for his name. They entered his name on a list and added a number to it. They told him to remember that number because he "needed" it. At that moment he missed why. Later it became clear to him: only numbers mattered, and names were unimportant. He was searched. His luggage, including the worst mattress from home, was inspected. Then he received a signal that he could continue. He looked around, wondering where to go. One of the other prisoners told him to find shelter "somewhere" and set up his place there.

"It doesn't matter where you lie down. Find a sheltered spot. Try to find something near a window or a door. Then you have some fresh air now and then."

He thanked the man and was fortunate to find a spot near a door. Other men sat on their mattresses, staring into space. Their eyes were vacant and they did not respond to his greeting. After he had put down his mattress, made his bed, and put clothes and things he had brought along at the head of the bed, he looked around. He expected anything to happen. But there was nothing. He asked one of the other men what the intention was.

"Nobody knows. Keep quiet. If there is food to be distributed, a call will be made. For the rest, you have to keep yourself busy."

"Shouldn't we work then?"

"No, you are free to do whatever you want. You are just not allowed to leave the grounds. If you do try, you will get into trouble with one of the Javanese policemen who are guarding the place. Twice a day a Japanese officer comes to pick up a report, and be especially wary of 'Jan the swatter,' who has rather loose hands and smacks people, even when nothing is wrong."

# Jan

*June 30, 1942*

Once they got back home, his mother broke down. She was devastated and kept repeating, "How are we going to carry on?"

The more she lamented, the more the girls distanced themselves from her. She was inconsolable. Piet, Gerard, and Jan remained with her, and Piet, the eldest of the boys, addressed her. "*Mama*, the girls need you, and we need you. Show that you are not going to give up and trust that it will all work out."

He had never heard Piet speak to her so sternly, and looked at him with admiration.

His message helped. His mother drew Piet to her. "You are right, son. This way I'm no help to you, and it's great that you are the oldest. You have to take over from *Papa*, okay?"

From that moment on, Piet tried to take the place of his father, and became a bit like the head of the family.

Fortunately, they were not abandoned. Help and support came from all sides. They received a lot of attention from the clergy and doctors, who did not have to be interned, and someone came regularly to see if they needed anything. Piet grew into his father role. He took care of many things, including finances, and began to make decisions. Everyone, even their mother, accepted this and considered it normal. From the church members, they received food such as flour, sugar, and rice. Every now and then their cook came over to cook. The boys, Piet,

Gerard, and Jan, could enjoy a warm meal once a week at hotel Matalaram. The owners were close acquaintances of their parents, and felt they should help them.

Every day Jan walked to the fort with his mother or with one of his brothers or his sisters. Only once did he go alone. They would take a pan of food and fruit, made daily by Chinese friends of theirs. His father would appear behind the bars of the gate, and they would talk briefly. Jan noticed that his father always had positive words to say and always sent them home with a glimmer of hope. Nevertheless, they grew sadder by the day, and especially Mother found things very difficult. She could not bring herself to go to the fort every day and therefore skipped regularly.

Concerned, Father asked Piet, "Is Mother okay?"

Piet, who was a bit like his father, would always answer, "It is not easy, Father, but she is doing well. She will carry on, as long as you also carry on."

"Then it is good; give her a kiss from me and God's blessing."

Jan became more and more rebellious when he heard that. Why God's blessing? "Then if we are God's children, why is he abandoning us?"

His father had looked at him with understanding but also anger. "Jan, that's why we are sinners, because we have no faith. You should never doubt His purpose, no matter how understandable the doubt is, and how serious the situation."

Jan looked down, not because he was ashamed of what he had said, but to hide his unbelief from his father. Jan found the faith of his parents difficult and that bothered him.

# Father Jaan Willem

*July 1942*

During the first days of his internment, he gathered information, bit by bit, about the comings and goings in the camp. Some of the Japanese soldiers looked warlike, with huge samurai swords. The camp commandant had a small mustache, which quickly earned him the nickname "Hitler." He turned out to be okay. If he saw that he was not understood, or if he didn't understand the men, then he turned and simply walked away. Jaan learned that for the big roll call, they had to line up in rows of five. He made a mental note not to stand in the front row, because he'd have to shout numbers in Japanese. It would be better to learn them first.

Within a few days, he was also able to call out *ichi-ni-san-shi-go-roku-shichi-hachi-kyuu-juu.* At one such session, everyone began to laugh at him, and he didn't understand why, until one of the men told him that he had shouted *"ni-kitja-shi,"* and that, according to them, meant "don't tickle." The Japanese soldiers had paid no attention.

From time to time a doctor came by and examined them. The point of this escaped Jaan, but there nothing else to do, so he just went along with the examination. Someone told him the examination was done because the Japanese were terrified of disease. Soon it became apparent that the doctor recognized only two complaints: chest complaints and stomach complaints. His prescription was always the same: milk for chest complaints and fruit for stomach complaints. You didn't receive that, but you could request it from your loved ones who regularly came to the fence for a visit. It was also a way for the prisoners to feign a complaint to get extra food from home. With the prescription from the doctor, the food was not confiscated at the checkpoint. When his wife Johanna told him that it was at the expense of the children's food supply, he stopped his "complaints."

Occasionally, if there was something wrong with him, he would still go to the doctor's office. He had trouble with constipation and his heart. Once again he was prescribed milk and fruit.

"I need *sajoerans,*" by which he meant vegetables. The doctor ignored him and kept repeating that he needed *boeah boeah djoega*—fruit. Once again he got a Japanese prescription for milk and fruit. He passed it on to Jan, who came to visit him. The next day he received the milk and fruits from Piet. Less than he had hoped for, but the food continued to come for a long time and with regularity. The advantage of this was that he could speak to his wife and children at the fence for a little longer than normally allowed, to ask them how they were doing. Even though his wife had told him that his request for extras was at the expense of the children's supplies, he was too preoccupied with himself and missed it. His wife had resigned herself to the situation.

"When can you come home?" asked Johanna one day.

"That won't take long, Jo. Rumors have it that by the next full moon, the Americans will invade and we will all be liberated."

His wife smiled incredulously. "How often have you said that already? You do see that it still hasn't happened, right? "

"Have faith in God, Johanna. He will send our rescuers in His time."

Within several weeks, the camp was jam-packed with steadily increasing numbers of prisoners. Every time he thought that no one else could be added, another load came. By now, there were already over eight hundred prisoners and the flood continued. Two hundred men were crammed into one dormitory, which had been divided into compartments for twenty people each. They slept on iron bunk beds that had previously served in the old barracks. Next to the bed was an iron cabinet for clothing and kitchen utensils.

Sitting in a small wicker chair in a secluded spot, Jaan was staring out into space. He was overcome with self-pity and doubt. Would this ever end? He often wondered about this, and when his wife visited him with food at the fence and asked such a question, he would admonish her. "You must always continue to have faith in God, Johanna. If we don't, we are lost not only here, but also for eternity."

Now he himself was in the same state, filled with doubt about the integrity of many things: *He had seen the skepticism in her eyes but had ignored it. Johanna had always expressed her doubts. In his thoughts, he went back to 1930. Even then, she doubted the suitability of his decision to take a job in the Dutch East Indies. Their future, as he saw it then, in this country, had begun with strife and disunity. Had there ever been a blessing on it? The first ten years, to be sure, had gone well, and Johanna seemed to have resigned herself to his choice. However, from time to time, she voiced reproach. A single remark that sometimes led to short or long periods of silence, or the pining for her family in the Netherlands. When they returned to the Netherlands in 1936 for a family furlough, she had asked him to see if he could find a job there again. He had ignored that request and reminded her once more of her wedding vows. What had it profited him? Had he ignored her too much? Wouldn't he have been wiser to listen to her? Then they would have been in the Netherlands right now. To be sure, in a country occupied by the Germans, but possibly with peace between their families. Now he was in a prison camp and, although he tried to cheer her up with stories of an early release, he knew that this might be just the beginning of more misery. What had they gotten into and would they ever come out unharmed?*

So, in a somber mood, he sat in that quiet spot in the camp and felt the same doubt and all those questions well up. Praying, his method of coming to terms with his thoughts and achieving an inner peace, did not help. At this moment, he felt forsaken by God.

*Was there really a God? And if so, why didn't He help them?*

Suddenly, he heard all kinds of sounds, the banging of a hammer, the violin playing of a violinist. He even heard people laughing in one of the halls. Then it was as if a voice spoke to him.

"Shame on you, Jaan Willem. If you sit here like this and do nothing, then you will become a victim and will never leave this camp alive. Go do something! Fill your time with whatever. Do something!"

The voice made a big impression on him and he looked around to see who had spoken to him. He knew that it was the voice of God in his mind. He had to work. Just do something; it didn't matter what, as long as he was busy.

"Idle hands are the devil's workshop," he said to himself and stood up. From that moment on, he would be busy and stay busy. No matter what.

The next day he searched the fort's archives and found all kinds of medical records. He tore off the cardboard wraps and made boxes from them, using glue that he made from potato starch, and then covered them with decorative paper. Making one little box took about eight hours, hours during which he didn't think of his situation but was busy concentrating on something else. Time passed quickly. Moreover, the boxes were seen as a memento of the camp, and he could sell them for one guilder.

An acquaintance taught him how to knot hammocks from rope: seventy knots long and fifty knots wide. This took up even more time. Because he himself was being creative, he noticed what others were making. It varied from bags to dolls carved from pieces of wood. Primitive figures that improved by the day. During the early years in the Dutch East Indies, he had made little clay figures. So he asked his son, who had come to visit him, if he could bring his pottery wheel and a lump of clay. That is how he picked up his old hobby again. Gerard took his vases to a Javanese potter who baked them and sold them at the local market. In that way, Jaan provided for his family, even at a distance, with a little extra money. From his wife he had heard that their money was nearly gone, and that she had already begun to sell some of their things. His vases were an extra source of income.

Relatively speaking, Jaan had a lot of freedom of activity in the camp, so he decided to organize a choir. In short order he found thirty men who were eager to participate. At the beginning of the evening, after the evening meal, people would sing. He adapted Dutch songs and church hymns. Sometimes they organized an open-air concert in the camp, which was supplemented by others with story-telling and other performances.

# Mother

*Friday, November 27, 1942*

In the middle of November, notices were put up here and there. Jan was the first to see them. He stormed inside, panting from running. "We will be imprisoned, or something like that."

My heart stopped. Who could tell me where this war was going? Frozen with shock, I couldn't utter a word.

Piet, who wanted to find things out for himself, went to investigate, and returned with more information. My son sat at the head of the table, just like Jaan. Gerard, Aafje and Willie also came closer. Controlled, Piet told us what was going to happen. No, we weren't going to be imprisoned; we were going to be interned. It was not as bad as it seemed. We had to be protected from the native Javanese people.

I said nothing, but my thoughts were whirling in my head. Who was inciting the population against us? Weren't those the same Japanese? Piet continued quietly. So, we will not be imprisoned, but interned.

*How can you stay so calm? Explain that to me.* There would be information meetings. Food would be provided in the camps; wasn't that nice? That undeniable confidence, was that my son? That food would be supplied would be a good thing, because it was not easy to put food on the table. But to be honest, I didn't expect too much. Until now, everything had just gotten worse.

"We have no choice," I hear Piet say. Yes, yes, Jaan had said the same thing days before his forced departure. "We have no choice, Johanna. We must trust in the Lord."

No choice, no choice, how often do I have to hear that? What do you mean, we have no choice, and who are "we" in this case? We should never have gone to the Dutch East Indies; regret overwhelmed me. To begin with, I should never have left Driebergen. And with this thought, I felt the anger mushroom. Like a submissive sheep, I had let myself be led to the slaughter. If only I'd had the courage then to say no. But I had lacked daring. I lack courage. That is the naked truth. In my lap, I clench my hands into fists.

# Jan

*November 1942*

When Jan came home with the news that they, too, would be imprisoned, Piet corrected him.

"Interned, you mean. That is different from imprisoned!"

"Just like Father, who is still behind bars!"

Angrily, Jan left the room and headed outside. He felt misunderstood. When he returned a little later, he heard the whole story from Piet, who had gone to find a notice with more information.

"All women and children with Dutch blood are to be transferred to protection camps to be protected and guarded by the Japanese against the indigenous population. There we will also receive food. It may sound crazy, but in fact, we can be relieved, because it is growing steadily more difficult for us to obtain our own food, and there we won't have to worry about it anymore."

"And all our things?" asked Mother. "What's going to happen to them?"

" That I don't know, but informational meetings are being held, and the Japanese will answer all questions there."

They all went together to the meeting. Jan looked around. The hall was jam-packed, and to his amazement, there were Japanese who spoke Dutch. They gave detailed answers to questions from the audience. Nothing was too much for them to answer satisfactorily. They painted a rosy picture of everything. The Dutch would thrive in the camps and there was more than enough food for everyone. Protection was in everyone's best interest, "because we can't guarantee that the indigenous people will leave you alone."

Several days later, they received an internment number: J-185, where the J stood for Djokdjakarta. The following days were filled with preparations. When their father heard the news, he was completely despondent. Piet, he told Jan, had to promise not to tell their mother. Father said he understood that resistance did not help, and that protection and the rhythm of regular food might be a good thing.

"The worst part is that I won't see you again for a while, but I've heard reports that the Americans are steadily coming closer and will rescue us. Then we will be together again."

Jan had just looked at him. How often had he heard him say this? He hoped it was true, but he didn't believe it. He said nothing. In his heart, he knew it wasn't true, and he suspected it might take much longer. Their future was more uncertain than ever. He didn't often agree with his mother and was at odds with her on many subjects, but he shared her opinion that they should never have gone to the Dutch East Indies. "Then we would have been in Holland now, with our own family! Rather there than here! Anything is better than here!"

# Father Jaan Willem

*December 2, 1942*

There were all kinds of rumors at Fort Vredeburg. All white prisoners were summoned to appear before a Japanese officer on Monday, December 7: not the Indo-Europeans but only the white prisoners. There was a lot of speculation about this summons. Some thought they might be released. Still others reported that they would be taken to a labor camp.

Resignedly, everyone stood around the officer, who looked at them with an amiable smile. He began his speech in Japanese. An interpreter translated into Malay.

"It has pleased His Majesty the Emperor to protect all white women and children. We will bring them all together in suitable camps. You don't have to worry about them, because we'll take good care of them."

Everyone looked around in confusion. When the white men were imprisoned, it was expressly promised that the women and children would be left untouched. With this announcement, that was reversed.

"If you have questions, you may ask them, but only in Malay," added the interpreter. A few asked a question and reminded the Japanese of the promise made earlier, to which the Japanese officer reacted angrily.

Without emotion, the interpreter passed on the answer: "Don't you want them to be safe? To guarantee their safety, it is better that we put them together and have them guarded. You can't trust the Javanese. We cannot assure their safety if we do not place them in the *Tangsi*

*Perlindoengan,* the protection camps. Under our guard, they will be safe."

Everyone became quiet. There was no sense in angering the Japanese with protests or questions. There was no choice.

That evening, Johanna went to the fence to talk to Jaan about it.

"What you say is true, Jaan. We have received a call to prepare for departure. We will be locked up in prison camps."

"Protection camps, Johanna. We heard from the officer today. It is for your protection," and he repeated what he had heard that morning.

"What should I do with our things? Do you know where we are going; did they say that too?"

He couldn't answer her questions and she left uncertain about the future. A few days later, Johanna reported that a Japanese officer had visited their home and had indicated which items she could take. They had to label the rest. "They say they will store everything for us until this is all over and everyone can return home."

Although neither one of them believed it, they told each other that they were glad. "Maybe it will all work out in the end."

In the days that followed, Johanna brought him all kinds of things, ranging from his leather briefcase to diapers. The diapers came in handy, as a towel or as a panel to reinforce the back of his threadbare shirt. At first he didn't know what to do with his leather briefcase, but later it turned out that he could use the leather in many ways. He re-soled his shoes and cut leather clog straps which, in turn, he could sell for sixty cents each. Johanna told him that a friendly Chinese family had taken care of his harmonium and their bicycles. As a thank you, they had a basket of Indian dishes brought.

Just before Christmas, they said goodbye. The moment had come for his loved ones to leave. At the fence, there were heartbreaking scenes. Then they walked away from him, and the image of his weeping wife, his three sons of sixteen, fifteen, and fourteen, the twin daughters of eleven, and the youngest daughter of four, would remain with him for a long time.

"My God," he prayed, "I must not doubt your grace. I hereby surrender my wife and children to Your care and love. If there be anyone who can take better care of them than I can, then You are the one."

His mouth spoke this prayer. But in his mind, he thought otherwise.

# Mother

What does one take along to a place of uncertainty? What does this person take? At the meetings where the Japanese gave us details about our new life and in which the future was presented as a ridiculously rosy one, lists were distributed, stating what was allowed. For days, sighing and worrying, I sat among my things. How difficult it was to keep thinking practically. What do you need for a stay at an unknown place? The list was clear: household goods, such as beds, linens, pans, dishes, clothing—all items necessary for a longer stay elsewhere.

But it was nowhere near enough. How about sewing supplies, important documents (you couldn't leave them unattended anyway), photos, jewelry (the precious bracelet with matching earrings that I had received from Jaan on the occasion of our pewter anniversary in 1935, as a symbol of a new start, in the hope that our love would gain strength). My indecision didn't make it any easier. Which clothes? What kind of weather would we encounter? How long would we be gone? All sorts of things passed through my hands; I kept sorting, and new and smaller piles kept forming.

All those things had given me security, and had previously helped me to accept the situation. I must admit that ultimately, I became quite integrated into life here. Then came the moment when nothing else could be removed. This was it. What was lying there, came along. When Gerard saw it, he immediately began to grumble. It was too much. How would it be transported? Had I thought of that? As if he were talking to a child. No, I hadn't thought about that. But no matter what, this was going along; it had to work. An unexpected moment of determination.

"Many hands make light work," was my firm answer. I heard my mother say it. What could not go along, I considered lost.

Four days before our departure, the boys are already bringing the heavy stuff to Lempoejangan station. They had arranged the use of a delivery bicycle, God knows how. They are good, independent boys. On the street, for a long time I check the delivery bicycle piled high with goods. Where will we find our things? Will we find them again? How will this work out? I am closer to crying than laughing.

When they are gone, the house at 2 Sindorolaan feels like an empty shell. The image of disrupted order, the order I am specifically so fond of, unsettles me. Strangely enough, only the sight of our luggage—the suitcases and bags in the hallway, ready for departure—provides peace of mind.

All over the neighborhood, groups of women are talking, gesticulating, and chattering restlessly. But what is there to talk about? Do I have to let all the rumors drive me crazy? About Japanese raging like beasts, raping women and girls, and many more awful reports? I can't yield to these rumors. I don't want to know. My thoughts drift to Driebergen. How is it over there? With Father, Mother? War in the Netherlands. A little while ago, Mother had written that there is relatively little fighting. How would her family be now? Is it still quiet there? I don't want to think about anything happening to them. Can anyone actually explain to me why they are there, and I am here?

I feel someone tugging at my dress. It's Annie.

"My little one, *Mama* had almost forgotten you."

"*Mama*, don't be angry. "

"Hey, what? Angry? Why should *Mama* be angry?"

"Annie sweet."

"Yes, Annie is sweet." Her bottom lip sticks out and I know immediately that she has soiled her pants. Unusual, because she has been toilet-trained for a long time. It must be the situation. She also has trouble sleeping through the night. Anyway, no time for further reflection.

"I can see it; it's okay, honey; a little accident. It can happen. We'll do something about it." With her little fist in my hand, we walk to the bathroom. My happy little girl. Barely four years old, and so much tension around her. The rotten war. How will things go in the future? Come on, first clean up. I must keep myself in check, and not speculate now about the future.

Until our departure, some nerve-racking, anxious days remain. I allow myself as little emotion as possible, but my tears fall unchecked. I am afraid, withdrawn. I don't want to feel this way; I shut myself off. I don't know how we got food on the table, by God. I do remember that our boys had a warm meal with our friends at Hotel Mataram, on the way back from seeing their father at Fort Vredeburg, where they had brought him some food. When they got home, I heard one of the boys, I think Gerard, say that Father is worried about me.

"Your mother can't handle all this. You must take good care of her." So, it seems that's what he said. True or not, I can't get those words out of my mind. How can Jaan say that? I'm here, right? Is this situation not living proof that I can indeed handle it? I survived the *fait accompli* or done deal with which Jaan presented me. Not wholeheartedly, but nonetheless. Even if I gave in to my inability to intervene (I just can't act), you don't hear me talk about it. I keep silent. Jaan doesn't understand. Jaan doesn't understand me. Do I understand it myself? Who am I really?

# Jan

*Early December 1942*

They had to make choices about what to take and what to store. He had seen his mother moving and sorting beds, bedding, a cupboard, a small table, clothes, some crockery, a few pans, and personal belongings such as papers, photo albums, and jewelry. Those things weren't on the list. Not taking them along was not an option, and that also applied to the little money that was left.

Jan found it difficult to choose, and kept moving things back and forth. Will go, won't go, will go, won't go. At last he seemed to know and packed his toys that he couldn't take with him. He had no faith in the "storage," and wanted to prevent his valuables from falling into the hands of strangers, so he hid them in the farthest *goedang* of the outbuildings, in the attic of the servants' bathroom. Nobody knew about that place he had discovered on one of his explorations of the house. He resolved to gather all his things when the war ended.

Finally, they got their date of departure: Sunday, December 27, 1942, right after Christmas. On Wednesday, December 23, they brought their belongings on a flat cart to the station in Lempoejangan. The rest of their belongings had to be left behind. Contrary to the promise of storage, it became the property of the new leaders "in exchange for the shelter and food they would receive in the protection camp."

The Christmas days that followed were spent in an empty house. Nothing indicated that it was Christmas.

# Mother

*Sunday, December 27, 1942*

This morning the streets are flooded with people. Children, Dutch women, Indonesian women (who are married to Dutch men), all on their way to Lempoejangan station. The children see it as a great adventure and run after each other, crisscrossing the crowd. But I really don't want them to do this, so fearful of losing them. And mind you, we have our hands full: Aafje and Willie have the evacuation bags, the boys carry the suitcases fastened with belts. Heavy as lead, but if they become too heavy, they can be dragged along by those belts.

On my right arm, I have Annie, strangely asleep in all the excitement and confusion. A bag hangs from my left arm. I can't carry any more than that. Since it is quickly growing warmer, I put my wide-brimmed sun hat on Annie's head for protection.

It is fortunate that we were able to obtain a vehicle, so that we don't have to walk the whole distance. Via Mataram Boulevard, where our friends run the hotel, we pass the swimming pool. My stomach tightens. Will we ever come back here? We ride past the Mohammedan orphanage where stones are thrown at us. Many Javanese are standing along the road. Many hostile looks. Sensitive as I am to their reactions—aren't we still friendly nations? —I keep every friendly gesture in my heart.

When we arrive at the station square, there is a flurry of activity. Armed Japanese soldiers and indigenous police have cordoned off the area. Here, too, are many Javanese behind barriers to watch the departure of the white people. Again, hostile looks, which I just can't get used to. How is this sudden about-face possible? Most of them just watch. Are they afraid of the occupying force? How do they view their former female employers?

Suddenly, out of nowhere, our *kokkie*—cook— appears and quickly presses a loaf of bread into my hands. She looks at me with tearful eyes, says nothing and just disappears again. Although I am standing in the sun, I feel cold. A lump in my throat, congealed tears from last night, make it difficult to swallow.

The station grounds are now filling up with women and children from everywhere. Children start to cry and ask for water. But there is almost no water left. Trusting that the Japanese would provide food and drink, many women have set aside their frugality and, on the way, allowed children to drink to their hearts' content, and even to snack. The crying scares me. Where is the promised care? But I force myself to stop. Don't think about this now, I encourage myself. Are you afraid? You aren't the only one. I do my best not to show it.

As usual, Piet takes the lead. He urges us to hurry; we must get checked off the list. The sooner, the better, because then we have the best chance of a seat on the train. Number J-185 reports. We are successful.

Do you hear the shouting of the Japanese soldiers? I just can't get used to it. We're sweaty, stuffing the luggage into the racks. We sit. Never thought that I'd be so happy with a seat on the train.

The train leaves slowly. We leave behind everything we know. Through the windows, we see women at work in the rice fields. How enviable. The heat and the monotonous sound of the wheels are numbing. The boys are standing on the outside balcony. They regularly let us know where we are. I don't really care. We're heading north; what difference does it make? Past the twin volcanoes Merbaboe and Merapi, the mountain of fire, one of the most active in the world. The last major eruption was in 1930, when volcanic material was heaved up more than a kilometer and a half. Then barely six months in Java, I was deeply impressed by it. Thirteen villages destroyed, almost fourteen hundred people killed, and many evacuees. But what about that? Now it is the Japanese who are active, and we are the evacuees. Look, residents of the camps wave to us. Some even make the V-sign.

There is singing on the train. *"En van je hela, hola, houd er de moed maar in*, take heart..." Unwavering, as if to ward off fate, they start song after song. *"En wat doen we met Soekarno, als hij komt, als hij komt?"* "And what do we do with Sukarno, when he comes, when he comes?" *"Als de moed er uit is, dan pompen we hem d'r in, pompen we hem d'r in, pompen we hem d'r in..."* "If our courage is gone, then we'll pump it in..."

The train stops in Magelang. Is this where we need to be? No, we may not get off. We all have to use the toilet; the toilets on the train are clogged; there is no toilet paper; the children whine because their pants are wet. No Japanese soldier in sight. We have to continue, presumably towards Ambarawa. Next, we take a bus. We arrive at the plateau of Ambarawa; we arrive in Banjoe Biroe and stop at a rejected barracks. On the other side of the road, we see the high, depressing walls of the large prison for Javanese. From the shouting of the Japanese

74

soldiers, we conclude that this is our destination. The rejected KNIL barracks will be our camp. It doesn't really look like a protection camp; why doesn't that surprise me? We follow the people in front of us. Number J-185 has arrived.

I am dead tired, almost succumb to the heat. I'm afraid of the barbed wire.

Through the gate, we enter the grounds, as if we were going through a dark tunnel. We have to put all our bags on the ground and may not touch them.

The waiting has begun.

# Jan

*December 27, 1942*

Jan and his family had slept restlessly, tense with anticipation of their departure. Nobody knew where they were going. Jan, who had slept next to his mother, had heard her sigh and cry softly all night. He had noticed that he was more annoyed than sorry for her. His irritation was exacerbated because she was more attentive to the girls than to the boys. She wasn't much concerned about them either. Piet had taken over that task, and kept Gerard and Jan under his wing, although both were very independent and found their own way in the crowd.

Jan thought it was an exciting and adventurous idea: the journey by train to an unknown place. He was very curious and kept a close eye on everything, impatient, awaiting their departure. He felt watched, especially by all the native Javanese who had thronged to the station to observe the departure of the whites. Japanese and indigenous policemen kept them at a distance and had cordoned off the yard with crush barriers. There were also pastors there. They did not have to be interned. He saw Pastor Rullman talking to his mother. She had been crying again and was seeking comfort from the pastor. He spoke to her intently.

"What are they talking about?" asked Gerard.

Piet replied, "I think he wants to comfort her and maybe he has another message from Father. We won't be seeing him again for a while."

While he spoke, Jan noticed that there was not much emotion involved. He looked sidelong at Piet, but little could be read from his face.

"Come," Piet said, beckoning them to walk with him, "we have to report at those tables." He gestured to his mother, who came quickly. "We have to report, otherwise we will have no seats."

At the table, Piet gave their names and their internment number, which were checked off a list. Then they received the signal that they could board the train. They could sit wherever they liked. Immediately upon entering the train, they took seats on three benches. They put their hand baggage in the racks above their heads, and then they waited for the train, puffing at the platform, to leave.

Finally, commands were given, and the platform was deserted. The whistle sounded, the steam locomotive hissed, and the train slowly began to move. They headed towards Magelang, but they didn't know if this was their destination.

"If we go to Magelang, then we aren't so far away. That is only forty kilometers," said Piet.

"Who says we're going there? We won't know until we are there," responded Gerard moodily. Since Jan had no desire to talk to his mother, brothers, and sisters, he had walked to the balcony of the train. There it was deliciously cool with the wind blowing around his ears. At first he still saw the familiar neighborhoods of Djokja, and when they had passed them, the train ran parallel to the road to Magelang. In front of him to the right, he saw the silhouettes of the twin volcano Merbaboe and Merapi. To the left, the *sawas*—rice fields—and *dessas*—villages—

were shimmering in the hot sun. Near the *kampongs*—native areas—groups of native Javanese were waving, and some made the V sign with two fingers. It did him good because it showed that not all native Javanese were happy with their departure.

Jan re-entered the train car and told them what he had seen. He was unable to lift the somber mood. The whining of children and crying of babies made it no better. Here and there he saw groups of people busy talking to each other; in other corners people were silently staring into space. Everyone was trapped in his or her own grief, with his or her own questions.

When they arrived at Magelang, hoping to disembark there, they were prompted to stay seated. For a long time, the train stood still in the hot sun and the temperature in the train cars continued to rise. Jan and Gerard walked to the outside balcony because it was cooler there, and they could also take a better look at what was happening. The locomotive was disconnected and replaced by a cogwheel locomotive.

"We're going into the mountains." Jan nudged his brother excitedly.

"Then we'll go to Ambarawa!"

"How do you know that? We can go anywhere, right?"

"No, because then they wouldn't need that cogwheel locomotive. We are going into the mountains and that means Ambarawa!"

He said it so firmly and looked so certain that Jan had to believe him.

And indeed, in the course of the afternoon they arrived in the small garrison town of Ambarawa. Jan had never been there. The train came to a screeching halt. The small platform was teeming with Japanese soldiers and indigenous police, forming a cordon around the station to prevent any of the passengers from daring to escape. For at least twenty minutes they sat in the stationary train, until a Japanese soldier gestured for them to get out. Between a hedge of soldiers, they were led to waiting buses.

"We're going even farther!" muttered Piet, looking around to see if they were all still together. For the last hour, Jan's mother hadn't spoken, and she looked frightened.

Mother, Piet, Gerard, Aafje, Willie, Annie, and Jan were the last to board a bus. Behind them, the door was slammed shut, and the bus left immediately. They barely had time to take care of their luggage. They rode through the old town, at one point passing a complex of barracks where they saw women and children walking around. They drove past and left Ambarawa behind. The ride was not long, at most five or six kilometers until they arrived in a hamlet called Banjoe Biroe. It turned out to be a barracks with only a few houses around it. It was near Rawan Bening, an immense swamp area surrounded by low mountains. They saw white buildings completely walled. The bus passed through a large gate. It was an old, rejected KNIL barracks, which had been given a new function.

Not until they got out of the bus did they see the size of their group: more than three hundred women and children. Mother and the girls were assigned a room in Block 1. The boys were housed in a boys' ward, near the kitchen. They were pleasantly surprised that their furniture had also arrived. This allowed them to settle into their new accommodations. First, Piet helped his mother and the girls, while Gerard and Jan arranged a little bit of their place as best they could. They had to share the space with other boys their age. The mattresses and their own things they had brought made it feel like home.

At the end of the day, they found each other to share experiences. The girls chatted excitedly about their room while Mother was still sadly staring into space. In a fatherly manner, Piet spoke to her: "Mother, you have to make the best of it and have faith."

The next day, Jan and his brothers "went to explore," as they told their mother. The girls pushed to be allowed to come along, but Piet declined. "When we've seen everything and know how things work here, we can show you around. The three of us will go first."

They discovered that the camp consisted of eight stone, whitewashed barracks, four wooden and bamboo sheds, and a guardhouse. A few hundred yards from their camp, they found a large building. It turned out to be a high-walled prison that was not yet in use. When they had arrived the day before, everything looked small-scale. In the months that followed, the number of internees would rise above four thousand because the Japanese had calculated that a space of 45 centimeters per person on the shared "bed of planks" was enough.

At the beginning, life in the camp seemed to be okay. This was because the number of internees was still reasonable in proportion to the available space, and there was initially enough food. However, as the number of internees rose, without a corresponding increase in the amount of food, the fare became scarcer and had to be shared and rationed.

Jan and his brothers were housed in a separate wing of the camp. There the older boys supervised and were in charge. Later that task was taken over by older men, often former KNIL soldiers. Sometimes clergy. The rule was that when a boy turned seventeen, he was transferred to a men's camp. That also happened to Piet when he reached that age in January 1943. On his birthday, along with a number of other boys of that age, he was transferred to camp Djoen Eng in Salatiga, about five kilometers east of Banjoe Biroe. Another year later, Gerard, as the second of the family, was also transferred to that camp.

Jan had to adjust to the camp. Everyone was too close together and there was not a shred of privacy. At home they had had their own room with their own things. Here it was one big dormitory where they remained in close proximity. As much as possible, he tried to stay outside of the barracks. Although he didn't find what he was looking for there either: space. He found the high fence the most oppressive. The fence around the camp was built on a wall. On top of that was a high barbed wire fence. And standing against it was a bamboo fence, making it impossible to see anything outside of the camp. The outside world was completely closed off, except for the holes in the fence where trade with the native Javanese took place. That's why he had no idea what was going on in the outside world and had to depend on the stories of others.

Most of the camp commanders were Japanese officers. These changed regularly and so did their behavior. There were "friendly" people among them, but most were aggressive, cruel, and strict, and some were even extremely cruel and had no qualms about getting their way by force. Beating, kicking, and issuing burdensome

81

community service were the order of the day. Because the Japanese guards were required in military operations, they were gradually replaced by militant native youths, the *heiho* soldiers, who had been trained by the Japanese. Not only in guarding, but especially in aggression. Their equipment consisted of a wooden rifle, soon the butt of jokes by the camp inmates, who were immediately punished by a beating with said wooden rifle; that made the prisoners more cautious. Every week there were bayonet exercises that were dangerous and real. There was loud and aggressive shouting to impress and to arouse fear.

The one who made the biggest impression on Jan was a small, hateful Javanese, who could invade a barracks at the most unexpected moments, sometimes in the middle of the night. Then everyone was chased outside and had to line up at the assembly point in anticipation of one of his infamous speeches.

"You white people have enslaved us for three hundred years and let us do all kinds of dirty chores. You have plundered our land and taken advantage of our girls in order to live in beautiful pavilions and houses yourselves. We had to do all the dirty jobs for you while we were exploited and considered inferior! We will now rectify that by punishing and exploiting you. We will punish you for what has been done to us. We will cut off limbs and use your women and girls. We'll make them scream so loudly that the wild animals of the valley will be silent."

He carried on until foam appeared around his mouth, and dead tired, with bloodshot eyes, ordered everyone back into the barracks. Then we had to be careful to avoid being beaten with bamboo sticks. Everyone was terrified of those punishments because they were unpredictable and occurred at the most unusual moments. Later, Jan heard that women had indeed been abused and beaten, so he asked his mother and sisters if it had happened to them too.

"Fortunately not, Jan, and I try to do everything I can to prevent it. But it is definitely happening around us."

And if one of the girls had disappeared from her sight, his mother would almost panic and ordered Jan to look for her.

When he found her, he scolded her for running away. "You have to stay near me! Otherwise, I can't protect you!"

Then the girls glared at him. "You go on your own too, don't you?"

How could he explain that it was different for boys?

"That's because we're boys; they don't do anything to us. For girls, it is too dangerous to go out alone. If you want to wander through the camp, ask me and I'll go with you."

However, the speeches of the little Javanese sowed seeds of doubt in Jan. Until the occupation, the Dutch had ruled a country that was not theirs. It belonged to the Javanese. He asked his mother, who responded, "It's the Dutch East Indies, isn't it, Jan, and then it's ours, isn't it?"

"And when we weren't here three hundred years ago? Whose was it then?"

"Yes, it was their land then; we conquered it."

"Just as the Germans are doing now in the Netherlands?"

His mother looked at him and realized that Jan was no longer a little boy. He thought about things. She responded awkwardly. "Yes, if you put it that way, then you might be right. But that is now, and we have occupied the Dutch East Indies for three hundred years."

"But that doesn't make it any different, does it? It remains their land, that has been occupied by the Dutch. In their eyes, we don't belong here."

She looked at him and he saw sorrow in her eyes as she said softly, "I agree. We don't belong here. I have said that to your father so many times, but he thinks we have a duty here."

"What kind of duty? And if they don't want us..."

At that moment, their conversation was cut short by Annie calling him: "Jan, will you go for a little walk with me?"

He smiled. For a moment he had forgotten about the camp because of this domestic question. He looked at his mother and she nodded her head. Then he took Annie's hand and walked away with her.

# Father Jaan Willem

*February 1943*

They had to hand in their money. The order appeared in the camp. Everyone had to report. It was an order from the Japanese government that needed money for its war effort.

"We provide you with housing and food, and from now on, you have to pay for it. Hand in everything you have in one shot."

On that particular morning, all eight hundred prisoners reported and lined up in rows of four. There was a police force of at least two hundred men, who divided themselves among the prisoners. The transfer of the money could begin. Jaan stood in the front row and received a signal to hand over his money. He took his wallet and let a guilder and twenty-one cents drop and roll on the ground, instead of giving them to a soldier. When he moved to put his wallet away, it was snatched from his hands by an officer, who then managed to shake out a two-and-a-half guilder note. In addition, a newspaper clipping fell from his wallet, drawing more attention from the officer than the bill. On one side was a crossword puzzle and on the other side something that he didn't understand. He turned the document over several times, and then handed it back to Jaan, who breathed a sigh of relief. On the back of the newspaper clipping was the Queen's radio address, which she had given when the Dutch East Indies declared war on Japan. Jaan looked around and saw that many of the prisoners were fooling the Japanese by not surrendering all their money.

With money, you could buy extras, food or clothing. No money meant you had to trade or exchange. After a while, the Japanese were done, and they could leave. Jaan knew someone who had hidden thirteen hundred guilders somewhere and advised him to hide the money in a ball of clay, but the man didn't do it. Everyone who had turned in money received a receipt from the Japanese on presentation of which one could withdraw fifteen guilders from the Japanese bank every month. In turn, you could use that to order something from the city. However, Jaan missed out on this because the amount they had taken from him was less than ten guilders. When Jaan objected, he was reprimanded. He shouldn't whine.

"Look at everything we do for you. Rather be grateful." With that message, he got a hard slap in the face for insulting the Japanese. The officer also pricked him in the stomach with a samurai sword. The warning was clear, and Jaan stopped talking, bowed before the Japanese, bade him farewell, and left. Punishments were meted out arbitrarily, often dependent on the mood of the Japanese. Jaan had to learn to stay in the background and adhere to the instructions, whether they were reasonable or not.

# Mother

**March 1943**

This morning at roll call they were at it again. Naturally, it had to do with the constant and repetitive bowing; it makes me sick. And you never get it right. If you bow at a 30-degree angle, it should be 45 degrees. If you bow at a 45-degree angle, it should be 90 degrees. Today I bow only halfway; it looks more like a nod; I think that's good enough. So, I bow a little. Aafje, who is standing next to me and has noticed that the *hei-ho* has his eye on me, urges in a barely audible whisper, "Try to bow a little deeper, *Mama*; otherwise you will be beaten."

But my body refuses. Everything that I have, again and again, admonished my children to do—take care that you don't attract attention, do what they tell you to do; I disregard it all. All the commands and the rules: bowing to every Japanese soldier, bowing to the *hei-ho's*, counting correctly in Japanese—*"ichi-ni-san-shi-go-roku-shichi-hachi-kyuu-juu,"* which often goes wrong and has to be repeated, making no sound during roll call; it doesn't stop. The *hei-ho*, a real flea bag, kicks me with the point of his boots and hits me in the face. He pushes me to the front, where I stand erect in front of him, a head taller than he is.

*"Saikeirei!"*—"Bow!"—he roars, taking a bamboo stick in hand. So, bowing down to apologize, from the hips, that is, with your back straight, I'm ready for the flogging. Even my calves are covered with red welts. For punishment, kneeling with hands behind my back and a sharp bamboo board between my thighs and calves, I have

87

to sit in the hot sun for two hours. A momentary lack of control. It could have been worse, but I don't regret it. Something in me took over. The lyrics of the melody being sung in the camp come to mind. *"Hei-ho,*sit on the pot, the pot falls over, *hei-ho* completely twisted."* Really distasteful, and I never sing along with it, until now. Inaudible to the rest. The constant attempt to keep me on a short leash, and to enforce commands and prohibitions, has summoned up resistance. No regrets, rather a little bit of pride. And besides, I'm used to punishment from home.

Lack of respect for the *Tenno Heika,* the Heavenly Emperor, lack of respect for my father, lack of respect for the *hancho,* the commander, for the teacher, for Jaan. What's the difference? Just a moment of rebellion, meaningless right? Why now? Why here? No chance of success. I can't win.

*Tidak boléh,* it's forbidden. *Tidak boléh* this, *tidak boléh* that. Gatherings are no longer allowed. No contact with the opposite sex. Evening devotions are discouraged. Singing is no longer allowed. Roll call twice a day. If you are absent without good reason, punishment will follow. And then the screaming. There's another raging Japanese soldier standing on a wooden box, yelling in that short, tight, staccato language. A blow with the butt of his rifle on the chest should strengthen everything. Ridiculously normal.

Pay attention.

While standing, place your little finger on the skirt seam.

If you see a Japanese, give a signal to the others. When he approaches, bow 30 degrees: *Keirei.* If you hear *Naore,* the bowing is over, but stay standing. Only with *Jasmé* is it all finished. The same ritual every time. And there is always something lacking, culminating in a punishing chore or a beating.

My strategy is not to be noticed. If you are not seen, then you can't be punished. But the boys play pranks, pass a guard with a whole group at a time, stop abruptly and loudly break wind. I warn Jan to be careful. "Don't make them angry. Don't say anything, don't look. Avoid them as much as possible. Be careful."

As a rule, I do exactly what needs to be done, on automatic pilot. A hundred times past a guard post. Bow a hundred times. Sometimes ten times, just as long as the Japanese thinks it necessary. Today is an exception. I can hardly tolerate hearing the word "forbidden" anymore.

Another thing: the clandestine trade, the *kedèkken*, the exchange of goods at the fence. The item of clothing you can spare for eggs, the gold jewelry for a bunch of bananas; you have to, the food from the kitchen is not enough. It was still always tolerated. They turned a blind eye, but suddenly it is forbidden. When the latest threat was carried out the first time—the clothing would be ripped off and the offender shaved in public—we were forced to watch. We felt powerless. With a bayonet, a soldier tore the clothing off her body, took a pair of scissors, and cut the hair roughly, leaving only irregular tufts. The woman was injured. Her green eyes, continuing to follow the soldier, didn't blink. What a heroine.

She demonstrates that all the rules, commands, and prohibitions do not turn us into exemplary camp detainees. She had that courage. But I don't have that courage.

I close my eyes, try to shut out the world, and cease my resistance.

# Jan

*May 1943*

It took Jan a while to discover who was in charge of the camp. In his eyes, everyone in uniform was in charge until he discovered that the camp had a commander. He was the one who made the rules. Since the commanders often changed, the rules changed with them. Still, he rarely saw the commander because much was delegated to the internees. Often, the oldest internee or the one with the most influence was appointed as the camp chief, who, supported by the block chiefs, was in charge of some barracks or dormitories. The surveillance and supervision of the implementation of the regulations were in the hands of the Javanese or Japanese guards. Everything the camp chief presented actually came from the commander, and if the camp chief did not do what the commander demanded, then the camp chief was easily pushed aside for another.

The position of camp chief had certain advantages, such as better housing, but above all, more food. And that was the reason why the camp chiefs were stricter than some guards. Moreover, compromising between the wishes of the internees and the demands of the Japanese didn't make the task of the camp chief any easier. This was an additional reason for being stricter, causing some to be hated by the prisoners. Still, the guards were not outrageous in their interpretation of the rules, so that every day in the camp was a challenge to avoid punishment, especially for boys like Jan who tended not to take the rules too seriously.

His mother could warn him every day to be careful, but every day new rules were added. Everyone in the barracks kept his eyes and ears open and informed the others of what he had seen and heard. If you didn't know the new rules, or if you didn't follow them to the guard's specifications, you were punished with caning, intimidation, incarceration, and even deprivation of food. Sometimes such a punishment was also collectively imposed, in which case an entire barrack was given no food for a day.

One camp chief made a deep and frightening impression on Jan. That was the strict Mrs. Van Riessen. She always wore a white tropical dress, had snow-white hair, and wore glasses. Hygiene was very important not only to the Japanese but also to her. Sometimes, she suddenly stood in front of you, checking for cleanliness. Despite all the boys' cleaning and polishing, she could explode terribly: "Do you think this is clean? Do you really think this is clean? I wouldn't want to keep pigs in here. Do it again! And if it isn't clean when I come back, then all of you will be punished, and I don't mean a few strokes of the cane, no, real punishment!"

Then she strode out of the barracks, and everyone began to fetch water quickly and polish everything again. When there was still enough water, the boys didn't have too much trouble; later the bullying started. Even though there was less water, extensive cleaning still had to be done. This was short-lived, because as the water continued to be rationed, the attention to cleaning lapsed. And then other matters came under scrutiny. Together with the block chiefs, the so-called *hanchous,* recognizable by two red stripes on a badge, Mrs. Van Riessen formed the daily camp administration responsible for what happened in the camp. Besides the *hanchous,* there were also the *kumichos,* the elders of the camp, who could be recognized by a badge with one red stripe.

At the beginning of their internment, the portions of food were reasonable. Due to the increase in the number of prisoners, and the fact that the total amount of food remained the same, the individual portions became smaller. What you could do without, you could always exchange at the gate with indigenous people who were eager to sell or trade for textiles. Near the guardhouse was a small shop where the nice Mrs. Cohen held sway. For beans and money, you could get your hands on soap or candy. Eggs, milk, and bouillon were scarce commodities and were saved, as much as possible, for small children and the sick. Meat and fresh fruit were very difficult to obtain and were rarely distributed.

The assortment of vegetables consisted of *sawi,* a sort of endive, cabbage, and *krot,* a kind of purslane. The staple was *ketelah,* an indigenous cabbage crop, albeit of the worst kind. For breakfast, everyone was given just a ladle of rice gruel supplemented with coconut milk, and at noon they received a cup of rice with a scoop of vegetables and very rarely a small piece of meat. Sometimes there was a scoop of brown beans. In any case, you did not get enough, so that the feeling of hunger grew by the day. Everyone lost weight and gradually became malnourished.

Jan was regularly chosen for work assignments. His task was to walk through the camp, to beat on a tin can with an iron bar, and then, loudly, to call the blocks to come and eat. He had to be careful not to call them too soon or too late. If it was too soon, everyone started to push each other where the food was distributed. If it was too late, the kitchen crew was angry that the line was not moving. The more he did this, the more Jan developed a good rhythm that satisfied everyone. He always tried to get work assignments, because then you regularly got extra food. Distributing food, a task that everyone was given from time to time, was a thankless job. The one who handed out the food was always blamed for giving too little. The trick was to give an equal share to each person, in such a way, that at the end, you did not run out of food. Otherwise, you would have to say that the food was gone, which meant that the person standing in front of you had nothing to eat. You could never do it right. The consolation was that if someone received nothing one day, he was the first in line the next day, and then someone else would leave with an empty plate or with just a scrap of food.

You yourself had to cook your food on an *angelo,* a small Indonesian stove made of baked clay and heated with *arang,* or charcoal. Extra food was obtained illegally, by *kawatten,* trading with the indigenous population, for textiles or clothing. With a little luck, you could get hold of coconut oil in which to fry. *Kawatten* was officially forbidden and was severely punished with a horrible beating with a stick. Nevertheless, everyone did it when it got dark. A beating was taken for granted in exchange for some food.

To amuse himself, Jan and other boys of his age made catapults to shoot fruit and animals from the sky.

There were also corrupt guards who eagerly participated in the barter trade, often for their own benefit. They always charged commission in return for their negotiation.

With the increasing number of prisoners, the individual rations steadily decreased.

The first time Jan had kitchen duty, he received an extra bowl of rice from a certain Maartje. That was a feast because, for once, he could eat until he was full. He discovered that he, as kitchen help, was allowed to scrape the rice remaining at the bottom of the pans. This food became so sought after that new rules were introduced for it. The food from the bottom of the pan, often burnt, was still so nutritious that you gladly ate it. It was soaked off with water and eaten or taken away as much as possible. He couldn't please his mother and sisters more than with these scrapings. As the scourge of hunger grew steadily worse, people began to catch and eat stray dogs, the *kampongladakkers*. The Indonesian Agatha snail—slug— was also secretly eaten, extra popular because of the protein. Officially, you had to take it to the kitchen for the sick people. Jan often felt guilty after he had eaten one, because that meant that a sick fellow human being was being deprived. Still, if he got the chance, his hunger overcame his conscience.

If you were lucky, you could work a small piece of ground to cultivate tomatoes, beans, or *kangkong,* a kind of spinach. You had to be vigilant to prevent others from running off with your crop.

Naturally, food was stolen, exchanged, bought, and smuggled. People who did the heavy physical labor, such as carrying, nursing, and maintenance, often received a double portion. Yet everyone was hungry. For Jan and his family, there was rarely, if ever, enough to eat, and the tiny bit of food they did get did not satisfy their hunger. It only made it worse.

Jan saw mothers looking around desperately as their children cried with hunger, powerless to get more, powerless to give their children more. Knowing that you would be hungry tonight, tomorrow, the day after tomorrow, all week, a month, the next year, was the worst of all.

In fact, food became so scarce that tapioca flour—made from cassava and used as a binding agent—began to be distributed for breakfast. Everyone got a wooden spoonful. Sometimes you got some squeezed-out grated coconut or *goela djawa*—a kind of brown sugar—added. At noon you got the rice ration, just a small spoonful, and in the evening tapioca flour again, sometimes with *krokot* leaves. Then it was soup. Everyone ate it eagerly; it remained food, but it fed and did not fill. Jan saw only skinny people who started to look more miserable by the day.

"You know what I'm in the mood for?" asked Gerard. "What?"

"In a big plate of sauerkraut with bacon and sausage!"

"Yes! And then semolina pudding with butter and cinnamon in a soup bowl!"

"And then we'll go and get an ice cream at the corner for one cent!"

"You treat, Jan; I already paid yesterday!"

They laughed and felt better for a moment. It was a favorite subject to talk about. People told each other great stories about what they were going to eat once they were released from the camp. Conversations about food didn't just kill time, but also, if only for a fraction of a minute, took the hunger away.

Recipes were written down and exchanged. Stories about home, what was being eaten at the time, circulated in the camp, and some people knew how to present it even more beautifully than others. They filled imaginary tables with an abundance of dishes, after which they usually made their way to their wooden beds (or slats) to dream on, to feel a little better, and to forget their empty stomachs for the night.

# Father Jaan Willem

*April 1943*

There was excitement in the camp. Nobody understood what was going on. It was rumored that they would be released. That rumor had reached Jaan's ears too, and he silently thanked God for liberation and for showing the Japanese that people cannot be locked up in a camp against their will.

At the morning roll call, the camp commander came out personally. Normally you never saw him because he left all the chores to his men. People looked at each other. If he came to tell it himself, it must be special news. Jaan's heart pounded with the excitement. The commander raised his hand in the air, and everyone looked at him expectantly. Then he began his speech in Japanese, which no one understood. After a few minutes, he looked at the interpreter delivering his message in Malay.

"Today is April 29, the birthday of the Holy Emperor of Japan, the Tenno Heika. The emperor has decided that on the occasion of his birthday, he will release one hundred Indo-European prisoners. These will be designated later. They may pack their things and leave."

Buzzing erupted among the prisoners. The Indo-European prisoners became excited by this announcement, and the white European prisoners looked at each other in disappointment. After the hundred lucky ones were appointed, the morning roll call was over. Among the fortunate ones was a man Jaan had befriended during their imprisonment. Jaan found him at the place where he slept and congratulated him on his release.

The man did not seem happy, and that surprised Jaan.

"Aren't you happy?"

"Of course, but also sad that you have to stay. It's not fair!"

"War is never fair. I am happy for you and you will see that our liberation will not be long in coming either. The Japanese will never keep this up."

"I don't think so either. You're right. Is there anything I can do for you once I'm out of the camp?"

"If you are willing, I'll give you a letter for my wife. Then I can write her how I am doing. The cards we receive from time to time don't have enough space to write anything. On top of that, they are censored, so anything you write is a lie."

The man told him to write his letter quickly and to give it to him during the day. He would leave at the end of the day. "I'll see if I can find her."

Jaan hurried to the place where he slept, picked up a pen and paper and wrote a long letter to Johanna, which she would receive three months later.

That evening, Jaan retired to his "secret" spot. That day had clearly affected him and he felt himself sinking back into a feeling of listlessness and exhaustion. This morning had seemed to herald a joyous day, but it ended in a bitter disappointment. Now that he had written his letter to Johanna, it felt almost like a farewell. And although he had expressed hope that their liberation was imminent, he knew it wasn't. He was tired of hoping and waiting.

*Why had he chosen the Dutch East Indies? At least they would have been together at home in the Netherlands, whereas now, his family was separated. His dream of a beautiful life in the Dutch East Indies had turned into a nightmare. In his heart, he agreed with Johanna that they didn't belong here. There was nothing here that you couldn't find in the Netherlands. She was right that they would still have been with their family. He had gotten his own way, put her on the spot, almost forced her to go to a place where they didn't belong, and where they had found nothing but misery. A misery, the end of which was nowhere in sight, despite the encouraging words that he had written: keep trusting and hoping for God's help. Why had he written that if he no longer believed it himself? Why had he not been honest, and why had he not expressed his doubts? Perhaps that would have benefited her more than his lie and show of confidence.*

"Are you hiding here?"

Jaan was startled from his contemplation when he was interrupted by one of the few pastors imprisoned with him.

"I don't know anymore, pastor."

Without being asked, Jaan blurted out his doubts.

"Shouldn't I have been more honest with my wife, writing her my feelings? I feel like a traitor now, while I doubt if we'll ever see each other again."

The pastor looked at him, and Jaan was almost ashamed of his melancholy complaint. The pastor was no better off than he. He was just as emaciated as Jaan, and his wife and children were also somewhere else.

"You know, Jaan, doubt and self-pity are bad counselors. You wrote what was in your heart, and that is

100

good. Perhaps you will encourage your wife. In any case, she knows you are still alive and are fighting to survive. That will give her the strength to fight too, and not to give up."

Jaan looked at him. He hadn't looked at it that way.
"And you know, Jaan, if you've written it and you're not willing to keep fighting and holding on, then you are betraying her. You don't want that, do you? Hold on, and trust the deep strength within you. God really cannot do it alone. You will have to cooperate a bit and never give up."
At that, the pastor stood up and walked away. It was as if his words had brought relief to Jaan. Jaan felt his energy return.

*I must hold on and never give up, not just for myself but for her and our children. I cannot disappoint them.*

With a smile on his face, he got up and walked back to his barracks.

# Jan

*March 1943*

"You know what I don't understand?" whispered Jan one evening to his brother and a few more guys with whom they were hanging out.

"No, what?"

"How is it that most of us are losing weight because there is too little food, yet there are people who don't seem to be getting any thinner?"

Gerard and the others immediately looked around at the assembled people in the large field.

"Like that one over there?" pointed Erik. Gerard slapped him on the arm.

"Don't point, stupid; he'll know right away we're talking about him."

They kept their eyes on a well-fed person standing among them.

"Next to that one, there is another one; do you see that?" whispered Willem.

"Darn it, yes, you're right. How is that possible?"

"I think they are stealing food or being provided with extras by guards. Otherwise, how can it be?"

"There is only one way to find out," said Gerard. "We just have to keep an eye on those people for a few days to see what happens."

They agreed and divided the "heavier" people among themselves for observation.

"Do it in an inconspicuous way, okay? We are not interested in punishment!"

It was not just Jan who had noticed. Later in the day, he overheard others talking about it. He stayed away from the stupid ones. He didn't want to get involved in the backbiting, the gossip, the jealousy, envy and irritation. There was no point in paying attention to the issue if you didn't know what was going on, and that is what they were going to find out together. He thought it was quite exciting.

After several days, when they were back together, they exchanged their observations. It seemed that considerable numbers of people, including respectable folk, had turned to pilfering and bribery. In exchange for money, jewelry, or other things that could be traded, they arranged extra rations with guards. These rations were stolen from the kitchen by the guards at those moments when no one was working there. Sometimes it was also mothers who did it for their children, and one of the boys had even seen one of the women being touched by a guard under cover of darkness, in order to receive something extra.

On the other hand, there were prisoners who sacrificed themselves for the benefit of the young people.

Gerard said that he had seen an old man at the food distribution. He was very skinny and you would expect he needed food badly, but he called to the men who were distributing the food and said, "Give that to the boys. They still have their lives ahead of them! We already have much of it behind us."

"Did he really do that?" asked Jan, almost incredulous.

"Really! He denied himself for the sake of others."

That story made a big impression on Jan, who suddenly understood the meaning of sacrifice. In church, he had often heard the pastor speak about it and his father also used the word quite often. But he had never really understood what it meant, until now.

Eating patterns changed. Previously, people had dinner together, now each person separated himself from the others by going to a safe spot to prevent the food from being stolen from his plate. Preferably as close to the kitchen as possible, to stand in the front in case there were leftovers or anything to scrape from the pots. If that were the case, it was important to get to the pots first. That went well until the guards forbade fighting over leftovers and scrapings, with the threat of beating.

To counter the trading of food, and also, perhaps, to dissuade guards from it, regular and unannounced dormitory searches were carried out. The goal was to find money, jewelry, or other valuable things: anything that could be used in the illegal trade within the camp. The searches were seen as humiliating; the Japanese and the Javanese guards were very rude and aggressive. They dealt blows right and left. The loot was usually great. Then it remained calm for a while in the camp. Some people, and this astonished Jan, were so creative at hiding their valuables, that, after a few days, they happily resumed their illegal trade.

The Japanese camp commander did not concern himself very much with the running of the camp, because this was left to the camp head and his committee. Yet the Japanese had instituted strict rules on order, tidiness, and hygiene, because they were themselves terrified of contagious diseases. And when high-ranking officials came, which happened regularly, the entire camp had to be cleaned. En masse, the prisoners were forced to tidy up the whole camp and remove blades of grass and weeds, even when there were hardly any to be seen.

All the chores were done by the prisoners, from cleaning vegetables to unloading the trucks that brought the supplies.

Jan gladly helped clean up the camp despite the hard work. The camp rubbish was gathered in large baskets, and those baskets had to be carried by two boys to Rawah Bening, outside the camp. That gave the boys a feeling of freedom, if only for an hour. Jan enjoyed those outings.

# Mother

*November 1943*

*I'm going to die,* was all that I could think of in the beginning. *How do I survive this day?* I can't abide being locked up. I live on autopilot and am amazed at what I am able to endure. I'm not dead yet. I do what needs to be done. But I don't participate. I am inaccessible, self-absorbed, empty, and without wishes. I can't escape from myself. I conduct myself as an aloof witness. Other mothers around me are much more active, helping their children pass the time, doing things together.

One internee created a Game of the Geese board game on a large piece of cardboard. You had to be clever, though, to find such a big piece. She used obstacles from the camp to fill the squares. There are plenty of them: the watchtowers, the camp store, the well. A big, mean goose—the Japanese, naturally—steals all the bread in front of the geese—that's us, the interned Dutch. The finish is magnificent: an imposing beautiful house with occupants inside, that ends well, all's well. A hopeful drawing, I admit.

Play is one way to escape the misery of the camp; I totally agree. You can be lucky in the game or unlucky, just as on the days here when there is little or nothing to eat.

But doing something myself, coming up with an activity, making something—I can't do it.

There is a lively exchange of books. My twins read *Afke's tiental* for the umpteenth time, which they don't mind. Anything to escape for a while. I don't read to them; I'm not the mother who reads aloud. I don't participate. And that is a thorn in the side for some. People try to encourage me; it feels uncomfortable, but that's how it is: thanks, but no thanks. The unreachable cloud that I am makes people uncomfortable and sometimes angry.

"Get over it, Johanna; think about your children." Just stop it. What are you talking about? I do what needs to be done. That's it. There's something eating away at me, and I'm not talking about it. The all-consuming, constant feeling that my family in Driebergen has forgotten me. That feeling cannot be suppressed. Is that selfish? The anger it evokes, over and over, holds me captive. That is my struggle. I really don't want that. Much of my energy is lost. I hardly dare to say it, but it is somehow more intense than hunger.

Despite everything, I am vigilant. You have to be, because in the camp there are plenty of women who are after someone else's things or food. There go the tomatoes that have been grown with care. The instinct to survive.

We learn tricks from each other. If you suck on little stones in your mouth, it reduces your hunger. Every day, we press on our ankles and arms to see how long the little dents remain.

But no matter how passive I am, I find it difficult to tolerate negativity or pessimism from others. Such as, "It can still take yeeeears," that is repeated annoyingly. It drives me crazy. Or, "It will be over soon, because nothing is too big for God, and the minds of men are small. He will judge." What good are such mantras? I have no feeling for it, and no understanding of it. For me, they are hollow sounds. Tell me where that God has gone. I don't feel His

107

leading at all. How long will it take before "our" God intervenes? He just judges. And then I feel guilty about that. I can't escape all the confusion. I can't relax. Rage lies like a sandbag at the door, interferes with my thinking.

To all appearances, I'm alive, but I'm not. I'll do whatever it takes. Every now and then, I conjure up a frozen smile. I help with the digging of a vegetable garden, which is certainly necessary, because the rations are nowhere near enough. And the rhythm of the work, rooting with my hands in the soil, gives me peace.

I haven't even mentioned the murderous heat, that terrible tropical sun. The Japanese gladly torture us with it. Worst of all is the roll call for punishment, standing in the sun. Because of some stupid offense, someone has been obstinate, or just because the guard wants to order it, we sometimes have to stand in the sun for hours. No water. Sweat leaves a layer of salt on your skin. There you are, bent in the sun. And again, as always, there is the excessive kicking.

When I surmise that Jan, young and brash as he is, has been careless, I repeat my warnings: "Don't make them angry, Jan. Try not to attract their attention."

He often visits us in the women's barracks. He is growing up quickly, beginning to ask questions. About faith, for example. He doesn't want to say much about it. I tell him to keep praying, keep his faith. Naturally, that feels hypocritical. I have a nagging feeling of unease. A kind of homesickness. For my home, for my family, for my familiar surroundings, where faith contributed to a place of rest. For Jan, I wish that anchor, that defense. The knot in my stomach is steadily growing. I wish I could find that place of peace again. Not the vacillating, not the doubt, but support.

# Jan

*December 1943*

The beatings, the regular strokes of the cane, and the hard work that had to be done made the internment more difficult and almost unbearable. Worse, most people died of dysentery and hunger edema. Dysentery was a nasty bowel disease that caused your body to lose a lot of fluid. It was contagious, and if anyone suffered from it, he or she was immediately taken to hospital for treatment. Often it ended in death.

In the beginning, Jan was shocked by the news of all these deaths. Over time he got used to it, and if someone with dysentery were taken away, you didn't expect to see him again. During the daily contacts with his mother and his sisters, he asked about their health.

Hunger edema, the number two cause of death, was caused by a long-term vitamin B deficiency. You could quickly see if someone were suffering from hunger edema because then the feet began to swell up due to an accumulation of fluid which would slowly creep up the legs. Once that process had begun, you would not have much longer to live, because once the fluid reached the cardiac region, you would be hopelessly lost. In young children, the whole process was much slower than it was in the older men around him. The food in the camp was too one-sided, and there was little or no grain or milk. Hence, it was difficult to combat. Nobody seemed interested. Jan noticed that usually it was only elderly people who fell ill and died.

Children also had illnesses, but they were the usual childhood illnesses, from which they recovered after a while. Every child suffered from a vitamin C deficiency, which you could recognize by the red spots on arms and legs, although they could also be caused by the bedbug.

His mother kept a close eye on her children.

"You must pray a lot!" she admonished them regularly, "because people who pray a lot receive the protection of our Lord."

Jan looked at her in surprise at those moments. He wondered if she really believed that, because he had heard her regularly express her doubts about that protection. In her words, he heard his father rather than his mother. She just said something, against her better judgment. Jan no longer believed in that protection, and found his mother weak that she now echoed his father's language. He had found his own method of surviving this camp, and that was by not giving up, moving around as much as possible, picking up odd assignments for extra food, and fighting.

Privacy in the camps was impossible. Everyone in the dormitory had a wooden bed with the least possible space. If you wanted to have some privacy, you had to create it yourself, by closing off your own space with rags or sheets which you hung from the ceiling with strings.

Most of the day was spent on odd jobs and chores assigned to them. Sometimes, and if they didn't fall onto their beds exhausted, there was still some time left for recreation.

The boys even had music in their dormitory, because someone had a suitcase gramophone. The spring was missing, but with their finger they could still turn it at the 78 rpm that it required. Nobody cared that it moaned and echoed; the main thing was that you could listen to music. The records were a variety of waltzes, dance music by Victor Silvester, and jazz. For Jan, this was his first encounter with jazz. At home, he was not accustomed to this, because only church music was listened to there. "Worldly music," as his father used to call it, was "a temptation from the devil and bad for your soul." Jan had noticed none of that in the camp, and deep down in his heart he thought it was nonsense. Music was music. What could be bad about that?

Tine Pruijs, a former teacher with a lot of initiative, organized recreational evenings, where she taught the young people how to dance. At the beginning of their internment, this was still possible in an empty barrack, but due to the influx of more and more prisoners, it shifted to the open terrain. Everyone participated because there was not much to do, and games made the children forget the hardships of the camp for a little while. Also, it was something to look forward to.

When it came to Christmas, Jan was asked to play a role in a Christmas tableau that was to be performed. That happened on Christmas Eve, 1943. Jan had the role of butler, a comic role with the line: "It's going to be all rrrrrrrrright!"

That brought the house down.

"I am going out with Greetje!" Gerard told his brother excitedly.

"And she with you too?" asked Jan, wittily joshing.

"Yes, it happened while we were dancing."

"Have you kissed yet?"

"What do you think? Of course not, that is not proper."

"Then how do you know that you're going out?"

"Because I asked her, and she said yes!"

Gerard's story made a deep impression on Jan. Naturally, he also looked secretly at the girls, but he had never noticed that girls looked at him too. Usually they lowered their eyes or turned and walked away. Privately, he was a bit in love with a certain Wil. He didn't know her last name. She smiled back when he looked at her, and that fed his infatuation. During the dance evenings, he often danced with her, and she never said no when he came to get her. Every courtship was, in fact, doomed to failure for lack of privacy. Even though Jan never told Wil that he was secretly in love with her, he still assumed that if he got out of the camp, he wanted to marry her. For him, it was an additional reason to want to survive the camp.

"Look, dear Jan, now you can completely accept that what the Bible says about creation of the world is accurate. However, if you think about that very deeply, do you really believe that the world and the human being were created in seven days?"

Jan and a number of boys were sitting and listening attentively to the stories of Mr. Gisius. He had come to them in the camp and was a master storyteller. All the boys listened eagerly to his stories and his teachings. For not only did he tell splendid stories, but also, he instructed them in paleontology, the study of fossils resting in the earth. And he let them look at a piece of stone with fossilized fish inside of it. "How old do you think this is?"

They looked at each other and no one dared to say anything, because they knew that regardless of what they would say, it would not add up.

"This fish is already millions of years old. And this stone was found somewhere in a mountain."

"How is that possible?" asked a boy.

"Because millions of years ago the mountains of the world were under water and after the earth dried up, all these fish remained, died, were encapsulated and became fossilized."

Mr. Gisius began to introduce fun. He eagerly told his stories to the boys because he knew that they would divert their attention from the misery in the camp.

"That is definitely not in the Bible!"

And thereupon he got the reaction from Mr. Gisius.

"But everything in the Bible is true, isn't it?"

"Who says that?"

"My father, the pastor, and people in Sunday School!"

"And you believe everything that is being said?"

Jan really had to reflect on this question. "I am told that everything in the Bible is true and that applies to the story of creation too."

"But doesn't it say in the Bible, also, that you must investigate everything, and retain that which is good?"

Jan nodded in the affirmative, because he had often heard his father read that text.

"If you believe that too, then I have a question for you, Jan, that requires further study. If the earth existed for barely 24 hours, then man should have appeared in just the last three seconds. Should you believe that?"

Jan began to think and to calculate, and then spoke spontaneously:

"That can't be, can it?"

"No, indeed, that cannot be, and the Bible wants us to believe, that everything around us was created in one week, therefore, in seven days. And you believe, because your father and the pastor have said that, that the world with everything on it and in it was created in those days, right?"

Jan and the other children, who, also, were raised in a Christian home, nodded in affirmation. That was ingrained in them; therefore it was true. Then Mr. Gisius again took the stone with the fish inside and held it up:

"How is it possible then, that we are living in 1943, and according to you, the world is not very old, that nevertheless, I have this fish that is already millions of years old?"

With open mouth and big eyes they looked at him, fascinated and amazed, but also full of doubt and disbelief. Yet nobody doubted the veracity of Mr. Gisius's story. He finished his story:

"Think carefully about these things, and in the coming period, observe closely what is around you: the mountains, the clouds, the sky, and the trees. And also look in the gravel because I found this stone with the fish here. We call that a fossil, and there are many to be found, if you look closely. And then next time, I'll tell you a new story."

Jan wanted to tell his mother, whom he saw every day, what Mr. Gisius had told him, and he actually wanted to analyze with his father what he had heard from Mr. Gisius. His father was not there, and although he had never had such a close relationship with him, he really missed him now.

The stories of Mr. Gisius and their plausibility changed Jan's view of the world. Jan had always assumed that what his father said or what the pastor said, and what he heard at the Christian school, was true. However, those stories could not withstand the logic of Mr. Gisius, and the latter's stories slowly crushed Jan's Reformed faith. For the first time, Jan became aware of other and equally logical views of life and creation. Views that could be explained. Insights that you could test yourself. And because there was no systematic and organized education in the camp, he had to make do with these stories.

Apart from being in the group that received lessons from Mr. Gisius, Jan was also in a sort of math group. All classes were held in the open air and without teaching aids. Improvisation was the order of the day. The pastor taught German, and Jan taught himself a little English by reading. Also, from other internees, some people received private lessons, varying from history and geography to Dutch. Attending classes was a pastime that was eagerly pursued, in order to forget everything in and about the camp, especially that gnawing and perpetual hunger.

Besides attending these "lessons," or going on an adventure, or doing his work assignment, Jan was also drawing skillfully. He had taken his drawing box, with plenty of pencils in it, to the camp. He was talented, especially in sketching portraits. Mothers even asked him to sketch portraits of their children in exchange for something he could trade for extra food.

One day, while he was sketching, the Javanese watch commander unexpectedly came up behind him and ordered Jan to follow. Jan was shocked, wondered what he had done wrong, and already feared the punishment.

116

Punishment was meted out for everything and for nothing, and the punishments were significant. With trembling knees, he followed the watch commander. People were eyeing him with curiosity, and Jan saw pity in the eyes of the bystanders. He had to wait at the guardhouse. His legs were shaking. The door opened, and he was called in by the watch commander, and then ushered into an office. There, behind a desk, in an immaculate white uniform, sat the Japanese camp commander. Jan made the obligatory *hormat*, the bow, and remained in that position, afraid of the judgment that would be passed on him. Suddenly the Japanese began talking to him and pointed to a table in the corner of the room. The Japanese spoke broken Malay, but Jan could nevertheless understand him. On the small table lay a Japanese bamboo pen, a pot of ink, and a stack of small boards. He indicated to Jan that he had to paint Japanese letters on them because those boards would later be hung all over the camp as signposts for high-ranking Japanese visitors to the camp. Jan was surprised and could finally relax:

*"Sajan tjobah itoe toehan,"* he responded. I'll try, sir. He felt honored with the assignment. He bowed deeply to the camp commander, who actually smiled at him, and followed the watch commander to a side room, where he set to work, using the examples he had been given. After a few hours, the Japanese camp commander suddenly came in, picked up some boards that were ready, and then said:

*"Baik itoe!"*—"That's good!"

It gave Jan two days of work and diversion. Above all, he wanted to do it well and not disappoint the camp commander. His efforts were rewarded with compliments, and even better, he was allowed to eat with the guard, delicious *nasi* that filled his empty stomach and alleviated his hunger for a few days.

When he told his mother and sisters and the other boys in his barracks, he was met with envy and jealousy. At first they had feared that he would be punished, and instead, he got a pleasant assignment and extra food. In their hearts, they were jealous of his artistic talent that had earned him more food.

With his ecumenical sermons every week, Pastor Van Hoof managed to alleviate the hopelessness, isolation, nagging nostalgia, sorrow, and above all, the lingering hunger. In his first year of imprisonment, Jan, his brothers, sisters, and mother regularly attended church services. Soon enough they were banned, and could take place only during the evening prayers of the Muslims on Fridays, and only in Malay.

The latter stipulation was not always strictly observed. There were many women who organized such things as evening worship, Sunday services, and vespers. There was also a pastor, but he suffered from mild dementia. None of them was able to replace Pastor Van Hoof. Many a Friday evening, he presided over an ecumenical service. He preached without notes with his eyes closed, and Jan was fascinated with watching him and listening to him. Offering comfort and encouragement, he gave wonderful discourses on the parables of Jesus. When he spoke, you could hear a pin drop; that's how quiet it was then. And he always ended his sermon with:

"In the name of the Father, the Son, and the Holy Ghost, Amen."

In doing so, he made the sign of the cross, which Jan watched with fascination.

Then it remained quiet, because his audience really didn't want to return to the harsh reality of the camp.

The pastor's sermons raised questions for Jan again, and then he tested them with Mr. Gisius.

"What the pastor says is sometimes at odds with what you say; whom should I believe?"

Mr. Gisius had looked at him for a long time. He didn't want Jan to start doubting his faith, but at the same time, he wanted to get Jan to think for himself.

"Dear Jan, it is not important what I or the pastor say. How you deal with it is important. You don't have to rule out one view in order to embrace the other. If the pastor's stories bring you comfort, and my stories offer you knowledge, can't they comfortably co-exist?"

Jan was pleased with that answer. Comfort and knowledge! Especially because he was at a sort of crossroads in his life. Despite his doubts, he was sensitive to religion, and that was why he daily read his devotional book. Few in the camp did that, but he needed to hold onto something. And he was hungry for factual knowledge. Once, when an old monk read over Jan's shoulder from his daily devotional, he muttered:

"What you are doing is very good, my boy. Dare to hold on to what you believe and that will help you tolerate all the misery."

Jan asked him to teach him how to make the sign of the cross.

"Watch carefully and follow my movements."

Jan saw how the monk joined the fingers of his right hand in a point. Then he brought it to his forehead, stomach, left breast and then right. He followed the movements and discovered how simple it was.

119

"It always goes so fast that you hardly see it."

"Now you know it."

"I am not Roman Catholic."

"You don't have to be Roman Catholic to make the sign of the cross, Jan. Anyone can do that, especially if it gives you comfort."

From that moment on, Jan regularly made the sign of the cross, always when he was alone, and no one could see him, and that gave him "strength," as he called it for himself.

For Jan, his "rituals," reading the Bible and making the sign of the cross, were important. They helped him cling to life. So much had already been taken from him, and continued to be taken. If the question of survival dominates daily life, and you actually have only this to hang onto, then you have no other choice. This did not detract from the fact that he regularly wondered where God actually was and, above all, what He did for you. The main question was how long it would be before "their" God would intervene. They had been in the camp for quite some time now, and the war went on and on, but there was still no intervention. His father's words echoed in his head.

"Keep trusting in God because He will save us."

"Where is God when you need Him most?" he wrote in his diary that he had kept for some time. A question he often asked himself, and that heightened his doubts about the existence of God.

# Father Jaan Willem

*February 1944*

The Japanese feared a breakthrough by the Americans in the Philippines or a direct attack on Java. These reports came to the attention of the prisoners. They sparked rumors in the camp that the war would soon be over. It was the flickering flame of hope. Without these rumors, they wouldn't be able to carry on. You had to believe that the war would be over some day.

The prisoners were ordered to prepare for a possible departure. Everyone was allowed to send a suitcase and take one with him. It was not checked; some had packed eight to ten suitcases to send. Jaan, who usually followed instructions, became over-confident, and also packed more suitcases. He even managed to pick up a charcoal iron that someone had left behind. Also, on the cart, he placed the trunk organ that he used at church services.

During the night of February 18, 1944, they left, and so the imprisonment of more than eighteen months in Fort Vredeburg came to an end. No one told them where they would be taken. Late in the evening before their departure, they were served a hot meal, extra bread for their journey, and a bottle of coffee. They left in the middle of the night, so that the civilian population would not notice, under heavy surveillance by nervous Javanese policemen, for Toegoe station, half a kilometer away. There, a blinded train awaited them. Although the train cars had only forty-five seats, ninety men with all their luggage were squeezed in. Because things were not going fast enough, they were pushed and shoved inside.

Jaan had found a small spot near the wall where he could barely move, with the result that for days afterward, he was still stiff from the one-sided posture which he had endured throughout the train trip. The journey took almost twenty-four hours, and eighteen hours later, they arrived in Tjimahi, a few kilometers west of Bandoeng, where they were lodged in Camp 4. It was a large building complex that had served as barracks before the war. The walls of the camp had barbed wire at the top, and four-meter-high bamboo fences attached to the walls. Jaan considered himself fortunate that it was not as hot as Fort Vredeburg.

The camp was located on the Bandung plateau where the temperature was pleasant. The buildings in which they were housed were more modern than their residences at Fort Vredeburg. The worst were the gutter toilets, long trenches in the floor, through which water flowed. No cleaning was ever done, which contributed to the dysentery that lurked everywhere. The sleeping places were barely eighty centimeters wide. You did not get more space, in order that the more than nine thousand prisoners that were thrown together could be housed. Jaan felt privileged to be housed with eleven other men in a twenty-eight-square-meter room. That made it easy for them to keep it clean. But it didn't help them eliminate the bedbugs, even though they pulled hundreds of them out of their mosquito nets every morning. During the day, the "wall bears," as they were called, were not a major annoyance, but at night everyone was attacked by bedbugs, and many were constantly scratching themselves. Then there were cockroaches that hid mainly in their suitcases. The good fortune of having cockroaches in their suitcases was that then there were no bedbugs in them. Apparently, these were eaten by the black monsters. Worse than these two pests were the white ants that devoured everything in their path. Jaan's mattress was already half-eaten. Nothing could mitigate their gluttony.

Due to the large number of prisoners, food was drastically rationed. The day began in the morning with half a liter of porridge made of sweet potato flour. At noon they received a loaf of bread weighing no more than one hundred and sixty grams. Like many others, Jaan cut his bread into very thin slices to make it last longer. Sometimes they received a supplement of yeast chemically made from *dudduk,* a kind of rice husk, brood yeast, sugar and ammonia. The latter was extracted from their own urine, which was collected in large drums set up in the camps with the text: "No full drums, no bread!" Not only were the prisoners fed with this bread, but also the Japanese and the Javanese guards. At the end of the afternoon, around five o'clock, they got their hot meal. This invariably consisted of one hundred and sixty grams of rice with *sambal,* an Indonesian dish of mashed Spanish red pepper with vegetables, or *sajoer,* an Indonesian vegetable soup. Sometimes there were some extra vegetables in the soup, and on rare occasions, such as certain holidays, a piece of chicken or something else that looked like meat but was of unknown origin. On very rare occasions, fruit was distributed, the quality of which left much to be desired. Since you got nothing else, everything was eaten as if it were a delicacy. Once a month, you were allowed to order extra food, such as brown sugar, coffee, tobacco, and biscuit flour, for a fee of one guilder and fifty cents. Despite the extras that could be ordered, the consequences of the strict rationing were, nevertheless, felt.

Prisoners were visibly losing weight, and there were more skeletons with sagging skin than well-fed people. This situation gave rise to many cases of dysentery. It was a very contagious and severe disease of the colon and claimed many victims. The cure for this dangerous disease was fasting and more fasting. Jaan had heard a doctor say this, and when he became the first in his room to contract the disease, he decided to fast.

Living on only weak tea and the occasional cigarette, he managed to do it for sixty hours. His daily ration of food was divided among his roommates to shouts of joy. When he began to eat again after this period and ventured into eating some rice porridge, he immediately got sick again. He was transferred to the ward where all infected patients were. After about ten days, limp as a dishrag, but "recovered," he came back to the room where he slept. He was greeted with cheers, glad that he had survived. It took him days to regain his strength. Yet he considered himself fortunate, because all around him, men were dying like flies, of dysentery and hunger edema.

A few weeks later, Jaan was hit by dysentery again. Within a week, through his renewed and even stricter fasting, he was back on his feet, albeit rather shakily.

The men around him asked him where he found the strength to survive. Then he told them about the conversation he had had with the pastor at Fort Vredeburg.

"If I concede to doubt and self-pity, and I am not willing to fight and persevere, then I am betraying

Johanna, my wife. I don't want that! I can hold on because I trust in the deep strength within myself. God really cannot do it alone. And if I don't cooperate, He won't succeed either. 'Never give up' has since become my motto."

# Jan

*March 1944*

It was the middle of the night and the barracks were pitch black. A small light was burning at the entrance, but this was insufficient to see the entire barracks. It stank in the barracks, a stench caused by people huddled together and stacked on top of each other on long wooden bunks. Each day hardly allowed enough time for the foul air to dissipate. All individual bunks had been eliminated and replaced by long sleeping bins with barely forty centimeters of space per person. The Japanese had done this to create room for even more prisoners. At the beginning, each person had still had his own cot. With the constant influx of more prisoners, these had been replaced by the long bins of tens of meters, which were stacked on top of each other in three levels. The cubicles had been hammered from wall to wall and on both sides of the barracks. Long tables stood in the middle of the barracks. There was no private space.

All around him, Jan heard the other boys snoring and turning. Above all, he heard many boys scratching, just like him. Despite the presence of insects that Jan did not know, he had the greatest aversion to, and the most problems with the bedbugs and the body lice. Then you had the malaria mosquitoes, and if things went badly, and you were bitten, you would catch malaria, a sickness that often recurred, after just one mosquito bite.

You also kept encountering other vermin, such as *tjitjaks*—geckos, spiders, beetles, cockroaches, and

126

*kadals*—lizards. Yet their presence was dwarfed by the invasion of bedbugs and body lice. The arrival of the bedbugs in Banjoe Biroe, the camp where Jan was, coincided with the massive introduction of the teakwood wooden beds they now slept on, which had been installed by an army of indigenous carpenters in one day. In Jan's camp, the bedbug had multiplied into an immense plague. They were small insects, brown in color, resembling ladybugs, and feeding on human blood. If you were bitten by them, the itching would drive you crazy, and you were always left with a small wound. The only way to get rid of them was to pinch them to death. That seemed hopeless, because they continued to multiply. Moreover, the bugs reeked of rotten camphor. The itch, pain, and stench deprived you of the sleep you desperately needed. The fight against the little beasts was almost impossible because they multiplied at lightning speed. During the day, they hid in the cracks and crevices of the barracks, and then, as soon as darkness fell, they appeared en masse, dropping like paratroopers from the ceiling joists and beams. They feasted on the bodies in the wooden beds. Sometimes Jan and the others dragged the bunks outside during the day and then left them in the tropical sun for hours, in an attempt to kill the little pests. The bedbugs could not tolerate that, and in the evening, when the wood was whacked, thousands of dead bedbugs fell onto the ground. The eggs remained; therefore, the conquest was only short-lived. And if, after many nights of fighting and scratching, you fell asleep exhausted, despite the bedbugs, you were surprised in the morning by a multitude of bites and wounds. Unlike the bedbugs, the body lice crept into your clothes and your bedding. They lived on textiles. Every day, Jan and his companions were busy inspecting their clothing for body lice, picking them out and pinching them to death between their fingernails.

# Jan

*June 1944*

"We get extra food and soap when we volunteer!"
His camp friend Henk whispered this to him, and both boys immediately ran to the watch commander.

"We are reporting as volunteers!" they called out, almost in unison. Several more had come with them, so the commander could choose. An indigenous guard took ten boys, including Jan and Henk, who felt fortunate to be chosen.

"I am curious to know what we'll have to do."

They didn't have to guess long. It turned out to be a very dirty job. Camp 11's two baths and latrine buildings were built in a semicircle above a small *kali* or river. The stream carried all human excrement and bathwater to a more distant swamp area. The rapidly growing camp population and the increase in the use of latrine and bathing facilities had created a clogging problem. The long grass, the *alang-alang,* along the banks of the stream, had grown very quickly due to the quantity of human excrement. From time to time, the grass had to be cut, and the *kali* under the latrine building completely dredged. All the boys were given a *patjol*—cleaver—and a *golok*—machete. Jan and his friend were assigned the filthiest job, dredging the stream beneath the building. They stepped into the stream with bare feet, sank into the muck, and walked through the sewer tunnel with bent back. At first it was dusk, and as they walked deeper into the tunnel, it became pitch dark.

"Dammit!" grumbled Henk. Jan urged him to hush.

"You signed up. Think about the soap and the food while you're busy! Think of something cheerful."

The rough stone walls were slippery and filthy, but there was no choice other than to become soaked en route to the last hole in the latrine. The worst part, thought Jan, was that people just continued to use the latrine, which meant that Jan and Henk had to jump away regularly, in order to avoid being soiled by excrement from the users above them.

They began to shovel. The stench hit their lungs and it was almost impossible to breathe, although their exertion required extra breathing.

"Work hard, Henk, then we'll be done sooner!"

And that's exactly what they did. After a while, everything began to loosen up, and through their effort, the *kali* began to flow nicely and more powerfully, which made their work much easier. Not long after, everything flowed normally, and they could leave the tunnel to rejoin the others. There they saw that the other boys had not been sitting still either; the grass was much shorter.

Jan looked at his legs and those of Henk. Alongside all the other mess, their legs swarmed with red maggots. It was disgusting to see. They quickly jumped into the *kali* to wash and remove the filth. It didn't matter that their clothes became sopping wet, because that meant they had also been washed. And in the sun, everything was soon dry.

When they were done, the soldier gathered the boys around to distribute the soap: a measly, flat piece of white soap. Still, they were happy with it. When the boys asked for the promised extra food, he shook his head.

*"Tida bisa,"* he said. It's not possible. Then he turned and walked away. That was what they had looked forward to the most. Grumbling was pointless, because then you ran the risk of punishment. Disappointed and feeling even hungrier, they walked back to their barracks, past the guard room. Along the way, one boy picked up a rock, and out of anger, threw it on the roof of the guardroom, a foolish and ill-advised provocation that led to the Javanese watch commander's running outside, and shouting insults. Jan remembered him from his drawing assignment, but now he seemed a lot less friendly than he had been then. Already scolding and wishing them ill, he ordered the boys to come to him. They had to stand in line in the gallery section of the waiting room. The short-tempered guard began to yell at them and demanded to know who had thrown the stone. He threatened all the boys with a beating if they didn't tell him. Frightened, all the boys kept silent. The quieter they became, the more furious the watch commander became. Jan felt his knees beginning to tremble. He kept staring straight ahead. Everyone knew who had thrown the stone, but no one would betray him. The increasingly angry watch commander walked to the first boy in the row and unexpectedly slapped him very hard in the face. Fortunately, that was it. Finally, he arrived in front of Jan, who had already braced himself. After all, there was no way around it. The watch commander had a furious sneer on his face and an aura of brute force. Although Jan was half a head taller than the Japanese, that didn't seem to bother him. He lashed out with his right hand just as Jan moved his head sideways, causing the blow to hit his neck, which burned red with pain. To Jan's relief, there was no second blow. He

131

breathed a sigh of relief, and ignored the speech the watch commander made to the boys, after which the Japanese indicated that the incident was closed. The boys ran to their barracks and told what had happened. They had escaped a worse punishment, and when all was said and done, they had at least kept a small bar of soap.

When Jan related the incident to his mother and sisters, his mother warned him.

"Don't make them angry, Jan!"

"I haven't done anything, Mother. We could hardly say who did it." And proudly, he handed the bar of soap to his mother, who was very happy with it. A bar of soap was worth its weight in gold.

"Tonight we'll wash our hair with it!" she announced happily, and it seemed as if the day had received an extra ray of light.

That night, when most of them were half-asleep or scratching themselves, they heard someone walking on the roof of their barracks. They quickly went outside to see a boy doing breakneck stunts. It turned out to be someone from a different barracks. He staggered over a little wall, towards the ridge of the kitchen roof. The patrol guards thought he wanted to escape, waited for him, and took him to the guardroom. Those outside were warned to go back to their barracks. Jan was standing at the rear and was the first to return to his cot.

"Did he want to escape?" someone asked.

"It looked more like sleep-walking," replied an elderly man.

"What will happen to him?"

The next morning, when Jan neared the guard, he saw the boy kneeling on the grass. He held his arms outstretched sideways and held weights in his hands. Every time he lowered his arms, he was hit or prodded by the soldier behind him. Jan closed his eyes because he could not watch the horror of the spectacle, and walked away from this place of contempt.

# Jan

*September 17, 1944*

Jan followed the nurse to the sick bay. In fact, it was forbidden to visit the sick for fear of spreading the disease. He wanted to say goodbye and had been given permission.

It was dim and swelteringly hot. The beds were pushed close together. There was hardly any personal space. The odor of sickness met him, but he managed to get through it. He had to do this. The nurse followed him and pointed to the bed where his mother lay. She lay with her eyes closed, and Jan was shocked. How terrible she looked. Her arms and legs were thin sticks. The severe typhoid attack had exhausted her, but had fortunately not yet consumed her. Her beautiful, thick hair had been thinned greatly by her illness and lay limp and untidy on the pillow.

"*Mama*?"

When he softly called her name, she opened her eyes and looked at him sadly. He pulled himself together and leaned over to give her a kiss.

"Son?" she whispered, apparently surprised that he was standing by her bed. "Jan, I want the Lord to take me away..."

Jan was shocked by the statement.

"You may not say that, Mother. What will happen to the girls? The boys will manage, but the girls still need you."

"Why did you come, son?"

He swallowed, knowing his announcement would cause her even more distress.

"I've come to say goodbye, Mother. We are being transferred to another camp."

"Transferred?"

Then she began to cry and repeated what she had said before.

"What will I do now if you aren't here either. First Father, then Piet, later Gerard, now you."

She cried softly, and Jan handed her a handkerchief.

"Why are they taking all of you away from me?"

"I don't know, Mother. They don't tell you that. You do know, though, that they'll do whatever they want with us."

"Where are you going?"

"They don't tell us that."

A few days earlier, on September 15, 1944, Mrs. Van Riessen had informed the heads of each block that all boys aged ten and older would be transferred to another camp in a few days. The heads of each block had told the boys to report for transfer in three days. The only things they were allowed to take were some personal belongings and their bedding. On the day itself, it became apparent that, along with the boys, some nuns would also go to the men's camp.

It happened rather often that there were rumors about transfers and relocations. They usually came true. The camp was overcrowded, and to make at least a little space for the influx of new people, further selections took place. Jan was now sixteen, and it didn't matter to him. They had been told that they would go to a better camp with more space and more food. Such promises were made more often, but you couldn't verify them—those who left never came back. Still, the group leaving now wanted to believe it. When Jan checked in for departure with about thirty other boys, it was very busy. In the days before leaving, he had already said goodbye to the twins Aafje and Willie, who were now thirteen and a half, and his youngest sister Annie, who was only six and a half. He had urged them to take good care of their mother.

"Will *Mama* get better?" they had asked.

"Yes, *Mama* will get better. You just have to believe that!"

"And when will we see you again, and *Papa* and Piet and Gerard?"

They were questions of desperation that they regularly asked, and Jan always gave the same answer. "When this is all over, we'll see each other again."

"Promise?"

"Yes, I promise you; hang onto that, stay together, and take care of each other!"

"Will I ever see you again?" whispered his mother with difficulty.

"Mother, when it's all over, we'll see each other again. You must believe that and tell me you're getting better and not giving up. The girls need you. Don't leave them alone; they have only you."

"Write me to let me know where you are."

"I promise, but I have to go now; they are waiting for me."

For just a moment, he pressed her hands, then, glancing back one more time, he slowly moved away from her bed.

*Would he ever see his mother again?* He pushed that thought away. Sadly he walked out and joined the other boys who were already in the truck.

The entire camp population had gathered to say goodbye to the boys. There were mothers weeping at the departure of their sons, some of whom were barely ten years old.

"Take good care of them," some of the mothers urged Jan and the other older boys. They promised, knowing they could offer only hope, nothing more.

Despite the farewell, Jan was very curious about the new location. Imagine if the promises were true, and that things would get better there?

Shortly after, the truck started moving, and, waving to those left behind, they rode out of the gate.

# Mother

*Sunday, September 17, 1944*

I remember being infected with typhoid. A week ago, or is it two already? It began with a splitting headache. Then came the diarrhea. I dragged myself, in great misery, to the latrine, again and again. No desire to eat.

Slowly, my fever had risen. Until that moment when things became unbearable, and I, very disoriented, was taken to the sick bay.

There were moments when she no longer knew where she was. She knew that Jan had come to see her, to say goodbye. Suddenly, he had been standing there, her sixteen-year-old son, skinny as a rake. *God, how could you let this happen?* Her brave youngest son.

Cleaning up the filth in the camp had left its mark. His face was full of ugly little wounds, dear boy. Bedbugs, of course. Fortunately, they didn't bother her here in the sick bay.

"Mother, I've come to say hello."

"Hello, son. Did they just let you in? Don't touch me, or you'll get sick too. Then who will take care of the girls?"

"You're here, aren't you?"

"So far, Jan, but if it pleases the Lord, it may be over for me." *Come and get me, Lord, come; let it be my time.*

"But Mother, listen, I'm being transferred."

"Transferred? Where are you going?" But Jan didn't know. The last of her three boys to another camp? Resurgence of anger over another farewell. I could not have stopped Jaan Willem. Forced to go along, first to

Bolsward, and then—God forbid—to the Indies. I hid my feelings, which wasn't difficult. I couldn't do anything about it, and I had no strength. I listened to what Jan said, but I didn't really hear it, felt no sorrow. If it had to be so, then I was resigned to it. Nevertheless, I wept. Jan even gave me his handkerchief.

"Mother, listen, you must not say such things. You must get better. For Aafje and Willie, and for little Annie. She misses you so much." I said nothing; I simply stared.

"Mother, do you hear? You may not give up. Think about the girls. They need you now more than ever. God knows what will happen to them otherwise. You have to promise, Mother."

I nodded; it was barely noticeable. There was nothing to promise; it was no longer necessary. I had no idea if I would ever see my son again. It was no longer up to me. The other, mechanical part of me asked him to let me know where he would end up. He would. He had to go now. Brief pressure of the hand. Red, mutilated hands.

"Don't give up!" A last backward glance. As he walked away, his gaunt and bony legs, sticking out of his shorts, drew my attention.

Then she sank into oblivion again.

My skinny, dried-out hand, where the imprint of the farewell can be recalled, lies expressionless on the white sheet, like parchment. My wedding ring dangles on my ring finger. It's a miracle that I haven't lost it yet. Perhaps a sign from God? A reminder of my wedding vows? My damaged and battered marriage that has become tedious. Lifeless metal. For the umpteenth time, I wonder what the point of all this is.

In the sick bay, the beds are close together. Emaciated patients lie side by side. I am certainly not the only one. The nurses do their best, but there is simply not enough. Not enough medicine, overflowing latrines, not enough of anything.

A woman is moaning in the bed next to mine. The nurses are whispering. They know that the woman won't last much longer. A screen is placed between the beds. The shadow of a human in a last mind-boggling attempt to sit up. A fierce stab of jealousy. When will the Lord come for me? I long for it. I am disconnected from this life, ready to leave. Waiting...again waiting...forever waiting.

I hope that Aafje, Willie, and Annie end up in good hands. They have grown up quickly; they will be fine. There are plenty of women who feel called to help. I've seen it before. I am sorry, but I can't bear it anymore. Besides, the Lord can lend a hand too. That is the least He can do. Forty-eight years is a good age.

I'm tired. The ring is heavy. Sleep is all that matters.

"When I'm dead, I'll never have to travel again, thank God."

# Jan

*September 17, 1944*

How often had Jan already said goodbye? First to his father, to the house on Sindorolaan, to Piet, followed by Gerard in February, and now to his mother and sisters. He stared straight ahead, wondering how often he would still have to say farewell. Lost in his thoughts, he didn't see much on the road, until one of the boys nudged him:

"We're going to Ambarawa!"

Jan looked at the road and saw that they were indeed heading in that direction. They passed Camp 6, which they knew housed only women and children, mostly from Djokja. Hoping to see an acquaintance, he peeked over the fence of the camp, but they rode by too quickly. At the railroad crossing, they turned left onto the road towards Magelang, and soon, on their right, they saw a building complex looming behind a bamboo fence, just as in all camps. They turned into the yard and were amazed at the modern appearance of the buildings. At the main entrance, they stopped and were able to get out. It proved to be the Roman Catholic boarding school Saint Louis, now renamed Camp 8. The prisoners there were mainly old disabled men, boys, and nuns. The camp was guarded by the indigenous *hei-ho* soldiers.

It was very busy in the front yard because more transports had arrived from various directions. The head of a block beckoned them to follow him toward the front door of a building which looked like an auditorium. There were more boys, and they all looked curiously at each other. They were told to find a place for themselves and lay their mattress there. The auditorium had something familiar and cozy about it and the boys looked at each other, pleasantly surprised. This was better than where they had come from. Smooth gray tiles lay on the floor. Colorful sunbeams fell through a number of small stained-glass windows, creating distorted figures in the room.

Jan sank down on his evacuation bag, felt waves of emotion coming over him and began to cry. No one paid any attention to him. From time to time, everyone had moments of weeping, and they knew it would be transitory.

He experienced immense grief over everything and everyone that he had left behind, without any assurance that he would ever see them again. He had not spoken to others about his secret hope of being reunited with his father and his brothers. Now that those hopes had not been realized, he was overcome by a tremendous feeling of loneliness and abandonment. Maybe he would never see them again. Big questions arose in him: Why do people do this to each other? Why can't you just live your own life? Why? Here I am, he thought, all alone, no father, mother, brothers, and without my sisters. What's the point of my life?

After sitting like this for some time and weeping freely to assuage his grief, he stood up, looked around, threw his bag on the mattress, and decided to explore the camp.

# Father Jaan Willem

*September 1944*

A concert was organized by a group of prisoners. The ensemble of the famous violinist Szymon Goldberg had been imprisoned by the Japanese during a tour of the Dutch East Indies. Jaan was one of the last to hear about it, and with his folding chair under his arm, he went to the place where the concert would be held. They played Beethoven's violin concerto. Jaan enjoyed the magnificent performance. It deeply moved him and for a moment he forgot his situation in the camp. The music uplifted them all, and Jaan was surrounded by the splendor and tranquility of the tropical evening. When the last notes faded, many sat in tears, staring into space. This is what music could do in situations like this.

Although everyone was struggling in the lonely fight for survival, there was also concern for each other. When Jaan returned after the concert, he was noticed and addressed by a fellow prisoner.

"Mobach, I think you have been looking absolutely awful lately." But before Jaan could respond, the man continued, "Here are five guilders. Go buy some *hoen kweemeel*—flour— and *goela djawa*—Indonesian brown sugar—to regain your strength."

Jaan thanked the man and followed his advice. With the money, he was able to buy extra *goela djawa* with the monthly order. The palm sugar gave him new strength. He had to survive to be able to provide for his family again. Food wasn't the only thing that would help him do that.

It was important to keep moving, and for that reason he signed up for the outdoor work detail, with the added benefit of temporarily escaping the camp. There were groups who went to Andir Airport near Bandoeng. Regardless of the work and the movement, such a work detail always provided food so that he could regain his strength. And he received wages of fifteen cents per day, and you could come into contact with Javanese citizens with the possibility of exchanging clothing for food. Jaan's first work detail was the so-called "Toontje work detail." Toontje was well-known because you could always get food at his place. With a group of twenty men, they had to clean the garden of the Japanese camp commander. Jaan was seated at the sink where he asked a Javanese servant if there was anything left to eat because he was so hungry. The servant did not answer, and Jaan threw himself diligently into his task of removing blades of grass, always as close to the house as possible. You just never knew. An hour later, the servant returned with a tin of liver paste. *"Ini babi?"*—Is this pork?—the servant asked him.

Jaan saw the quandary of the servant because the question of whether it was pork would get him in trouble, for his faith forbade him to eat it. Jaan looked at the tin and saw that the liver paste was made of pork, and he confirmed that, indeed, it was pork. With a gesture of disgust, the servant handed the tin of liver paste to Jaan. It had been a long time since Jaan had eaten this, and he thoroughly enjoyed the servant's gift. During the day they also received extra slices of bread, which made up for the day's work in the garden. How long had it been since he'd had a full stomach?

# Mother

*Wednesday, September 20, 1944*

Nurse Winfrida brought the postcard. I immediately recognized the slanting, regular handwriting as Jaan's. From Tjimahi, Camp 4, the former prisoner-of-war camp. Written in blue ink. Fortunately, Jaan still had his fountain pen. In all likelihood—just as it was here—he was dictated what he could or couldn't write. A message without a message. He did outdoor chores, the food was reasonable, his health was good. Positive messages. No date.

The card brought me back to the here and now. For the first time in a long time, a sign of life again. The important thing was that Jaan was alive and was thinking of me. I clutch the card against my chest. I feel a slight hope. The mail is coming through again; could that possibly mean the end of the war?

It starts with a stain. Later that night, I suffer terrible cramps, too long and too many. My last remnants of energy disappear. The gloomy face of Dr. Heimans does not bode well. He administers medicine. God knows where he got it from. I feel a stabbing pain in my stomach; I can't stand it anymore. The ink from the card has left a stain. A big spot on the card. As my abdomen relaxes a little, my attention is drawn to the stain. Wait a minute, am I seeing it correctly? That stain is alive. I look again. Must be a message from Jaan. I gesture to nurse Winfrida, who comes running immediately because of my

145

worrisome condition. Excitedly, I try to explain to her what I see, and push the card under her nose.

"Nurse, look at the faint lines here. Can you see them too?" I wave the card feverishly in front of her face.

"I can't see anything that way, Johanna. But please stay calm; you are in bad shape, and can't endure much more."

"I'm fine, nurse. No cramps now. But look, don't you see the contours?" I point to the stain again, but nurse Winfrida doesn't understand what I'm talking about.

"It's really better if you don't work yourself up so much. You are extremely sick."

"I just want to know if you see what I see, nurse. Oh, never mind." She looks at me with compassion, and before walking away, she strokes my hair for a moment. Speaking takes a lot of effort; I sink back into the pillows and look at the card one more time. It is not a question of being able to see well; I do see it, don't I?

The spot is alive. I turn the card a quarter turn. It looks like *The Last Supper*. Wait a minute, how many people? I count one, two...eight people. So, not *The Last Supper*. I can still count. When I tilt the card, so that the light falls on it better, I see it. Wait, there are eight Mobachs, the complete family. Oh, Jaan!

She closes her eyes, and a final image appears before she is taken to the sick bay.

"*Mama*, don't be sick." Crying, Annie calls her. She doesn't remember how long ago that was. Do I love my girls? I grab my midriff; the cramps are returning. How quickly they have matured in this war. Ouch, another wave in my belly. I can't stand it anymore. I can't leave my girls alone. Not now.

These conflicting feelings drive me crazy. Do I want to die? I'm done. Something in me wants to live. Hope? I'm choking up. Another wave of misery. Nurse, is there blood in my stool? Maybe I should stay. Leave my ugly longing for what it is. Hey, there's Jaan. He hardly dares to tell me that we are leaving for the Indies. He thinks I'm falling into a big black hole. It doesn't matter, Jaan. My God, what's going on here? I don't care which way it goes. Just say it. Something is dancing before my eyes. Nurse, can you take that away? Is this my hand? It's boiling hot in here. Could you turn the stove down? The endless emptiness within me feels less painfully empty. Jaan is in control; a man decides what happens. Why actually? Nurse, is it good that I'm so angry? Mother, help me, it hurts so much. I can't go on. No more pain, please. I am afraid of falling asleep.

# Jan

*September 19, 1944*

The first days in Camp 8 were busy and chaotic. Once he got used to his situation in the new camp, and now that the large influx of new detainees had more or less been processed, a bit of a pattern began to emerge.

Jan was introduced to the new camp head, Mr. Refuge, a Belgian merchant. When he left Banjoe Biroe, he was happy to have said goodbye to Mrs. Van Riessen. Inexplicably, the Japanese were keen on precise administration. The identity of prisoners in the camp was a number, but if you were transferred to another camp, you got another number, while they thought it also important to indicate which camp the prisoners came from. For example, Jan received number 9907 in Camp 8, followed by serial number 350, to indicate that he had come from Banjoe Biroe.

The Japanese camp commander Tadaka, a fierce person with a stern, red face and loose hands, led the camp. If things didn't go the way he wanted, he started hitting people, so everyone tried to stay out of his way.

The halls of the complex were packed with men, boys, and nuns. Indeed, the promise of a better place proved to be a lie. The former boarding school was so full that even the chapel became a sleeping quarters. Jan considered himself fortunate that he got his own place there. The chapel was better than the other rooms because it offered a little more space. During his "tours of discovery", which he took because his curiosity to know how everything was

148

laid out overruled his loneliness, he discovered that the buildings were connected by open galleries, so-called *empers*.

The buildings were made of stone, and he hoped there were no bedbugs, or at least fewer. In the beginning, that was the case, and he rated this place as better than Banjoe Biroe. However, it remained that way only temporarily, because due to the excessive influx of prisoners, the lice also flourished in such a way that the lice infestation became worse than he had ever experienced. Strangely enough, and that surprised Jan, you seemed to become accustomed to them, and you didn't even notice the times when there seemed to be fewer.

On his tours of discovery, he noticed also that sick men were kept in hospital wards, under the care of doctors and nurses. This increased the chance of recovery and reduced the risk of infection.

The promise of sufficient food proved once again to be unfounded. The kitchen was operating at maximum capacity, owing to the number of prisoners. The rations here weren't bigger, certainly not better. There was only one water source for the entire camp, although there was plenty of water in the vicinity. To bully us, the Japanese had set it up that way, resulting in long lines at the tap to fill all the buckets. The kitchen always had priority, so it was a long wait.

Washing one's body was the exception rather than the rule, and when Jan did wash himself, usually without soap, he rinsed his pants in the residual water, and that's how you had to make do. Most of the boys, like Jan, had dark, speckled patches on their skin, the result of increasing filthiness and neglect. When Jan saw them for the first time, he was shocked and began to scrub them very hard. Only then did the dirt loosen, and just as with burned skin, he could peel it off in little curls. Later, he didn't bother with the spots, just leaving them alone, because he discovered that they formed a protective layer against lice and other vermin.

# Mother

*Thursday, September 28, 1944*

After last week Wednesday, it was still not over. The stomach cramps persisted and completely exhausted me. I became dead tired from all the thoughts that kept whirling in my head. Dreams took over from reality. Mother whispers in my ear that she loves me. I hug Jaan, just as we did at the beginning of our marriage. My little friend from first grade beckons me outside. "Come, come outside; we'll go for a walk. We'll see where we end up." And then things were good. But then the cramps come again. My belly aches.

The medicines from Dr. Heimans have done their work. Nobody knows where he conjures them from. That man is my salvation. On Saturday, my stomach is calmer, and the fever diminishes. For the first time in a long time, I can sleep through the night again. Very slowly, I recover; little by little I am getting stronger. My appetite is returning. That helps, but at first, I can have only porridge and dry rice.

When I have recovered sufficiently, I move to the ward for less seriously ill, where I may occasionally receive visitors. Children are not welcome. Seeing my daughters again will just have to wait.

My friend Paula, who comes from Utrecht and followed her husband to the Dutch East Indies (the same way I did), comes to visit. She walks in immediately after her last chore. I can smell that she has worked in the kitchen. Her dirty hands contrast sharply with the white bedding. Strange that I notice it. What does it matter?

Paula, always chatty like a verbal waterfall, and so different from me, immediately begins to prattle. The women have supervised her girls. It hadn't really been necessary, because the twins, of whom she can be very proud, have remained courageous. Annie misses her mother and cries herself to sleep every night. She has started sucking her thumb again. But Aafje and Willie are taking exceptionally good care of their little sister; those girls are such a blessing.

And then they still have time to participate in the clandestine educational clubs. Has she heard that all instruction for people under the age of twenty has now been banned? But a solution has been found; it has gone underground. The class for Aafje and Willie is held every evening behind the laundry tent, and the girls are taught at tables that have not yet been destroyed. Only card games are not yet forbidden, so bridge cards serve as camouflage material. There is always someone who can take care of Annie at that time. Johanna, it all went very well. Paula keeps on chattering.

But I can't digest so much information yet; I must apologize and ask my friend to slow down. "Paula, it makes me dizzy. I really can't keep up with you."

She was shocked. "Sorry, I should have known that. Sorry, sorry. You must recover. I am such a dreadful chatterbox." It's not a problem; stupid that she hadn't thought of that herself. She can hit herself on the forehead. But she is also so happy that I am doing better that she has completely forgotten that I am still weak.

The next day she returns with a Bible to read a few short selections out loud.

Today I can leave the sick bay. A nervous feeling. I haven't looked in a mirror for weeks. What do I look like? I weigh hardly anything anymore; my rib cage feels like a washboard; my cheeks are sunken. My skin is covered with red spots. As I was getting dressed this morning, I saw how sharply my pelvic bones stick out. Is this the body, I thought, out of which my children were born?

"You must stay calm for now, ma'am." Well-meant words, loving too, but the nurse must surely know that I cannot control that? I just let it go.

"You are still weak and should not get excited." I nod, thank the nurse for all the good care, and leave for the women's hall, which has increasingly resembled a shed with bunks that are 47 centimeters wide.

Being up is disappointing; in bed I felt stronger. I still have difficulty walking; my movements are unsteady. The heavy work, the long hours, I don't see myself doing it. Hopefully the head of the block is lenient. When she comes to check me out, should I exaggerate, heaving myself up laboriously? One, two, a little more. I'll practice for a while.

After their chores, the twins, who had meanwhile been notified of my return, come running up with little Annie in their wake. Jumping, laughing children. Malnourished and sloppily dressed.

"*Mama* is back. *Mama* is back, look."

Annie runs the last meters towards me and falls into my arms.

"Stop, stop, ladies. Your mother is still weak," I hear Paula say, just as she arrives. Here we are, the three girls

153

and I, a tangle of arms, grabbing each other and letting go. Completely overcome, I begin to cry, long, loud wails. Everyone is shocked. Am I not happy that we are together again? But that isn't it. Of course I am happy, even more than ever. It's grief over what could have been. I cry for everything I have missed. And it doesn't stop. Even though it's confusing for everyone, I can't stop it.

Later, I calm down somewhat. And then it is time for the surprise. Aafje and Willie will clandestinely perform a homemade puppet show. A scene from the Bible: Gideon and the Midianites. Talk about persistence. A cardboard box serves as a theater. It had become a truly collaborative project. Many women had worked together on the puppets, which were made from old rags. Others had helped to write the script. At the point where Gideon finds himself in front of the enemy camp and wonders if things in his nation will ever go well again, Paula, who is the lookout, suddenly gives a signal: the Japanese are on the way. Pack up, quickly. And in no time at all, everyone is on her own cot.

A new situation; I am missing something; the question is gone.

# Jan

*September 30, 1944*

"Who are you?"

Jan was approached by a friendly gentleman. He wore glasses, and insofar as Jan could make a good estimate, he was at least fifty years old.

"Jan Mobach, sir."

The man reached out his hand to him and said, "That's what I thought. I'm Mr. Grenzenberg and I am the head of your block. You remember me, don't you? Before the war, I lived across the street from you."

Jan was shocked for a moment when he heard that this gentleman was the head of their block, because by now he had learned that you had to be careful around the heads of the blocks.

Mr. Grenzenberg had seen his fear and calmed him down. "You don't need to be afraid, son, as long as you behave properly, and don't attract the attention of the Japanese, I don't have to step up, but if you do crazy things that make the Japanese angry, then I have little choice but to punish."

He said it in such a friendly way that Jan had to believe him.

Thanks to Mr. Grenzenberg, he occasionally got privileges that others didn't. When Jan looked desperately in his direction, he always got a wink as a sign not to show it. Besides Mr. Grenzenberg, he also got to know Alfred van Sprang. In Camp 8, he was one of the nurses, while before the war he had been an announcer for the Dutch-

Indies-Radio-Broadcasting Corporation Society. By virtue of that background, he regularly organized story-telling evenings for the boys, and then he told stories about his adventurous life.

Fascinated, they listened to his soothing low-pitched voice. They briefly forgot everything and were caught up in one of his many adventures.

Life in Camp 8 became a pattern: living in large groups of people who were all imprisoned in an overcrowded camp full of hardships. The absence of women and girls sometimes made it very boring in the camp. The only women in the camp were the two hundred nuns, who were more or less isolated from the rest. They lived withdrawn lives, and apart from their work details or their work in the wards, you saw them very little. Jan had a quiet admiration, that occasionally gave way to surprise, for this group. How was it possible that, despite the harsh conditions, they did not suffer physical decline, as you saw elsewhere in the camp?

From other camp internees, he learned that they were treacherous scoundrels who played a dubious role in the distribution of food. Not only were they corrupt, but they took good care of themselves. Food, according to the stories, intended for the starving and the sick, all too often went to themselves. And Jan had to admit that, despite the hardships, this group continued to look well cared for and nourished. He also knew that, just as with men who worked certain extra shifts, the nuns were given extra food for extra services and their work. They also managed to keep their habit and head covering tidy, something he certainly couldn't with his clothing. He decided not to engage in these stories. After all, nuns were also ordinary people, who, like him, if given the opportunity to earn extras, would take them. Didn't he do that himself? Why then shouldn't they? Everyone, if given the opportunity, was guilty of such practices. The nuns could not escape the power games that you had in every camp. If you were part of that, you were, by definition, living in a glass cage, and all your actions were constantly weighed and judged. Jan did not express his opinion, because then you would soon have to endure harassment from other camp internees. He always pretended to be stupid, and said he didn't know or see anything. Survival had nothing to do with taking part in angry conversations around you. It was best to stay aloof from gossip and backbiting. Then you did not end up in a difficult position.

"They are looking for people for a construction project in Bandongan. If you apply and are chosen, you move there and receive more food because it's hard work."

One of the camp internees whispered this to Jan, and told him not to spread the word too much, otherwise he wouldn't have a ghost of a chance.

Would it be true this time? The constant hunger and the prospect that by doing something, you could get more food, always enticed people.

Jan reported quickly and looked at the large group of boys ready for selection by Mr. Refuge.

"Everyone get in line and I'll see who is suitable. If I point to you, you can stand on the other side. Unfortunately, I need only sixty boys."

He walked along the row, surveyed each boy, and nodded whether he was accepted or not. It remained unclear on which basis he chose. When he stopped at Jan, he stood for a long time. Jan straightened his back to show

157

that he could handle a tough assignment. It took a long time for Mr. Refuge to make a decision. Much to Jan's relief, Mr. Refuge motioned for Jan to stand on the other side, and with that, he was chosen. For those who were not chosen, it remained a mystery why not. They knew deep down that there was a personal preference of Mr. Refuge in his choice. Disappointed, the others returned to their spots. No adventure outside the gate for them.

"Report here tomorrow morning at eight o'clock and take your mattress and *barang*—personal effects necessary—with you!" One of the boys asked how long they would be gone.

"I don't know. Expect it to take a long time. So take as much as you can."

Then he turned and walked away. The selected ones went to the area where they slept to gather what was most necessary.

The next morning, they were ready on time. Even boys that hadn't been chosen still hoped for a miracle. Someone could have gotten sick or dropped out during the night, but that was not the case. The sixty chosen ones were quickly loaded onto a pair of trucks. Then they rode out of the camp. For a moment it seemed as if they were free and there was no war. Through the streets of Ambarawa, past the houses, the Asian shops, and the fields, they wound over mountainous roads with magnificent views of beautiful and green panoramas, the rice fields, and along Rawa Bening, the marshland. A feeling of bliss enveloped Jan. He thoroughly enjoyed the trip. Higher in the mountains it became cooler, which reminded Jan of vacations with his parents in Kalioerang and Kopeng.

In time they arrived at their destination, and under the supervision of a few Japanese soldiers, they were ordered to settle into a house. Wooden beds had been built in the rooms, and together with fifteen boys, Jan ended up in the front room of the house, right next to the large veranda.

Then they had to report in front of the house for the division of duties. Jan indicated that he wanted to be a room attendant and got the assignment. He would take care of cleaning the house, the yard, and the kitchen. Some of the boys were a bit jealous because Jan outwitted them in asking for this position. Most of them were assigned to the cultivation of fifteen hectares of land with crops for the camps in the region. Mostly *lobak* was grown, a type of Indonesian radish, a white tuber rich in vitamins. Every day the boys left for the fields with a *patjol* on their shoulder, a hoe with which to work the soil and plant or harvest produce. It was hard work after eating only one ladle of tapioca flour porridge. They did not receive the extra food that had been promised. The starchy gunk filled their stomachs but did not satisfy their gnawing hunger. Above all, it was too little for the heavy work, with the result that many boys passed out during the day. Ultimately, this led to a slightly better food supply, but it was never enough.

In the morning and in the evening, Jan was responsible for the roll call, a way of checking whether everyone was there, and whether or not some were sick. As a room attendant, he had the task of getting everyone to stand next to his cot, and then the first one began to count:

"-Ichi-ni-san-shi-go-roku-shichi-hachi-kyuu-juu-dju. ichi-dju.-ni-" He had already heard the counting from one to ten, and even beyond that, so many times, that the sounds were etched in his memory. Everyone knew the number sequence by the sound of the person counting. It was difficult if you had forgotten your number or if you hadn't been listening to your predecessor. Sometimes you got away with grunting your number, but more often you were hit if you weren't paying attention. Each time it was a tough military drill with which the Japanese tried to keep you in line.

Bandongan was a small camp and considerably cleaner than the other camps. Given the cooler temperatures, they were not bothered by lice, which daily terrorized the internees of the other camps. An added bonus of being in Bandongan was the hotel in their vicinity, where many Japanese and German guests slept. There was a swimming pool with not very clean water, so the guests did not go swimming there. However, the boys were delighted with the possibility of swimming there, albeit naked, because no one had swimming trunks. The sight met with great hilarity on the part of the hotel guests who watched with amusement.

After six weeks, they were relieved of their duties. With the trucks bringing their replacements, they were taken back to Camp 8 in Ambarawa. Jan didn't understand why he had to go back, all the more because a number of his roommates were allowed to stay, and indeed, stayed there until the end of the war. Upon his return, he noticed that even more prisoners had been added, and that his old sleeping place had been taken.

160

You could not lay any claim to it. Only if you were actively using a spot, could you be sure of it. Otherwise, you lost it.

After Bandongan, life in Camp 8 quickly returned to normal. Bandongan had been a short, beautiful dream in comparison with Jan's situation in Ambarawa. In particular, the food shortages, the discomfort from the bedbugs, malaria, and the lack of proper latrines made life unbearably difficult.

Several times Jan had a malaria attack and diarrhea, which was the result of the poor quality of food or the food they took from the garbage heap. In the autumn of 1944, Jan, like many others in the camp, contracted jaundice. The advantage of that disease was that, every day, you got a small tin of sugar as medicine. After a while you would recover. However, Jan ended up in the sick bay because he developed paratyphoid fever as well. Alfred van Sprang, also stricken by jaundice, was his roommate in the sick bay. Jan thought that either Alfred wasn't that sick, or just pretended not to be so sick, because he had plenty of time for him and the other boys. His calm, friendly, and likeable manner made him a father figure.

Because of his illness, Jan fell into a comatose state, and one night he was overcome by the feeling of wanting to let go of everything. He was hallucinating. He was in bad shape, something he heard Dr. Bolke say at his bedside, "His pulse is only 35; he's not going to make it," after which Jan slowly slipped away into a feeling of surrender and bliss.

After hours or days, he didn't know which, he was awakened by Alfred's voice:

"Jan, you can't give up. You want to see your father again, and your mother, and maybe your brothers and sisters? Imagine if they would give up too? How would you like that?"

He was being called from afar.

Miraculously, he recovered from his illness and was even able to return to his sleeping place, which was now waiting for him. He was greeted enthusiastically, and as he was still weak, they watched over him and provided food. He was forced to rest and sleep until he had completely recovered.

One evening, Jan asked Alfred how he knew that he missed his father.

"Don't you miss him?"

"Yes, of course, but how did you know?"

"Every boy misses his father; you do too, don't you?"

Jan admitted that it was true.

"Were you and he close?" Alfred asked amiably.

"No, actually not. He was inaccessible to me, and to be honest, I don't have many pleasant memories of him. He was always strict and formal in his dealings with us. He hit me too."

"But you still miss him?"

"Yes, but I don't know why."

"Do you have any more brothers and sisters?"

Jan never found out why Alfred asked all those questions. But his interest helped Jan to talk about his mother and his sisters who were still in Banjoe Biroe, about his brothers in Djoen Eng Salatiga, and his father in Fort Vredeburg.

"And since then, you haven't heard from them?"

Jan was closer to crying than to laughing, and when Alfred saw that, he put his hand on Jan's arm.

"Don't be ashamed to miss them. Since you are now sixteen, you need a father as a role model, and he isn't here. Whom do you actually have here? Mr. Grenzenberg and me; what good does that do you?"

Jan burst into laughter and told him that he was happy with them.

"I will try to be your father a little, until you find him again when this war is over."

"Will I ever find him again? Maybe he's already dead."

Alfred had looked at him and said very slowly, "If you think that, he has no chance of survival. If you believe you will see him again, then you will see him again when this is all over. You have to hold on. It won't last much longer."

Then he changed the subject. "If you don't have time to think, everything goes faster. Do you know what you need to do?"

"Well? What?"

"Look for distraction. As soon as you are better, sign up for a work assignment. Then you are not only busy, but it offers you a chance for extra food from the nuns, which you need to become and to stay strong."

When Jan had recovered, he signed up for extra services. And so he was put to work in the kitchen of the boys' sick bay, under the watchful eye of a few friendly nuns. He spent every day with them, and Alfred was right: his work in the kitchen gave him regular extra food. Alfred had also seen that he missed his father, but because of the hard work, he did not have time to worry, and he was so tired that he fell asleep immediately.

Other boys were assigned to the heavy forage-transports to the various camps. Jan told one of them where his mother and sisters were, and asked him to look for them. In this way, he heard that his mother and sisters were doing well, and that, providentially, his mother had recovered from the severe typhoid attack. Before going to bed, he thanked God for this miracle, and resolved to distrust no more, and to cling to Alfred's words: "If you believe that you will see them again, then that will happen." His mother's recovery was proof of that. If she and his sisters persevered, as well as his father and brothers, the day would come when they would see each other again.

The time for being pampered was over. After his illness, his camp companions turned their attention back to themselves or to other sick people. If you were considered able to take care of yourself again, you should do the same.

To get enough food, you had only one method: *kawatten*. Smuggling, bartering, and trading were strictly prohibited, and if you were caught, resulted in severe penalties. Nevertheless, it was rampant, usually at night. The locals were always willing to trade food for whatever could be exchanged.

"Do you have something to trade?"

The question was whispered to him by a professional trader, a little blond boy from his hall. Jan's trading stock was declining rapidly. He did still have his barely worn black velvet Sunday trousers that their seamstress in Djokja had made for him at the time, and to which he was very attached. It was no time for sentimentality, so he offered the pants as an item for trade.

"I want hard-boiled duck eggs for them; otherwise, don't trade," he commanded. The boy took his pants, and after Jan passed an hour of longing and curious waiting in the pitch-dark room, the boy returned.

"Here, Jan, I was able to get eggs for them."

Jan eagerly took possession of the eggs. What a luxury, to have so much food in your hands. He didn't think twice, thanked the boy, and quickly crept to a toilet in the hall. There, in the dim lighting, afraid of being caught, he eagerly peeled his eggs. Greedily, he ate them all without feeling nauseous. After he had devoured them, he was overcome with a sense of regret. He could have enjoyed this much longer. Still, he walked back to his bunk with a full stomach and a grateful heart, and his regret was eclipsed by the pleasant feeling caused by this opportunity and a full stomach. How long had it been since he had felt like this?

Every day, wagons for corpses were driven into the camp. Nobody was surprised anymore. Coffins were the only items the Japanese let in. They were rough wooden boxes, sloppily assembled from poor, unshaped wood. Sometimes they came apart just after being hammered together. The internees of the camp were not surprised. Not by the number of coffins, neither by their daily appearance. Every coffin represented a corpse; every corpse a funeral, that occurred not once, but several times a day. In the beginning, people still cared, especially if it were someone from their own vicinity in the camp. As the number drastically increased, the sense of compassion and pity decreased.

"Another one who has been released from his suffering and is now at peace," was a common comment, and death became a friend rather than an enemy. The Japanese responsible for this was the enemy.

The number of sick people had recently increased alarmingly, and there were many victims, especially among the older men. Often children had to board up the dead men's coffins. Apparently it didn't affect them. It was a task you were given and performed, regardless of who was lying inside.

The lack of food and medical care was the cause of all the illnesses and deaths in the camp. Hunger edema and dysentery were the most common diseases and the main cause of many deaths, especially if you were unlucky enough to have both diseases.

"Cancerous Japanese! Unbelieving sinners! Destroyers of the world! Bunch of bastard idiots, Kraut-lovers!"

Jan was shocked by the many curses he heard coming from a sick bay. An old man suffering from hunger edema grumbled about his fate. To relieve his illness, the doctors had inserted a kind of catheter into his stomach to drain the accumulating fluid. It was thought that this could prolong his life, but after a few days, he died nonetheless. There was a lot of declining life in the sick bay, and Jan saw that everything was being done to help the sick and alleviate their suffering, but it did not benefit the patients, due to a lack of food and medicine. Jan got used to death, and yet, as he walked across the gallery, he glanced into the sick bay to determine that the number was only increasing. He observed that once you reached a stage that placed you in this ward, it wouldn't be long. When someone died, he was quickly taken away, so that someone else could lie there.

One day, he was apprehended by Alfred van Sprang.

"That's what almost happened to you, Jan! Be thankful that I called you back, and make sure you stay out of here.

You have given yourself a task and you must complete it. It is not good to look at this often. It is better to look at life and to repeat the assignment that you have given yourself."

Jan wanted to thank Alfred for his words, but strangely enough, Alfred had already left. Jan could still hear his soft laugh.

And Alfred's words stayed with him, because at a funeral, Jan seemed to hear his voice again. Life and death were closely intertwined in this camp. One night, when Jan dreamt that he was dying, he saw himself being sucked up into an inky black space. The world slowly slipped under him, and around him he experienced silence and saw a number of stars. He was overcome by a great sense of calm and peace. Surprised, he landed on a white stone staircase and looked ahead where a large gate had opened. He looked inside and saw plenty of light and human shapes. Beautiful music played in the background. He decided to obey the inviting music and go inside, but again, the voice of Alfred van Sprang called him back.

"It's not your time, Jan; come back! Think about your assignment!"

Jan awoke, and for a long time afterwards, he lay staring in the dark, listening to the sleeping sounds around him, and thinking about his peculiar dream.

When it was still dark, and he had just fallen asleep again, he was awakened by the head of the block.

"Get up, get dressed, and gather at the main building!"

With thirty others, he was hustled out of bed, not knowing what to expect. Nor would they be told. Their stomachs empty, they were ordered to board a waiting truck which left almost immediately. In the vehicle, they were all guessing why. That soon became apparent when

167

they arrived at the yard of the nearby station, which, strangely enough, was fully lit.

"Get out, and quickly!" was the harsh command. At the platform there was a long train, and around the station they saw a cordon of Japanese and native Javanese soldiers. A large number of trucks stood on the yard.

The platform was swarming with women, girls and children laden with all kinds of things. They looked exhausted and hollow-eyed. All around him, he heard shouted commands directed at the women, girls, and children, to board the trucks. They were to be taken to Ambarawa and Banjoe Biroe. When everyone in the trucks had left, the boys were ordered to board the train and unload the cars.

With other boys, Jan clambered into the cars where there hung a sour smell of food scraps, sweat, vomit, and urine. The women, girls, and children had been in the armored train cars from Bandoeng for almost two days. In Ambarawa, they had been ordered to get off the train and leave everything behind.

"It will be gathered and taken to you!" That was a lie.

The sudden confrontation with so many food scraps turned the boys into a grabbing, greedy, and appalling mob.

Everyone grabbed what he could, especially bread and rice. Yet they were also expected to throw everything— loose or attached—out through the small shutters. What was not yet broken, was now indeed being broken. In no time, both the platform and the area alongside the train were littered with an incredible pile of junk.

In a luggage net, Jan found a small pan. In it, he discovered rice gruel, and he greedily swallowed the rice.

168

The mash turned out to be sour, but that didn't deter him. He satisfied his hunger and that was more important than the quality of the food. In time, the job was done, and the train cars were empty. Everyone had hidden as much food as possible under his shirt, especially small and doughy bread that they sometimes got in the camp.

Like little Michelin-men, they stood on the platform; what a ludicrous sight. It was impossible to hide their loot.

A Japanese officer in charge of the whole operation saw immediately what was going on, and fiercely brandished his sword. He stopped in front of some boys whose shoulders he then struck with his sword. Jan too, and consequently, the bread fell out of his clothing onto the platform. With sad faces, the boys looked at their lost rolls. Then the officer made it clear that each one could keep one small loaf of bread, and with a smile, he turned and walked away.

It was a wonderful day. First, they could feast on the food on the train, which had satisfied their worst hunger for that moment. Then, as a reward, they were allowed to take another small loaf of bread with them.

They were driven back to the camp where they told their story of the day. Those who stayed behind had been astonished that the others had left so suddenly. In fact, rumors had been circulating that they had misbehaved and had been taken away, or that there had been boys who had stolen valuables from the train for barter. You were not told the truth behind these stories. Neither could you rule out that it was true. Everything that you could use to trade for food must be carefully stored. What if it were there for the taking?

# Father Jaan Willem

*October 1944*

After more than twenty-two months of separation, Jaan's two eldest sons, Piet and Gerard, came to Camp 4 on October 19.

"How did you get here?"

After this cool greeting, and the expression of his concern that they looked so skinny, it was time for this question.

They both laughed cheerlessly.

"When we received your 'sign of life', we immediately applied for a transfer..."

"...and got it. Isn't that amazing? We thought it wouldn't work..."

"...but within a few days it was done. They would rather be rid of us than be rich!"

They were prattling and interrupting each other.

"But how are you, Father?"

Concerned, they looked at him. He was skin and bones.

"I'm fine, boys. Since I can regularly participate in the outdoor chores, I get extra food. Sometimes it is so much that I can sell it, and that is how I can save again."

He looked back and forth from Piet to Gerard and saw from their swollen faces that both had traces of hunger edema. Their mood, however, conveyed a zest for life and a feeling of joy. They were together again, and that's what mattered.

"Have you heard anything from Mother and the girls?"

He owed them that answer. His wife's last message had been nine months ago, and he was worried about that.

"Don't worry, Father. They will be fine."

Piet wanted to reassure him, for which Jaan was grateful. The boy had grown up. Jaan realized that he had been alone for too long and was saddened by the thought that he might never see his wife and children again. The fact that two of his sons were here now belied his gloom. They were living proof that you will meet again, if you just keep believing.

That evening, as they unpacked their belongings, Jaan was amazed at the number of items they had with them. According to the rules of the camp, that was not allowed, but not too much attention was paid to those rules. To his surprise, they even had his old white suits and also a white cassock of a pastor.

"What are you doing with that?" he asked with surprise, and looked, almost with disapproval, at something from the Roman Catholic Church.

"Oh, we bartered for something, and who cares that it belonged to a priest? It's a beautiful fabric that you can always use for something..."

"...or trade for food," Gerard completed Piet's thought.

"That's great that you have gathered so much. You will soon have to trade. I have only sold. My fountain pen, my watch, and even my wedding ring, because I had absolutely no financial reserves anymore."

Piet noticed his father's dejection at the loss of his things and put his hand on his father's arm.

"It's just stuff, Father. The most important thing is that we are still alive. Things can be replaced, but you have your life only once."

His son's wisdom struck him anew. When he was interned, they were still children. Now they were grown men with their own outlook on life.

The boys were housed in a building opposite his barracks. It was full of bedbugs, but it didn't bother them.

"We've seen worse," was Gerard's laconic response, when Jaan nearly apologized for the pests and the filth.

The next day, hoping to be with their father, the boys signed up for the outside chores, but the camp leadership decided otherwise. They were young and had to do tougher jobs. This resulted in extra food that they could take with them to the camp in the evening, to share with their father and others. After dinner, with stomachs reasonably full, they sat cross-legged, tailor-style, on their father's straw mattress. While enjoying a rolled cigarette, they could sometimes talk for hours or just look straight ahead. *It was almost like home*, thought Jaan.

"If Mother, the girls, and Jan could be with us now, we would be a real family again."

"It will be fine, Father. Have faith. It won't be long now."

The next day, none of the three was assigned an outside chore.

To pass the time, Piet asked, "Father, should we be bosses?"

Surprised, Jaan looked at his son and burst into laughter. "What should I imagine that is?"

"*'Bazen'* is the camp word for selling clothes. We often did it in Bandoeng."

"Don't we need those clothes ourselves?"

"Not everything, and you know, when the Americans come, we will all get new clothes, so we can sell quite a bit of stuff."

They decided to sell a few things. There was a constant interest among the prisoners. Some even had more money than things. The "*bazen*" earned them over sixty-five guilders, which they divided amongst themselves. Unfortunately, the purchasing power of the money was not very great; one egg cost three guilders.

T he money was immediately converted into food. Hunger remained a problem, and although Jaan urged his sons to be thrifty, and not to convert everything immediately into food, the hunger was too great. Better to go to bed with a full stomach today than go to bed for days on end with a growling stomach. Anything that the boys received in food was immediately consumed, instead of being spread out over the days when there was less or no food. If they had eaten well, their strength increased, but when the food was gone, it decreased just as quickly.

Jaan saw with sorrow that almost no learning was going on. During the day, Piet and Gerard were usually on a work assignment, and when they came back, they were too tired to study. On Sundays, there were church services in Tjimahi, which surprised the boys, because in their camp all church services had been forbidden and were conducted secretly. In Tjimahi, they were permitted. The Dutch Reformed and the Reformed organized their services along with the Salvation Army. The Roman Catholics had their own services. In the midst of all the iniquity, cruelty, heartlessness, misery, and struggle for existence, there was still a place for consecration and devotion. For many, it was also the last shred of hope in a miserable existence. Jaan noticed that even unbelievers came to seek comfort and to profess their faith publicly during the services—the faith they had reclaimed in the ruins of their existence.

There were Japanese officers who didn't like any of this, and came to disrupt services. Sometimes the sirens went off, which meant that everyone had to return to the barracks as quickly as possible and close doors and windows. One Sunday, the pastor conducting the service decided to continue as usual and even to allow the organist to continue playing. A Japanese officer, hearing it, entered furiously and ordered that the service be ended. The pastor walked up to the officer and said, *"Tuan, ini adalah pertemuan doa,"* or "Sir, this is a prayer meeting." The Japanese gave him a vicious blow to the face, at which his glasses flew through the room. The pastor, who had fallen, scrambled to his feet and repeated what he had said the first time. Again, he took a few blows. With that, the fury of the Japanese had subsided and the service ended. Everyone slipped out of the room. Jaan and the boys took refuge in their own barracks. Yet, the exercise of punishment, started by the Japanese, was not ended. Prisoners were taken to the penal barracks, where punishment continued. They heard the screams of the victims. Anyone could be next. There didn't always have to be cause for punishment, which was arbitrary and disproportionate. Minor offenses were maximally punished, while larger offenses could be overlooked. Sometimes the entire camp was punished for an offense committed by an individual. For example, no food was distributed, or you had to work without wages.

Jaan urged his boys to stay away from the Japanese, and above all, to do nothing to arouse their fury.

# Mother

*November 1944*

Strange how life just goes on. When you are gone and when you come back. At first I am still weak and often dizzy. I can't wash myself, although I would certainly like to. Aafje or Willie help me and have no problem with it, but I do. The touching of my private parts, I can't get used to it. I can't move beyond the shame.

I spend a lot of time in bed...with the permission of the head of the block, Mrs. Riessen. I am fortunate. Sometimes she is less accommodating. I am obliged to do one thing: attend roll call twice a day. For the first time, I feel a slight connection with the women who have continued to believe in the good, who try to make the best of things, and who are the ones I used to avoid. I think about the resilience of children and their perseverance. They may have been robbed of their youth, their decency, and their health, damaged for the future, all true. But they are still here, and there will be other years, other dreams.

Life in the camp hardly changes. As always, the days are filled with chores. We have our hands full with keeping our clothes clean and repaired, organizing our living space, scrubbing, cooking over fires, and looking for snails. There is always something to do. Cultivate vegetables with a pickaxe. Clean vegetables. If you're lucky, you can slip a carrot into your shirt. Get hold of a leek. Our main concern is food, survival.

The normal chores are performed with a relatively positive attitude. The forced labor meant to harass is worse. The Japanese are very good at that. If it is clean inside the camp, we sometimes have to go outside to clean the grounds around the camp, the so-called blade-detail. Plucking blades of grass from between the fieldstones, in the hot sun. With our scissors, nail clippers, and table knives. Pointless work, especially in the rainy season, since the grass grows back just as fast. Exhaustion is the only goal. Once in a while, using old table knives, we have to chop down a banana tree: try it sometime. That's when we are taken from our cots. Goodbye afternoon nap.

My experiences are repetitious; I do what I have to do: wash, dress, eat, talk. I am who I am, but I experience things differently. How can I explain it? I have a greater underlying feeling of contentment, as if a layer of resistance has been removed. That makes a difference. I am better at hearing the questions. I am afraid in a different way. Not because of pettiness, not because of my dependence, but more because of the actions of which people are capable. I am less trapped in my own world, where I, as the unlucky one, would prefer to stay. How exhausting is that?

But there is something else. I have become more sensitive to what is happening around me. I think of the incident a few weeks ago during the roll call. As a rule, the man who wears a sash—the head of the block, with a wide sash diagonally over his shoulder, white with red stripes— is in charge of the roll call, and represents the Japanese. The bizarre result is that twice a day, a charade takes place: Dutch women bow to other Dutch women who are shouting orders.

But this day, there is a Japanese standing in front of the rows. Two Japanese guards walk along the rows and inspect the women. We are animals. One girl is picked from the row, and the guards drag her to the other end of the camp and disappear with her into a hut. With a loud bang, the door slams shut behind them. We must remain standing in the blazing sun. We all hear the cries coming from the hut. I feel embarrassed. The image of my lovemaking with Jaan comes to mind. Always a bit absent, aloof, and silent; I didn't know any better. I wasn't looking for pleasure. But it was normal. Something you cannot say about the sounds coming from the hut. It's heartbreaking.

A vicious smirk appears on the face of that nasty yellow slit-eye who keeps screaming unintelligibly in front of our rows. After a while, the girl is returned, pale as a sheet, with an empty look in her eyes. Tears flow down her cheeks. I look away, feel dirty, unworthy. I'm afraid. We are all scared. It's not the first time I've seen it, but without my armor of indifference, it hits hard. Now I'm participating, and I feel it too. Mind you, the next time, the only time that counts, it could be Aafje or Willie (fortunately, their femininity is not yet evident, and their breasts have not developed so far...). I really don't understand why it is only now that I am so worried about that.

Mothers teach each other little ruses. With zinc ointment, we put random white spots on the faces of our daughters and then sprinkle some powder on them. When the Japanese, terrified as they are of disease, see the girls, they immediately grab their masks. Then we feel pleasure and are happy even in degrading circumstances.

I'm also surprised that rape is such a common topic of conversation among the girls. They giggle about it. Strategies are devised. "We smear green soap on our

178

bellies, and then they slide out." Followed by contagious laughter.

Reality is flexible. But this goes much too far for me. Then I think of the bodies of the women at the well, who, after their rape, saw no other way out than to hang themselves, ironically right at the spot that keeps us alive, that provides us with water. Could it be any more cruel?

Anyway, my constricted heart has gotten a little more air. I don't have to keep my eyes closed anymore; it is no longer necessary.

# Father Jaan Willem

*December 1944*

His work assignment was a job in a factory in the blacksmith department. His boss was quite principled. At one point, the Japanese gave the order to make bayonets. For the soldiers. The material was so shoddy that his boss refused to produce them, and a discussion arose between him and the Japanese.

"You heard what was said, and you do what has been said. I also have my orders to carry out without question; therefore, you do too."

"I'm not starting this. Then you'd better have the men killed immediately."

He persisted in his refusal and the Japanese became angry. He had all the workers assemble in the courtyard, and began to tell a story that no one understood. Foam formed around his mouth, and as his argument progressed, he grew increasingly angry. He picked up a bamboo stick, signaled to bring the supervisor forward, and began to hit the man, systematically and skillfully. Harsh blows descended on the man, who staggered, and was then tied down. And again the blows fell on him until the stick broke. A new stick was brought and the Japanese repeated his beating. Meanwhile, the man's eyes betrayed his agony. The Japanese kept hitting until he could do it no longer and, utterly exhausted, he left the grounds. The bystanders took care of the victim and helped him to his feet. Someone said, "You will see the Japanese regret his behavior."

The beaten man came away with serious bruising and contusions. Fortunately, nothing was broken. He did not permit the bayonets to be forged. That was a win for him, and nothing more was said about it.

During the Christmas season, the Japanese allowed a banquet to be held for the factory workers. By pure coincidence, the supervisor ended up sitting next to the Japanese officer. At one point, the Japanese officer stood up and gave a speech in Malay, declaring that he had done wrong and promising to improve his life. So, he did have regrets.

The Christmas celebration was the end of Jaan's work in the factory. A reason was not given, and Jaan had to wait and see where he would be placed next. Working in the factory had increased his physical strength, but hunger remained a daily torment, and the search for extra food a challenge. For the umpteenth time, the rations in the camp were decreased, which compelled him to search for food every day.

One day he heard that Red Cross packages had arrived for the prisoners of war. Their arrival caused a riot of joy in the camp. But things didn't turn out as they had expected. First, the packages had to be inspected, and were temporarily stored. After several weeks, they were suddenly distributed. Much to their frustration, they received only a very small portion of the packages. The Japanese had kept almost everything for themselves. For the people in Jaan's room, there was a single one-man portion which had to be shared with all of them. Still, they were happy with it, because it was completely different from their normal food. Jaan thought the milk powder was the most delicious.

The biggest surprise was the heavenly manna, as they called it. They were flying ants, which, exhausted from their flight, fell from the sky in swarms. One evening, these *larongs* were fluttering around their camp lights. In just a few moments, the ground was strewn with these creatures, which were rich in protein and fat and had been eaten by the Javanese in all kinds of dishes for centuries. After an hour of rummaging, the men in Jaan's room had gathered a large number which they roasted and ate blissfully. There were prisoners who could not wait until they were fried, and put them in their mouths alive, swallowing them as the greatest delicacy.

# Jan

*March 1945*

The rumor spread quickly: "We are going to move!"

"The camp is being cleared!"

"We have to get out of here!"

No one knew precisely what was going on. What Jan had learned by now was that each rumor hid a measure of truth, although there were still people who shrugged their shoulders. And yes, a few days after the first rumor, it became reality. Within a week, they had to vacate all the buildings.

"We are going to another camp that is already so full!"

The fact that another camp was already overpopulated left the Japanese indifferent. According to them, more could always be added. If there were already two layers of wooden cots, a third or a fourth could always be built on top. They recognized no basic requirements, and as for hygiene, it was no longer considered or implemented. Was lack of hygiene meant to kill more people? The non-indigenous population had always been a major concern for the Japanese.

On moving day, an intensely sad and gloomy procession of men and boys passed through Ambarawa. They were in such poor condition that they could barely walk. Appearing distressed, but remaining silent, the native Javanese looked with pity at their heads, red with exertion and riddled with bulging blood vessels. You could read it in their eyes: a look of disapproval, pain, and compassion.

They had initially seen the Dutch as the occupiers of their country, and the Japanese as the liberators, but the years of the Japanese occupation had taught them that they had fallen from heaven to hell.

The sun shone unmercifully on the procession of misery: men in stiff suits, torn clothes, and threadbare pajamas. Some still had something on their feet: old worn-out shoes, tattered slippers, and wooden sandals, but many walked on bare feet which were dirty and bloodied.

Sick people who had still lain in a sick bay the day before, staggered through the streets. If you were lucky, you were transported in a truck whose chauffeur strictly controlled who could ride and who could walk. Anyone who could move in the slightest could not get in a truck. In the hospital of the abandoned camp, there were still a few hundred seriously ill people. People assumed that they would be transferred by truck. That did not happen.

"Carry on stretchers!" came the command from a Japanese. All patients with edema, heavy as lead, and more dead than alive, were transported on stretchers made of bamboo sticks and leather bags. It was a hellish torture, both for the sick, and for the starving and severely malnourished porters, who had difficulty lifting the heavy stretchers onto their shoulders and carrying them for two kilometers. The shaking caused patients to fall to the ground, their misery intensified by the rain. The Japanese hounded everyone to finish before dark.

And miraculously, everyone arrived on time, surviving the arduous journey. They were given a place somewhere in a barracks. The sick were taken to the "hospital," the old horse stables of the camp. Soaked to the skin, they were stacked up, while the infamous winds of Ambarawa blew through the wooden walls, bringing in the cold. There were no windows. The sick lay on the floor of uneven paving stones in four long rows. It was cold and damp, and moaning and weeping were heard everywhere. In a single quiet corner, prayers were lifted, against the better judgment of the suppliant. Salvation came when night fell, and the first deaths occurred. Many more in the following days. Although the move had been successful, the price was inhumanly high. Humanity was a word that did not exist in the vocabulary of the Japanese occupier.

Every day there were dozens of deaths. The move had been useful because death could do its work, and the culling could not be stopped. There was a lack of everything: no food, no vitamins, no fats, no medicines, no medical care, and no longer any strength or hope for the prisoners. Death became a welcome friend, a deliverer from sorrow, pain, and misery.

The new camp, Camp 7 Ambarawa, was a collection of old barracks made of wood and bamboo, and was many times worse than Camp 8. With a gloomy and painful feeling, Jan looked around when he passed the gate and saw this revolting, dilapidated mess. You wouldn't even house animals there. It was the residence of twenty-five hundred men, a thousand boys, and three hundred nuns.

Looking for a spot for themselves, hundreds of people thronged the area in the middle of the grounds and around the barracks.

Jan was placed in a corner of the horse stable, now barracks 7, not far from the gate. On both sides there was a sloping roof, supported by the outer wall. Holes served as windows without glass that could be closed only from the outside, to ward off the wind. In the barracks, there was a vestibule with a small room that served as a place for the oldest resident. Behind that was a large room paneled on both sides with three-storey bunks. Under the lowest part, the bunks were two storeys high. For each person there was a personal space of forty-five centimeters.

In the centre aisle stood long tables with benches. A light bulb with a blue shade hung on a wire from the ceiling. Jan was one of the seven hundred internees of their barracks. He had been appointed as *kumicho*, head of a section of the barracks assigned to about a hundred physically weakened boys. His assignment was to supervise the distribution of food and to accompany Dr. Bolke and a nurse on their daily rounds. With the help of a checklist, he had to ensure that his section of the hall was kept clean. As *kumicho*, he was given a badge with a red stripe above which his camp number, 9907, was shown. There was a daily consultation with the other *kumichos* and the head of the block, Mr. Dolman, about the state of affairs in the barracks.

Jan, who had great difficulty adjusting to the new living conditions, had to force himself to take his new duties seriously. If he didn't, someone else could be assigned, and he wanted to prevent that. Everything around him was revolting: squalid wooden shelters above a creek at the edge of the camp. It was filthy there, it reeked, and it was crawling with vermin. He missed his own nook, like the one he had in Camp 8, but above all, he missed his friends. They had come along with the move, but were housed elsewhere in the camp. In time, he did encounter them again, and they shared their stories. It became apparent that they were even worse off and were at the whim of the heads of their blocks and fellow prisoners. Some of them were put to work in the sick bay where they did their best to help the sick as well as they could, together with the nuns, who had the ultimate responsibility for the nursing care which had more to do with guidance to death than to healing. From experience, he knew that the sick bay was a place where you should not end up.

His imprisonment was gradually becoming worse. In each camp, despite the harsh and terrible conditions, there was still something to cling to: your own spot, forced labor assignments that gave you a chance for extra food. Even though they were often false promises, they gave you hope. Camaraderie with fellow prisoners gave you the feeling that you were not alone, and the ongoing rumors that it would be over before long, and that the Americans were coming soon, were encouraging. In the previous camp, that rumor reached a high point when they suddenly heard the sound of an airplane. It was early 1945. That was rare, and many heads turned skyward. A green airplane flew relatively low over the camp. It did not have the red circle of the Japanese as expected, but the tricolor of the Netherlands. Pamphlets were dropped from the airplane and were gathered by the Japanese in haste. In the pamphlets, the Dutch government reported on the state of affairs during the war. No one had been able to read what it actually said, but it did spark much speculation about an imminent deliverance.

"By the next full moon, it will be over!" Many whispered it; even more hoped it.

The Japanese escalated their inhumane reprisals. They instituted more severe hardships to quell this rumor. Jan experienced this period as the worst of his entire period of imprisonment. Everything worked against him.

They tried to keep their barracks clean by mopping every day, airing the bedding regularly, and fighting the bedbugs, for example, by sleeping on the floor in the centre aisle. The wooden beds were riddled with bedbugs, which, as soon as it was dark, emerged from all the cracks and crevices to feast on the sleeping prisoners. And if you weren't already being eaten by the bedbugs, chances were you had to run to the latrines several times a night due to constant diarrhea. Many did not make it on time, because, in the dark, they stumbled over the boys on the floor. This led to swearing, cursing, and sometimes even fighting among themselves. Tolerance had fallen to an absolute minimum, and due to sheer exhaustion, hunger, overwrought nerves, and anxiety, arguments broke out regularly. Then there was scabies. And yet another macabre practice:

On a pole opposite the entrance to their barracks hung a blackboard on which were recorded daily the names of those deceased the day before. The list grew longer by the day. Death was breathing heavily down everyone's neck. It began with a few, but soon there were more than twenty deaths a day on the list. Five to six hundred deaths per month. Jan initially tried to ignore the lists. "What you don't know doesn't affect you," he recalled Alfred van Sprang saying, but no matter how hard he tried, he couldn't avoid looking. His curiosity overcame his fear.

"As long as you're standing here, you're not on the list," whispered an older man, Mr. Stam, to him. "Make sure you stay on this side of the list; then there is still hope."

A few days later, Jan saw Mr. Stam's name on the list, and remembered the assignment that Alfred van Sprang had given him: "You have a mission!"

Later, when some prisoners renamed their camp the "death camp," the ominous and paralyzing prospect was complete, and you knew for sure: you were here in order not to survive. That was the intention of the Japanese barbarians and the reality proved their theory. The boys had the best chance of survival even though they were severely malnourished. With the death of so many people, their task became steadily harder as they had to haul the bodies outside and place them in coffins. There was no one else to do it anymore: not the men, not the nuns, only the boys were left. It was a disgusting job; the coffins were basically crates through which the edema fluid leaked out. Every day, death looked them in the eye.

Jan did what he had to do and forced himself to remain indifferent.

Usually he succeeded, except once.

During his stay in the camp, he had become acquainted with Mr. De Boer, a shipbuilder, who built small ships at Tandjong Priok before the war. Since Jan made many drawings of ships and airplanes and was interested in the shipbuilding trade, he had contacted Mr. De Boer through a nun to ask him to teach him the trade. Jan showed him his drawings, which Mr. De Boer examined carefully through his glasses. He was impressed and took Jan outside where they looked for a shady, peaceful spot, insofar as that was possible. Mr. De Boer took a small stick in his hand and drew the hull of a boat in the dirt.

"Look, Jan, calculating the center of gravity of a ship is always the hardest part. If you do that wrong, the ship won't lie well in the water."

He told him how to make these calculations, and because Jan continued to listen to him with great fascination, Mr. De Boer told him more and more. Jan saw himself becoming a shipbuilder, and they agreed to find a spot every day to continue the lessons.

Only occasionally did they discuss the situation in the camp.

"In your mind, you must daily tell yourself that it doesn't exist, but that you are living in a bad dream. You will see that one day you will wake up, and the dream will be over. You are still young and must hang onto that image of the future. My time is almost over."

A bond had developed between them, and it served as a distraction. Every spare moment, they looked for a spot, and Jan was allowed to ask a question. And although it was mostly about building ships, there was room for other things.

When Jan asked him about his family one day, he said that he was divorced, and that his daughter was in a different camp, but that he had not heard from her for a long time. He listened attentively to Jan's story about his father, mother, brothers, and sisters. And he consoled Jan in his loss and longing for them.

"It won't be long, Jan, and then you will see them all again. Keep believing that!"

One day, when they had agreed to meet again, Jan noticed that Mr. De Boer was very gloomy. He asked why, but Mr. De Boer shrugged and said it was nothing.

But Jan noticed that he was somewhat preoccupied, so Jan asked again what was going on.

A gray veil passed over the face of Mr. De Boer, who pulled up his trouser legs a little and pointed at his feet:

"Death is coming for me, Jan, look; I'm not doing well, and I'm afraid I will have to cancel our lessons. I am extremely tired and don't feel well."

Jan was shocked at the sight of his calves. He had often seen it in others and knew that Mr. De Boer was suffering from hunger edema. He knew what this meant.

They saw each other less and less, because Mr. De Boer had to stay in bed. Jan faithfully visited him. Then, Mr. De Boer was too tired to talk, and asked him to come back the following day.

After a few weeks, he was admitted to the hospital barracks. Jan continued to visit him and was shocked time and again by his bloated body. The man whom Jan had temporarily considered as his father was deteriorating right before his eyes.

"Jan, I don't think that I will make it anymore..."

It was a sigh that sounded like a relief.

Jan felt too powerless to say or do anything, and just sat next to his bed.

One night, several days later, a nurse woke Jan.

"Jan...Jan, Mr. De Boer has asked if you would come."

Even though Jan knew what this meant, he was still stunned. He got up and quickly followed the nun to the hospital barracks. Jan walked over to Mr. De Boer, sat down on the edge of his cot, and took the hand of his old friend, who was lying with his eyes closed.

"Mr. De Boer, I'm here."

For a moment the man lifted his eyelids and looked at him.

Jan felt restless and did not know what he must or could do. Mr. De Boer whispered, pausing to catch his breath, "Jan, I don't have much longer...I'm leaving...I'm going to God...would you read something from the Bible to me?"

It was lying on the cupboard next to him, but Jan did not know what to read. Then the psalm that his father had read just before his departure came to mind, and he looked it up, and softly read Psalm 23:

"The Lord is my shepherd; I will lack nothing. He leads me to green pastures..."

When he saw the small smile on Mr. De Boer's face, he realized that he had made a good choice.

He read the psalm calmly, while watching Mr. De Boer, who was listening with closed eyes. He seemed to be enjoying Jan's reading. Jan also saw that he sometimes cried, then smiled again. Sadness for the approaching end and joy for the peace and rest it would bring him.

When he had finished and closed the Bible, it seemed as if Mr. De Boer were asleep. Suddenly, he opened his eyes and whispered, "Thank you...Jan... that was beautiful."

Jan had trouble holding back his tears. He felt the pain this man was enduring, and was reassured when the nun came up to him and laid her hand on his shoulder.

"Come, Jan, Mr. De Boer must rest now."

Jan stood up and took Mr. De Boer's hand one more time. He squeezed it gently. With one last look, which seemed like a farewell, Mr. De Boer looked at him and Jan stammered, "Bye, Mr. De Boer...bye...," and walked away.

In the cool night air outside the hospital ward, he let his tears flow freely. He wept for Mr. De Boer and for all the other deaths that he had seen, but which had left him seemingly indifferent. In the east, he saw the first rays of the sun through his tears. A person died, a new day was born, and at the sight, he cursed God:

"Christ, if you really exist, why are you forsaking us? Why don't you intervene, if you are really so powerful? A God who loves mankind doesn't do this to His children, does He?"

When he returned to the sick bay a few hours later, the nursing nun told him that Mr. De Boer had died shortly after his departure.

"He fell asleep peacefully, Jan. You brought him much comfort in his final moments. Thank you."

Dazed, Jan turned around and walked away, too tired for grief, too empty to feel loss, and too full of longing for the end of this state of misery, pain, and sorrow.

The number of deaths continued to rise. Now, more and more boys as well. If death no longer had any respect for young people, then his name, also, could appear on the death list.

Pastor Klaassen, his gaunt figure in an oversized Sunday suit, prayed in an open-air service:

"Lord God, Heavenly Father, see Your children here at the hour of their death; we implore You for mercy and deliverance. Help us out of this hell of pain, grief, sickness and death, a hell where living is not allowed. Where are You now, when we really need You? We have had to say farewell so many times, and You have not intervened. Are You really going to allow our young people to be taken from us too? Don't You have a plan for them for the future?"

The hope of survival diminished by the day. If you spoke to someone, that person, in his heart, was already saying goodbye to loved ones and those dear to his heart, wherever they might be.

People gave each other assignments: "If you survive, will you tell my mother that I have missed her?"

Pastor Klaassen continued to pray and radiate hope. "If we give up, the Japanese have won! We don't want that! God doesn't want that either!"

He tried to bring comfort with the promises of God from the Old Testament. Waiting patiently for his turn, he also stood in line for food with his little pan. He continued to be a model of steadfastness and devotion, always having an uplifting word and a joke.

And it was uplifting. When he stood near the pastor, Jan smiled also.

# Father Jaan Willem

*June 1945*

The news came that Germany had capitulated. The assumption was that they too would now be liberated soon. Instead, an order came to select a squad of twenty-five hundred sturdy men to prepare for departure. The reason was not known. Again it was said that it would be better "there," and once again, it mobilized people who declared themselves willing. Piet and Gerard had registered, and Jaan, who was fifty-one and not necessarily strong, didn't want them to go alone, so he registered as well. To his surprise, he was selected, and within two days they left the camp to be housed in a pair of separate barracks where they would stay for two weeks.

During that period, they did indeed receive extra food: double portions of bread, extra sugar, and warm food to strengthen them. One morning, heavily loaded, they left for Tjimahi station. Each train car was crammed with twice as many men as space allowed. Thirty kilometers east of Bandoeng, the train stopped. The men were lined up in rows of three and then marched seven kilometers south. It was a sweltering day, and despite the extra food, the trip was very difficult. After a seemingly endless journey, they arrived at their destination, where they were housed in old sheds with tiled roofs. The roofs, supported by poles, were sealed off with bamboo mats. The floor was compacted dirt. A mat served as a bed. There was no light, so after sunset, you couldn't see a thing. The space between the mats was so narrow that it regularly caused irritation when, once again, someone stumbled over another's legs. Worst of all was the lack of water. There was one concrete tank for everyone present, which was more than five hundred meters away. They were sleeping close together, and in no time there was a plague of bedbugs and body lice, and scabies broke out. The morning started with a run for the meal distribution: for everyone a bowl of muddy porridge: a mixture of tapioca flour. With that bowl, you rushed back to your mat to eat it and then prepare for the morning roll call. You had to be there, because at roll call you were given a tool, and the trip to the workplace began. A railway track had to be constructed. They worked in groups of three men in an area demarcated by two posts. The work consisted of chopping, digging, and leveling, so that eventually heavy railroad ties could be installed.

The men discovered that they could work less strenuously with the same result, by stacking up clods instead of chopping and leveling. In this way, the railroad ties could be placed on a few clods of soil, and then covered with dirt, to make it look as if it had all been done as prescribed. It was not monitored anyway. Work was halted a few hours before sunset, followed by their return to camp. Despite their stratagem, they came home dead-tired. After that, they had to fight to arrive at the well in time to wash and fill a few bottles of water. Everything happened in great haste, because soon afterwards, the food was distributed. Then darkness fell, and everyone dropped, exhausted, into "bed".

Of course, all the promises made in Tjimahi about extra food and shelter were broken. There in Tjitjalengka, as before, everyone tried everything to get extra food. The ration, even less than in Tjimahi, was insufficient for them to do the hard work. All this gave rise to a busy trade with the neighboring Sundanese. Jaan noticed how clever Piet and Gerard were in their scrounging and trading. And they were creative with food. Deep in the mud, they looked for snails that they cooked in small tins. Once cooked, the snails were picked out of the shells with a needle or a piece of iron wire. They were not really tasty, but they were a source of protein, and there were prisoners who liked them and were willing to trade.

One day the boys were caught bathing in a nearby *kali* that smelled badly. A Japanese saw them and immediately made them step out. As punishment, they first had to stand in the sun for an hour, after which they were beaten in turn with a bamboo stick. Piet and Gerard got off reasonably well, apart from bruises and sore shoulders.

News did not reach them, but a sense of speedy liberation seized them. The railroad progressed quickly, and hopes grew that they could return to the old camp soon.

*Wednesday, August 15, 1945*

The people in the work camp prepared to leave for the railroad. In the semi-darkness, the men, including Jaan and his sons Piet and Gerard, were ready. A still morning breeze was blowing, and Jaan silently prayed that the wind would continue. It also felt chilly, and he wanted to start walking to warm up.

To their great amazement, a Japanese officer shouted: *"Jasmeeh!"* Rest.

There was some excitement among the men. Rest was nice, but that was never allowed at the beginning of a workday. "Forward" was usually the command at this hour of the day, for them to go to the railroad.

They looked at each other, not understanding what was going on, although they sensed something unusual was happening. What they heard from a Japanese was that a big conference was going on about ending the war. They were sent back to their barracks. There would be no work that day, only "rest."

To kill time, Jaan and the boys walked to the garbage piles near the kitchen, where they searched for food and vegetable scraps to cook "sajoer"—vegetable stew. The attitude of the Japanese was striking; they could go where they wanted. Normally, they would already have been sent away. But this was not the case now.

On August 16, the boys congratulated their father on their mother's birthday.

"Let's pray to God that all is well with her, and that next year we'll be able to celebrate her birthday together," said Jaan, and then walked with Piet and Gerard to the roll call area to leave for the railroad.

Even before they got there, they were sent back with the message that, again, there would be no work done that day. They saw that the Japanese flag had been pulled down, torn, and trampled underfoot. Then it became clear to everyone: the war was over!

Together with the boys, Jaan danced for joy.

"If that's true, then that is the most beautiful gift that your mother has ever had on her birthday!"

On Saturday, August 18, they were notified that they had to return to Tjimahi. Jaan did not feel well, and with that message, that feeling only increased. His erysipelas,

198

which he had previously contracted, reared its head, whereas he had no streptococcus tablets now. Piet and Gerard helped him load his luggage on the wagon, but he had to walk all the way to the station.

"Don't give up, Father. Not now. We have been liberated, and soon everything will be over."

They supported him as well as they could. They fell behind the rest of the group and were warned by a Japanese to keep walking. *"Tidah bisa djalan, kaki saja sakit,"* he told the Japanese. "I can hardly walk, because my leg hurts."

He hadn't finished speaking when his legs gave way and he fell to the ground. The Japanese ordered a male nurse to help him. The nurse offered him a strong arm and helped him to the train. They were able to board on time. In Tjimani, Jaan was immediately admitted to the sick bay, where he received American medicines. He stayed there for about ten days, which ended his plans to welcome their liberators with a choir that would sing American and Dutch songs. However, there was no question of a glorious entry of Americans or liberators, because no one came. Their liberation went almost unnoticed. The only thing noticeable was that the food supply increased. Airplanes flew back and forth, dropping food at the back of the field. Cigarettes, chocolate, cookies, and tins of meat were dropped in large quantities. In addition, they were inundated with rice, meat, fruit, and eggs. It had been a long time since they had eaten normal food. A warning not to overeat was in place, because this would be counterproductive. Some ignored this warning, only to suffer severe stomach cramps and be taken to the sick bay. Jaan saw to it that Piet and Gerard did not overeat, but after a few days, they were so used to it that they could eat everything. It seemed they would never get enough. Jaan, too, felt his strength returning. For many, the food came too late. People continued to die from hunger edema.

They were short of staff in the sick bay, and when Jaan felt somewhat stronger, he offered to help. With the boys, he was assigned to cleaning vegetables, and there they dreamt aloud about the reuniting of their family.

At the beginning of September, Piet and Gerard broached the subject.

"Father?"

He looked at them and saw that it was serious. They were smoking a cigarette after a day of work in the vegetable barracks.

"What is it, boys?"

"We want to go to Banjoe Biroe to look for Mother and the girls."

"But that is dangerous. You can't leave!"

"We are liberated, aren't we? The Japanese won't stop us..."

"No, maybe not, but the freedom fighters will. Here, at least, you are safe."

They were not to be dissuaded. The roles seemed almost reversed. They told him what needed to happen.

"I'm going along."

"That makes no sense, Father. Unfortunately, you are not strong enough yet, and that would only hinder our trip. Piet and I are going together and will come back later for you."

"     And money for the trip?"

"We will find a way."

They walked away. After a while, they came back.

"We sold two cartons of cigarettes for seventy guilders and have the money, so now you can't stop us."

Jaan could do nothing more, save to make them promise to be careful, and to come back. An Indonesian lady had arranged a so-called permit for them, allowing them to travel safely. Then, praying every day for the safe return of his sons, Jaan was alone in the camp again.

# Jan

*August 18, 1945*

A little more than a month after Jan's birthday, rumors circulated through the camps, sparking a wave of optimism. Apparently, a Japanese officer had said that they had capitulated, and that the war was over.

"We're going to get more food," it was said, and they all looked at each other. The rumor persisted, and as Jan walked through the camp, he saw groups of people talking excitedly everywhere.

Could it be true?

Around eleven o'clock that morning, they had to gather at the inner gate where the camp head, Mr. Ter Henne, would address them.

Curious and nervous, Jan walked to the meeting place. This had never happened, so it had to be something special. They didn't have to wait in suspense very long for Mr. Ter Henne to come with his assistant. He stepped up onto a bench, and everyone saw his well-nourished face. He looked happy and spoke with sober words.

"At the behest of Emperor Hirohito, the Japanese army has laid down arms and has surrendered to the superior forces of the Americans after a nuclear bomb was dropped on a Japanese city. This bomb has dire consequences and has caused unprecedented devastation, causing the Japanese to surrender."

A buzz arose among the camp internees. Disbelief, amazement, joy, and sorrow seized all who were listening.

Mr. Ter Henne paused and then raised his hand to finish his speech.

"Starting with your noon meal, you will receive double food rations. You may not leave the camp, and security is taken over by Japanese soldiers. This for your protection; know that you are no longer being guarded, but that they are protecting you from the indigenous population."

It was quiet for a moment, but once the news had been grasped, loud applause and shouts of hurrah followed.

*I am free!* thought Jan, joining the applause.

Jan fully believed the news of the liberation. He wondered excitedly what would happen next. Others debated what an atomic bomb really was. They had never heard of it. Some were saying that an atomic bomb pulverized everything and everyone on impact.

Only one thing was important to Jan: they had been liberated! It was finally over! Their misery had ended, and life would return to normal. The war was over! Yesterday it had sounded inconceivable; today it was a fact!

How cruel, he thought, would this message be for all those who were seriously ill, lying on their bunks, waiting for their liberator—death—knowing they had lost the race against time.

The same afternoon everyone got an extra portion of rice and *sajoer,*, which was enough to create a feeling of euphoria. Also, it was proof that Mr. Ter Henne had spoken the truth. Nothing more was said about the unknown atomic bomb because suddenly everyone was busy with other things. Bread debts, which had been important until that morning, no longer mattered. Jan still owed eight loaves of bread to others, but now it no longer mattered. The flow of extra food cancelled unsettled accounts. It turned out that a skinny boy still had food tins that he had been frantically saving for even worse times.

The change in regime also caused chaos in the camp. The camp administration had lost all grip on the camp, and even though people had been told to stay in the camp, many ignored this directive and left the camp in search of their family. Trading at the gate, still forbidden until recently, and severely punished, flourished again. Indigenous people with food stood at the gate every day to trade. Suddenly, there was such an abundance of food that it even took human lives, despite the warnings. Malnutrition could lead to death if someone suddenly ate too much. Most people heeded the warning, but a few ate themselves to death.

# Mother

Or is it August 23, 25? I really have no idea. Rumors are circulating that we are free. We live between hope and fear. We feel that something is about to happen. For example, yesterday the Indonesians heard that they could sign up to leave the camp.

We notice it in little things. Arguing among themselves and yelling at each other, the guards seem more nervous than usual. The viciousness toward us is gone.

But at the same time, a new area is being prepared for even more occupants. It concerns a few officers' quarters here on the site. So, the war is really not over yet. A hundred women from our camp have been designated as coolies for the prisoner transports from Moentilan. The occupants of that camp are being transferred here. There is a lot of enthusiasm for that work detail. The women are to be picked up in Ambarawa, five kilometers from here. Besides the fact that it is a nice walk, which is appealing, it is an opportunity to get food, which is strictly prohibited. If the Japanese notice it, a beating will follow.

I am dead tired from all the conflicting stories and my mood swings which vacillate with the flood of rumors. And from the maddening doubts whether this war will ever end.

Today, suddenly, in broad daylight, Javanese are standing at the *gedék*, as the trading is called, with bags full of foodstuffs.

Excitedly, the girls come running up.

"*Mama*, are we going to trade? Everyone is doing it."

I see it happening. Women and children arrive with their last possessions: bags full of rags, old clothes, whatever. It is a true witches' cauldron. Children are pushed near the barbed wire and help to pull, if the Javanese don't want to pay. A feverish excitement takes hold of us. A great many people come back with loot: eggs, Javanese sugar, and all kinds of food packages in banana leaves. Aafje and Willie are better at it than I am. It is this rag plus that old dress for a bunch of bananas and that bottle of soy sauce. Let others do it. They become so absorbed that they forget the Japanese, and know how to convert old rags into delicious food. I can't. I do participate— albeit awkwardly—but anticipate a blow at any moment from the guards passing by and cringe beforehand.

This morning a few planes flew low. At first we heard the distant hum. Then we saw them. A wave of excitement swept through the camp.

"Do you see those red-white-blue stripes?"

"O God, it's our boys."

"Hey, they're coming back."

"They've seen us; they've come for us."

"Look, they're dropping pamphlets."

"Could it be true?"

At four o'clock, we are summoned by the camp head. It is different than usual. There is no roll call. Instead, we listen to the news. The war is over. *This* is the end. The Heavenly Emperor of Japan surrendered on August 15. So ten days ago? So it is true! I pinch my arm. I'm alive. So, it is true. Thank God. Finally.

At first, it remains strangely silent, as if no one can believe it, as if we don't want to know the truth. We cry a little. And then someone reluctantly begins to sing the "*Wilhelmus*." Another joins in, then another, each at her own pace, everyone in her own key, and soon it is a jubilant racket. Women hug each other. Happy, sobbing women.

The camp commandant stands there with an expressionless face. We hear what we are now: the Republic of Indonesia. The Indonesians want their independence. There is unrest, anger, and resentment against the whites. We must remain in the camp "with some privileges." The Japanese guards are here to protect us. We are cautioned to be careful until our departure from the camp can be arranged.

But the message doesn't sink in. We are free. The Japanese have been defeated. Great God, we praise You. I shall see Jaan again, the boys. We are going back home. My face is wet with tears.

# Mother

*Thursday, August 30, 1945*

There is peace. The war is over. We've made it—flabby, half-starved, and emaciated. It just doesn't feel like peace. There is no end to our waiting. We receive conflicting instructions. The flag may be raised; the flag may not be raised. We may not leave the camp "for the time being"; then, suddenly, the gate swings open, and we are allowed to go for a walk in the vicinity. Naturally, that is a wonderful moment. To be able to go where I want to go. Seek shelter from the sun under the canopy of a banyan tree. With memories of times gone by, of family outings, when we could just plop down for a picnic. It is all true, including that we are in a camp.

The Japanese guards have been ordered to protect us. Finally, they are doing what they initially promised us. I feel satisfaction. It's strange to see how effortlessly they seem to switch. The enforced protection is tangibly necessary, for example, when a handful of hostile Javanese stare from a distance, eyes full of hate. Because sticks and rocks are thrown at anyone who ventures near the fence. I can hardly bear the animosity, and it scares me. I don't quite know how to reconcile this desire for revenge with the eagerness of their barter and the warmth of the broken *gedèk*, the longing with which they look at our threadbare clothes: worn-out dresses that are exchanged for coconuts, eggs, cucumbers, soy sauce, tomatoes, and so on. Our shabby rags seem to be more attractive than the rags in which they are enveloped. What has happened to this country? Something unimaginable has really gone wrong.

Little by little we receive more food: 50 grams of flour, a little more sugar, a double portion of rice. It still requires hard work to prepare the food, between the mess, a wisp of hair in our faces, and the buzzing sound of the mosquitoes around us.

Occasionally, parcels are dropped from an airplane with tins of food, treats, cigarettes, and medicine. Not nearly enough, but we're happy with it. Sometimes trucks drive into camp with luxury goods such as thinly sliced dried meat—*dengdeng*, eggs, soap, and toothbrushes.

The children are visibly more energetic, amazingly fast, actually. I can even detect gentle curves in the twins. I have to keep a close eye on us and see to it that we practice moderation. Getting sick is not an option. This requires control, because our feeling of hunger is bottomless. We have been deprived of so much.

My twin daughters are hardened and unmannerly. I perceive it, nothing more. If you have to fight for food, then you have to fight for food. Survival is what counts. Secretly taking potatoes from the plates for the sick? That temptation cannot be resisted. Is this done at the expense of others? I'd rather not think about it. Stealing from the camp kitchen? My daughters don't lose sleep over it.

They also volunteer readily to clean the sewage ditch, which gets clogged time and again with washcloths stolen from the line and used to wipe buttocks. They don't care about the filthy work; they care about the reward: a cup of rice.

Do I have to decide, is it good or bad? There is no easy answer.

It's different with little Annie. She has retained something childlike. At least that's what it looks like, and I hope that's true. Happily, she parrots her sisters, but she has no idea what she's actually saying.

"When *Papa* comes home, then..." But what does she know about her father? She hardly knows him. She is a darling.

The foremost question is, when can we go home? So far, there has been no progress. I crave some indication, no matter how small. If only I could see that something is happening. The pamphlets that the aviators are dropping give a little hope. "Take heart. We are not allowed to land." That little bit of hope disappears again when I think of those dangerous armed groups that we are being warned about: the rumors of attacks by rebels with pointed bamboo sticks. Camp leaders say it is unwise to leave the camp without protection. Suddenly, disaster now comes from the outside. The native Javanese want independence. Be ready—*bersiap*—is their battle cry. That applies to us too. I hope my boys are careful! It keeps getting more complicated.

Every now and then, men and boys arrive at the camp and a reunion takes place. Then suddenly, a couple, with arms around each other, wanders through the camp. An almost unreal image, even jealousy-inducing. Because where are my boys, my men? My worry, my anxiety, increases. There are all kinds of questions. What if Jaan and the boys don't manage to get here? Oh God, I so hope they are still alive. How can I find them? Do I have to look for them any which way I can, and am I able to do that? To begin with, we are not allowed outside; it is not safe. What if we can't find each other? Do I have to arrange everything then? Where do I get money? Having become so accustomed to war, how can I live as a free person?

We become bored, restless, and impatient. We want more.

My eye falls on Paula, still and straight as a statue. She is smoking a cigarette. With eyes closed, she lets the smoke escape. The image gives me peace.

# Mother

*Wednesday, September 5, 1945*

It is still early, and the girls have just left for Ambarawa. It's as though they're going on a school trip, coltish, uninhibited; they are on an adventure.

"Lord, let them return safely," I mutter to myself. "They are young girls. Please protect them, protect my girls." My brave, untamed Aafje. I wonder what we'll be arguing about in the future.

The announcement came the day before yesterday. During the kitchen work chore, I was scrubbing one of those impossible pans when someone tapped me on the shoulder. I turned around and there was Aafje. I was shocked. God save me, not bad news, hopefully? Aafje noticed.

"Don't be alarmed, *Mama*, I have good news; I'm going to get Jan." That was all, nothing more.

What do I hear? Get Jan? I couldn't believe my ears. True? And I just stood there, unable to do anything but stare dumbfounded at her.

"I'm going to get Jan." Again that calm, clear tone. There is no denying it. She didn't inherit that self-confidence from me. But it wouldn't happen; I was sure of that. It was an absurd plan. What had gotten into her? By no means is it certain that Jan is in Ambarawa, and if he is, then there's the question of which camp. No words came out of my mouth, absorbed as I was in my own thoughts. Aafje persisted.

"*Mama*! I'm going to get Jan." She turned and went back to her own duties. I just stood there, motionless.

"Hey, hurry up with that pan; we need it for cooking." A fellow occupant looked at me quizzically. I had to get on with my work. For the rest of my work duty, those words, "I'm going to get Jan," haunted my thoughts.

Aafje did not give up. Just back in the barracks, tired from the hard work, I wanted to lie down for a while. But bringing it up again, Aafje was already standing in front of me.

"*Mama*, it's really true, I'm going to get Jan; something has to be done." I could agree—something had to be done—but not this.

"Why don't you say anything?"

"Why not?" I searched for the words I couldn't find. "Because I don't know what to say."

"*Mama*! All you ever say is that you don't know. But I do know." She threw the words at me. I took a deep breath.

"Good," I began as calmly as possible, "I don't know how you got the idea, but what you want to do seems impossible to me. I don't like it. A girl alone, on the way to Ambarawa, that is asking for trouble. Where are you going to look? We don't know where Jan is. And what about all that unrest outside the gates? No, it can't happen; it's too dangerous." I got ready to lie down. But Aafje became angry.

"You haven't asked enough questions, *Mama*. First, listen carefully." Her abrupt tone, her fierce eyes...I didn't like it. It was clear that she wouldn't be quick to accept my "no." Since I didn't have the energy to deal with it, I postponed our discussion.

"Okay then, we'll talk about it later," and I let out a deep sigh. "When I'm rested, I can listen to you better. Okay?"

"Okay."

After ten minutes, she was already standing next to my cot, arms crossed over her chest.

"Can we do this now?" It had to be done now.

"Out with it."

"Well, some of us girls were sitting together and giggling, when—I don't remember exactly how it went—Manon, you know, that girl from the other barracks, suddenly asked which of us wanted to go to Ambarawa with her. We were instantly quiet. To Ambarawa? Why would we go there?"

"Good question. What do you want to do there?" My tone remained calm so as not to irritate her.

"Well, Manon had thought about it. She would go to the boys' camp to look for her brothers. Everything was taking so terribly long. They could easily walk to the camp; it wasn't that far. After that, we talked about it a few more times, and because there are more of us, we dare to go. Then at least, something will happen." As she spoke, I recalled the image from a few weeks ago, the enthusiasm of the women who returned with the prisoners from Ambarawa. The trip had given them new energy. Everything had worked out. They had so enjoyed being out in nature.

"Under normal circumstances it is quite doable, Aafje; it's not far to walk, and I've heard it's a beautiful hike. But these are not normal circumstances; it is war, and it's completely unclear why you should go there."

"Well, I'm going to get Jan," she replied impatiently, and immediately added, "Even though we don't know for sure—because you've been saying that the whole time—and even though Willie can't come, which is a shame, I'm going. At least we'll know for sure. At least six or seven girls will go along. So, I'm not going alone."

No, Willie can't go. She can barely stand on her feet, which are swollen due to hunger edema. Glad I don't have to think about that. But deep down, something shifted. If no one does anything, nothing will happen. At least, Aafje takes action. And the trip is not insurmountable, because there are seven of them, and it is only five kilometers. Aafje would go anyway...

Now I see the girls slowly disappear from sight. Like a bunch of young puppies, with the hope of good luck, off to Ambarawa.

# Jan

*Early September 1945*

At the moment of his liberation, Jan was seventeen and weighed only thirty-four kilograms (about seventy-five pounds).

His prospects were good, especially now that more food was available. In a relatively short time, he felt himself getting stronger. But not all of the inconvenience was gone. His diarrhea was ongoing, the lice were still there, but thanks to the availability of sulfur ointment which they did not receive before, the scabies could be controlled.

A lot of fruit was distributed, so the vitamin C deficiency was quickly eliminated, and the red spots on his skin shriveled up.

"Jan!" He was approached by one of the boys from his barracks.

"Jan, there are girls at the gate who say that they come from Banjoe Biroe, and your sister Aafje is there too. She's asking for you."

Jan's heart began to beat wildly. Without saying another word, he ran to the gallery, and there he saw her, barefoot. He ran to her and took her in his arms. Overjoyed, she greeted him, and both wept at the reunion. When the tears had dried, the questions came.

"What are you doing here? How did you know I was here? How did you get here?"

He overwhelmed her with questions; he was so nervous and happy.

"I heard you might be here, so I took the gamble and came to get you. Are you coming to see *Mama*?"

Despite the ban on leaving the camp, he didn't have to be told twice.

"Where's Willie?"

"She has swollen legs and can hardly walk; that's why she isn't here. Are you coming now?"

"Yes, of course. I'll quickly grab my things and my bag, and then we'll leave immediately."

He was back in a moment. He didn't have much to pack. He left his mattress and his worn flannel blanket behind. He no longer needed them. Also, there was no one to say goodbye to. He wanted to leave this horrendous time behind as quickly as possible. Besides, all his fellow sufferers in the barracks were busy with their own affairs and little attention was paid to the others.

Chatting busily and barefooted, Aafje and Jan left the camp together. The Japanese guard let them go unhindered, and briefly Jan had the urge to make the obligatory *hormat* as they passed. Suddenly, he realized that this was no longer necessary. As if the world were theirs alone, they walked toward Camp 6. It did not occur to them to wait for others who might be heading that way too. Jan turned around one more time to look at Camp 7. He saw the bamboo fence with the roofs of the old and dilapidated barracks above it. He could hardly imagine having been imprisoned there. That truth felt unreal.

After passing Camp 6, they followed the road to Banjoe Biroe, which lay five kilometers south. Ambarawa was now behind them. He looked around and his eye fell on the top of Mount Telemojo, which he had seen from Camp 11. In the rice paddies and the many fields, they saw farmers working the land as if there had been no war. Jan was no longer accustomed to the everyday scene. He felt alienated from the reality around him. In the camp, there had been a constant struggle for survival, and there was no awareness of a world outside.

Above the asphalt road, the warm air vibrated in the hot tropical sun. The sun was directly above their heads. Everything was so beautiful, so quiet, and so peaceful. It was too hot to walk, and yet, the sound of the crickets seemed to encourage them.

What a few days before had seemed like a dream and wouldn't have been believed, they now experienced: liberation.

Jan was unable to run. His condition did not allow that, and he had to gasp for breath several times.

"Are you okay, Jan, or would you rather rest a bit?"

His sister was worried, but Jan waved her worries away.

"No, it's fine. We will go to Mother, and maybe soon we will see Father and our brothers again, and we can go back to the Netherlands."

"Do you want to return to the Netherlands? Don't you like it here?"

He realized that Aafje had been born here, and even though they had been to the Netherlands for a year in between, her world was the Dutch East Indies. He glanced at her. Their reunion was still fresh, but it immediately felt natural to walk right next to her, and to be together.

"Yes, I really want to go back to the Netherlands. I have never really felt at home here. There we can build a future. You want that too, don't you?"

Aafje was not given an opportunity to answer, because someone was calling them. They were halfway through the

218

beautiful countryside. On the veranda of a house that they were passing, an Indo-European couple stood beckoning to them.

"Don't respond, Jan; just keep walking!"

Jan did not know whether to trust those people or not. Fear and distrust had crept in. He was no longer used to kindness and hospitality, and danger lurked behind friendliness. When he looked again, he decided to respond anyway.

"Come on, Aafje, I am dying of thirst and these people look trustworthy. We can always run."

With that remark, he offered an escape route, and that was enough for Aafje to be persuaded. Hesitantly, they walked to meet the couple who had greeted them. They could go inside and sit at the table. With eyes wide, they looked around. It had been at least three years since they'd been in a regular living room. It felt uncomfortable and at the same time familiar. The space exuded a sense of security and reminded them of their old home and the time before the war. They were given a glass of cool lemonade and the couple asked them about the camps. With open mouths, pain in their eyes, and horror, they sat and listened to their stories. They had not known what was going on inside the perimeter of the camps around them. Shame and sadness were visible on their faces.

Jan and Aafje were invited to stay for a meal, which they could not refuse. A delicious *nasi-goreng* was set before them. How long had it been since they had eaten such a meal, and on a plate with normal cutlery on a tablecloth?

The woman motioned for them to take as much as they wanted. And because their bodies, despite the increased rations, were still crying out for food, they could continue to eat.

When they were satisfied, Jan indicated that they had to continue their journey.

"We are eager to go to my other sisters and my mother, and we still have a distance to go."

"We understand that. Go now, and thank you for being willing to tell your story. We are sorry for what has been done to you. This was the least that we could do for you."

They waved goodbye to Aafje and Jan for a long time, until they lost sight of them.

"There still are angels," Jan concluded, and because they had eaten and drunk well, the rest of the journey was not too difficult.

After a while, they approached Banjoe Biroe. Jan recognized the contours of Camp 11, where he had spent twenty months with his mother and sisters. At the gate, there was a flurry of activity, because a *pasar* was underway. The market was full of stalls.

# Jan

September 5, 1945

The reunion with his mother and other sisters was emotional and strange at the same time. They fell into each other's arms, and asked repeatedly how the other was doing. There was no time to answer all the questions. Jan said he was happy that his mother had survived the typhoid attack on the day before his departure.

"I don't know from whom, but at one point I was given extra medicines, and I was able to recover."

"Also, you were not allowed to die, Mother. Exactly what I told you then. The girls needed you, so you had to live. Now we need you. It won't be long before we are all together again."

"Do you really believe that, Jan? I've had so much fear for you. How are Gerard, Piet, and your father? Are they still alive? You don't know that either, do you?"

"No, *Mama*, I don't know, and yet I believe we'll all be together again soon."

Nothing more was said about it. They couldn't convince each other. Jan was unable to dispel his mother's doubts, and his mother could not convince him of her doubts. And at that moment, they had other concerns on their minds, such as finding a place for Jan to sleep. That evening, Jan ate potatoes for the first time in a long time. He had completely forgotten how they tasted, and could not remember ever having liked them so much. During the days that followed, they found time to listen to each other's stories.

# Mother

*Wednesday evening, September 5, 1945*

Things have changed a lot since that moment in the sick bay, when we last saw each other. Then I prayed, even begged the Lord to take me. In retrospect, it is good that my request was not granted.

Jan has grown up, and is unimaginably thin. We fall into each other's arms. I can feel his ribs. We exchange awkward sentences.

"Son, you look so tired." A concerned mother. Jan tenses up. "Shall I get you something to eat?"

Jan looks at me quizzically. He doesn't understand. He doesn't know that now we are getting more provisions, and that it has become much easier to get food.

"Later, Mother."

"It's been a long time, son, since we saw each other." He avoids my gaze.

"You were not allowed to die, Mother, exactly what I told you then." It sounds grumpy, but I don't say anything about it.

Aafje is triumphant. Look who brought him! The bravado of a teenager. She talks exuberantly, glowing with pride. It was an exciting trip, and yes, she had been scared. They had encountered no trouble on the way. The surroundings were so beautiful; she had loved it, the rice fields, all that splendid greenery. What a contrast to the colors in the camp. She had been careful, she said, looking in my direction, also on the way back. Jan a little less. He had been terribly thirsty, and when strangers had called and motioned for them to come in, he had walked over without thinking. She had certainly warned him. Fortunately, it had worked out well. Jan quenched his thirst, and they had been served all kinds of delicious food as well. They were nice people who were ashamed of all the violence in their country. I couldn't get a word in edgewise.

I am simply happy. Aafje and Jan, both here safely. Willie, too, is visibly enjoying this. She has become a caring girl. While I was just nervously awaiting Aafje's return, she tried to reassure me.

"*Mama*, it will be fine. God is not taking my twin sister away. That would be very cruel. We need each other. I can't stand on my own two feet, can I?" She has her own logic.

Jan looks terrible. How many kilograms does he weigh, thirty? He constantly scratches his legs and hands, and between his fingers. He is covered with red bumps and has small wounds everywhere, with or without scabs. Scabies. There must be some remedy somewhere in the camp, I think; cream or powder, it doesn't matter what. I'm going to look for it.

We have to adjust. We listen to the stories which are equally horrendous. War is terrible—it hardens, numbs, blinds and paralyzes, all at once. Caution towards Jan is fitting. I don't discount our moving reunion, but there is something tangible between us; I'm not crazy. The intertwining of my previous severity, the hard kernel of being locked-up-in-myself, my longing for my parents, my nostalgia for something. The barrier to my heart.

Jan has always been a sensitive boy. And in recent years, we have also exacerbated, in each other, our struggle with faith, which is a shame, because the power of faith should not be underestimated. We've sold each other short. I readily admit that my own lack of conviction doesn't help. Do I really believe my own answers to his questions? I hope that we encourage each other. Fortunately, Jan has an optimistic nature.

"We're going back to Holland as soon as possible, aren't we?" That enviable trust—that the family will get back together—that self- assurance irritates me.

"I hope so, Jan. We must trust in the Lord." I try not to reveal my doubt.

"We have to look for Father. For Piet and Gerard." He longs for his father and his brothers. Are they still alive? I don't dare to hope.

# Jan

*September 6, 1945*

In the days that followed, they tried to regain some semblance of normality. They didn't have much privacy. That was not so bad. They had their freedom, and even though they were not officially allowed to leave, they could still exit the gate. Outside the camp, friendly native Javanese tried to trade their wares for money, textiles, or other valuables. It was a pleasant commotion, and they enjoyed the markets and the haggling. On one of their outings, they were startled by a black limousine moving slowly through the crowd. In the vehicle were young native people who looked at them aggressively. On their heads they wore black *topis*, the symbol of their nationalist and republican struggle for freedom. Through the open windows, they threw out pamphlets calling on the people to declare their country the Republic of Indonesia.

"Why would they want that, Mother?"

"Because they are tired of the occupation, Aaf, also the occupation by us Dutch."

"It's our country, isn't it?"

"That's how we think about it, Willie," said Jan, "but they think it's their country and that we're occupying it. That's why they want a republic, to be their own boss in this country. We *blandas* have to leave. That's how it is, right, *Mama*?"

He looked at his mother.

"That's how it is, Jan, and I understand."

The euphoria of liberation gave way to a new fear, to a threat that grew into a vague, unsettled sense of doom. The "being outside", as they had experienced it before the war, would never return, and strangely enough, the hated prison camp became a safe shelter. The hated Japanese now protected them from the freedom fighters. For Jan it was also the confrontation with a new reality that he would carry with him from that moment on: you could always lose something that you liked. There arose in him a fundamental distrust, that even though everything might seem to be good, it could always be in the shadow of something threatening, something that could dash your plans.

On September 8, 1945, Jan heard the sound of an airplane in the distance. With his sisters, he ran outside to see what was happening. They weren't alone. Jan, fond of airplanes, immediately recognized the aircraft: a twin-engine Catalina amphibious airplane skimmed low over the coconut trees. The plane wobbled its wings in greeting. Jan saw the crew sitting in the cockpit. The viewers on the ground screamed hooray. An old Javanese woman next to him tapped him on the arm.

"How nice that the Queen is coming back!"

The plane flew over and turned towards the fields next to the camp. There it dropped large containers and bales that landed in the fields with a soft thud. This happened a few times, after which the aircraft flew on. Excitedly, everyone ran to the fields to see what was in the containers. The oldest in the camp rushed to supervise the distribution of the booty, and to ensure a fair distribution. There were canned goods, snacks, chocolate, and cigarettes in the containers, as well as medicines.

Naturally, there was not enough, but everyone saw it as a gesture of compassion for their situation on the ground. It held the promise that things would get better and back to normal. Also dropped from the plane, and boosting morale, were pamphlets, printed in Malay and in Dutch, that said that they would soon be truly liberated. They were urged to stay inside the camps, because outside there was a new danger: the Merdeka or freedom-fighters.

The waiting was not easy. The longing for family, and the desire to know where they were, and whether they were still alive, was great. As more families were reunited in the camp, that desire increased. For some, the reunion was a first encounter with their father or their brother. For days, young people, asking about their families, roamed the camp. It was heartbreaking when they were told that a mother, brother, or sister was no longer alive. The horrors of the camp and the extreme suffering had sometimes made people unrecognizable to their own families. How moving it was to see Dutch men and boys walking through the camp with their rediscovered wife and children on their arm.

The Indonesian Red Cross was looking for children and women to tell them that a loved one had died in another camp or in a transport. Joy and sorrow went hand in hand. Jan now also began to doubt whether his father was still alive.

His mother, fortified by the reunions she had seen, answered with hollow eyes, "You know what Father always says, Jan. You must trust in the Lord. He will bring us back together."

Jan, in turn, was now reassured by her words. What he didn't see was his mother turning her head away to look the other way with tears in her eyes and doubt in her heart.

*September 13, 1945*

Less than a week later, Piet and Gerard were standing in front of them. Mother, the girls, and Jan laughed and cried at the same time. How was this possible? Where did they come from? How did they know they were here?

Piet, the eldest, said that they had come from Camp 4 in Tjimahi, and that they had travelled four hundred kilometers to Banjoe Biroe.

"We gambled that Mother and the girls would still be here, because we were all brought here first. But to find you here, too, Jan, we wouldn't have dared to hope that!"

To which Jan responded by telling how Aafje had gone for him. Piet went on to tell about their journey.

"We took the train from Bandoeng to Djokja and Magelang, and then came to Ambarawa. From Father we got..."

"Father? Is he still alive? Have you talked to him?"

Joyful and emotional, their mother interrupted Piet's story.

"Yes," laughed Gerard, "Father is still alive. Last October, when we were transferred to Tjimahi, we found him there."

"Thank God," sighed his mother, looking at Jan as she did. "Now, do you see that Father was right? You have to trust the Lord more, Jan!"

Jan swallowed his tears. "Father is still alive;" the words echoed in his head. This was his greatest gift.

For hours, they took turns speaking, and even when they had to go for a meal, they kept on talking. The stories piled up and intertwined because everyone was anxious to share his or her story. A place to sleep was prepared for Piet and Gerard.

After a few days, Piet and Gerard discussed with Jan and their mother their desire to take Jan to their father.

"He is the only one who doesn't know that we are all alive. And we have to tell him that. If Jan comes with us, then Father can already see him."

"The girls and I really want to see Father too. Can't we all go together?"

"No, Mother, that's not a good idea. The three of us can handle it, but with you and the girls, it would really become too dangerous, for you and for us. Officially, you can't even leave yet. Jan, Gerard, and I come from other camps and will not be stopped. You would be."

# Mother

*Friday, September 21, 1945*

My boys have conceived the plan to go to their father. It is unbearable, but we can't go along. Women and children may not leave the camp. Lord Mountbatten, Vice Admiral of the Allied High Command, insists on it. It is too dangerous. Slowly, messages are trickling in that things are happening. For example, the Allies have finally landed on Java as well. It has taken an eternity, enough to make you feel despondent.

Joy and dissatisfaction alternate. I am happy that Piet and Gerard are alive, and to have heard from them that Jaan, also, is alive. And now, another farewell. They leave tomorrow morning—Jan is going along too—and to be honest, it is gut-wrenching. Outside there is danger. Outside there is no freedom.

From the stories of Piet and Gerard, I understood that Jaan initially did not want to let them leave Tjimahi, that he looked for reasons why it wouldn't work. For example, the lack of money for the trip. The boys were able to sell two cartons of cigarettes (no idea how they got them). And with that, that argument was quashed. Finally, Jaan changed his mind. I made a mental note of that. Previously, Father's will was law. My Jaan has lost authority.

Anyway, we can't go along. It's really not possible. However, I do want to communicate something, so I'm sending a letter along with them. Yesterday and today, I have been working on it for a long time, because it is still difficult to decide what to write and what not to write.

*Banjoe Biroe*
*September 20, 1945*
*Dear Jaan,*

*This letter is being sent with our boys. Because no one is censoring this, I am going to write more personally. I am not able to put all my impressions down on paper; I will keep it short. So, it may have become a chaotic letter.*

*Camp Tjimahi is four hundred kilometers from here, but if you are reading this, I feel that we are one step closer to each other. Who could have imagined that?*

For a moment I feel my anger rising again, the bitter aftertaste of my forced move to Bolsward, and then to the Dutch East Indies. All of this could have been avoided. At the time, Jaan did not take me into account at all in his decisions. Why not? And who really does that?

I remind myself; hadn't I made a decision not to let myself be held hostage any longer by my own indignation? That is in the past. And as I reread this letter, I realize that the real question—why Jaan found it so necessary to go to the Dutch East Indies—has never been asked. That conversation did not take place. Apart from everything that we have experienced, what was Jaan actually looking for? Did restlessness drive him? Ambition? I am quite curious about it. Come on; carry on.

*Your card from a year ago was the last message from you and meant a lot to me. It sounds dramatic, but it triggered my will to stay alive. I was close to giving up. I was suddenly so happy to know that you were alive. I had*

231

*not dared to hope (and that lack of trust, Jaan, doesn't make me a sinner!).*

*Like all of us, you must have experienced some terrible things. Piet and Gerard said that they were kept calm in the boys' camps with reports that we were well taken care of. Is that also the case in the Tjimahi camp? In actual fact, it was unbearable, but I won't elaborate on that here. We've survived. I've survived.*

*Thankfulness predominates. We're still here. I have learned a lot, not least about myself. It is clear to me that I haven't always been a good wife and mother; I'm writing this in advance. Locked in my own grief at being cut off from family, from my roots, and my anger about it.*

Jaan could misunderstand. Should I leave it out? No, I decide, he may know that the situation has changed, that I have changed. Jaan will not be the same either, after three years of Japanese occupation. I'm leaving it in.

*I see things differently now, more nuanced? I see more clearly the part I played, and my own inability to deal with the situation (for which, by the way, I don't blame only myself). I hope that we'll be able to talk about this in the future. But first it is important that we get back together. Only God knows how quickly that will happen.*

*Take good care of yourself and the boys.*
*Hope to see you again, dear Jaan.*
*With the warmest greetings,*
*Johanna*

I can be satisfied with this. In the draft version, I tried to delve deeper into the state of my marriage, but to be honest, it unravels in all directions. This says what is important now. I put my letter in the envelope that Paula gave me. The adhesive edge has tiny hairline cracks. I carefully run my tongue along it and press it shut.

Now we have to wait and see.

# Jan

*Saturday, September 22, 1945*

And so, Piet, Gerard and Jan, three grown-up men of 19, 18, and 17, left the camp that day.

Saying goodbye was difficult after the joy of the reunion, and they knew there would be risk involved with this trip.

In tears, their mother was waving goodbye.

"Be careful, please be very careful, and go with God in your heart."

She handed them the letter she had written to their father.

They rode to Ambarawa station in a truck with more people. Piet took the lead, and Jan, meek, excited, nervous, and a little scared, followed. Naturally, he thought it was fantastic that he was going to see his father. After three years, he would finally see him again. But he had difficulty saying goodbye to his mother and his sisters. Always saying goodbye to each other. It made him sick and restless. He didn't want it anymore. His concern was compounded because they were leaving in a clandestine manner. So much could happen along the way.

They boarded the train, which ran on a rack railway through the beautiful landscape of Magelang. After slightly more than an hour, they arrived in Magelang, where they had to transfer to the slow train of the Dutch East Indies Railways to Djokdjakarta. It was only forty kilometers. In Djokdjakarta they had to catch a train to Bandoeng, the longest and most dangerous part of the trip.

Once they were in Bandoeng, it was still ten kilometers to Tjimahi. They found a place in the slow train. There were some other Dutch folks, but the majority was predominantly native Javanese, who left them undisturbed. The last time that Jan had made this trip was in 1942 when they were interned. They passed Moentilan, where Jan saw the convent that had also served as a camp. He turned his head away from the sight and looked the other way, at the blue silhouettes of the volcanoes Merbaboe and Merapi. He thought of their holidays in Kali-Oerang and Ngablak near Kopeng, when the land was still at peace and their lives were quiet and pleasant.

In the afternoon, they arrived in Djokdjakarta at Toegoe station. What an experience to be back there. The station brought back memories of 1936 when they had gone back to Holland for a year's leave and of their return a year later. Jan had not wanted to return to Indonesia, and remembered the crying fits of his mother, who also wanted to stay in the Netherlands. He could still hear his father's stern voice, which had shocked him as well:

"Johanna, our country is not the Netherlands, but the Dutch East Indies. If you don't want to follow me, you should have made a different choice a long time ago."

He had seen the fright in his mother's eyes, and had taken her hand to comfort her.

The platforms were busy. The boys worked their way through the crowd. There were Indonesian people, some of whom they recognized and greeted. Jan met his classmate Henkie Bronkhorst, who told them that he had heard that they were no longer alive.

"Then it must be very strange to see me here?"

They talked to each other for hours until another question arose, namely where they could sleep that night. Near the station was the Grand Hotel, and someone told them that there was certainly room there. They walked to the corner of Malioboro and Jonquiere Boulevard, to the hotel, where they reported to reception. To their surprise, they were taken to a room by a Japanese. There was no furniture in the room. On the floor, there were mats to sleep on. They paid very little for their bed and breakfast. Due to their fatigue from the journey and the tension, they fell asleep quickly.

The next day, Piet made every effort to obtain tickets for the continuation of their trip. That day they were guests of an Indonesian family in Lempoejangan, a neighborhood near the station. They knew these people from the time before the war, and their hosts insisted that the boys stay there for the night. They were warm-hearted people, concerned about the boys. They asked them innumerable questions about the camps, and with each question and answer, they felt more and more guilty about what had happened to the boys. Piet tried to make it clear to them that there was no question of blame, but they wouldn't hear of it.

That afternoon they walked around the neighborhood and passed the maternity clinic where Annie was born. A few hundred meters farther, they saw a group of boys chanting slogans, threatening them with sticks and spears pointing in their direction, and screaming *Merdeka*—freedom—and *Bersiap*—be ready. Jan became frightened and asked his brothers to go back, because there was no one around to protect them. What a contrast there was between this behavior and the hospitality and kindness of their hosts. To avoid trouble, they decided to stay indoors for the rest of the day. Above all, they didn't want to jeopardize their journey the next morning.

Jan just couldn't understand the boys' behavior. "We used to go to school and play games together. We lived in the same neighborhood and were friends. So why are they doing this?"

"They don't want us anymore, Jan. In their eyes, we are the occupiers. They want to be free!"

That night remained quiet, and they slept well. The next morning, they got up early, because the train was due to leave at seven o'clock. Their hosts provided food for the journey, warned them to stay away from the Merdeka fighters, and bade them a hearty farewell. A housemate escorted the boys to the station, where they again encountered a group of native youth. Their guide advised them to just keep walking and not to respond to this group.

They arrived at the station without incident. Jan breathed a sigh of relief. He had been truly afraid. There they saw many Dutch women and children, who, like them, were trying to join their husband or father. Hundreds of indigenous people also wanted to board this train. It was almost impossible to get through, but after much pushing and shoving, they were able to reach the train car reserved for Dutch women and children. A few men boarded as well, including a former KNIL officer and an ex-prisoner-of-war. The other train cars were packed with native Javanese. People were sitting even on the roofs, and others hung on the running boards. The train was overcrowded, and it was not pleasant to be on the train with so many people. On the platforms, many vendors were selling their wares. Even though the boys had been given enough food and drink, they still bought extra drinks. The train was ready for departure for the three hundred and fifty kilometer journey. Gerard and Piet found a place on the closed balcony, and Jan on the floor in the aisle between two open compartments. The space was packed with passengers and their luggage and whining children. It would be a tiring journey, but the coming reunion with his father made him feel positive. That was something Jan could cling to.

Creaking and groaning, the train began to move. For a moment, it seemed as if the locomotive was unable to pull its counterweight, but after the initial shock and some scraping of the iron wheels over the rails, it began to move. As the speed slowly increased, Jan felt the breeze entering the train through the open windows and the cracks, and the flow of air diminished his sense of suffocation. After a while, people fell asleep to the cadence of the wheels. Between all those people and luggage, Jan tried to see some of the surroundings, but that was difficult from the floor. In time, he too fell asleep.

He awoke as the train slowed and stopped at Tasikmalaja station, a town on the border of the Preanger Mountains. It was around noon. The sun was high overhead and the temperature kept rising. Many people disembarked to make room for new passengers. There was jostling, and in the pushing, native young people began to stir threateningly. Many of them had weapons such as the *bamboe-roentjings* that could be used for beating and stabbing. It was a fomenting unrest, especially because they began to shout loudly, chant slogans, and fill up the small space on the platform. Entrances and exits were blocked. The harsh cry of "*Merdeka*" sounded loudly throughout the station grounds. The front row of the group tried to enter the carriage where Jan and his brothers were sitting, and there they came upon the unarmed KNIL officer. His refusal to admit them became the fuse in the powder keg. The screaming and shouting of the group grew louder and more menacing. A violent uproar ensued, and like an oil spill, the uprising spread across the platform. They called for revenge, and trying to get in, began to hit the wooden doors of the train car. Murder was evident in their eyes. A wave of fear swept over the passengers. They were trapped like rats. To protect their children, women closed the wooden shutters on the windows. Children cried and screamed in fear. The atmosphere became more alarming by the minute. At first, Jan thought his life might be over. It was sad that after years of imprisonment in a camp, he would die here. There was no protection. Not from the Javanese. Not from a police force. Nothing good could be expected from these young people. This was their battle that broke out after the liberation from the Japanese. The pent-up hatred against every enemy, including the Dutch, went back for generations, and now received a hearing and space. This was their chance. They would unceremoniously kill anyone who opposed them in their fight, as they had already done elsewhere, according to the stories Jan had heard recently. Why would he be spared? Jan silently prayed for help, for a way out. That was his only hope, for a miracle to deliver them. Jan prayed for a gentle death, without much pain.

"Not my will be done, dear God," as he had heard his father often pray, "but Yours. I surrender into Your hand."

He regretted not listening to his mother, who had almost begged the boys not to leave. If they had stayed in that safe camp, this wouldn't have happened to them.

"Did I survive the camp in order to be killed here?" He spoke softly to himself and bowed his head in anticipation of the final blow.

Then...suddenly and totally unexpectedly...he felt a vibration going through the train. Was he mistaken? Was he dreaming? It was no delusion...it was true...with light thrusts, the train began to move. They were on their way!

The engineer had rescued them from the lions' den, pulling them away slowly from this terrifying place. The screaming outside faded into the background as the train picked up speed. Away from danger...away from the *Merdeka* fighters. The windows were opened again to let in the sunlight and fresh air. People around him began to talk excitedly. Many cried with relief. Two of the "freedom fighters," *pemoedas,* had taken cover on the running board. They turned out to be unarmed, and they were admitted to the balcony by the KNIL officer. Now they were quiet and submissive boys, who had been incited by their companions. Tasikmalaja became increasingly distant, but not out of Jan's mind. Even in the prison camp, he had never felt closer to death than there.

The train began to climb the hills and the mountains, and the heavy locomotive pulled its load towards Preanger. The magnificent landscape passed by: terraced rice fields, overgrown slopes and ravines. Like a slow-moving snake, the train wound its way upwards to arrive finally at the large station of Bandoeng. It was afternoon. When he disembarked, Jan feared to be confronted anew by the *Merdeka* fighters. To his great relief, there was no sign of them, and everyone could get off the train quietly. Women and children were directed to the school near the station, under the supervision of RAPWI, an improvised partnership between the Dutch and the British. Piet thought it better not to go there.

"It is still light and I suggest that we walk to Tjimahi."

"How much time do we need for that?" asked Jan.

"About two hours of walking. It is still light and I think that we can get there before dark."

Via the *"Grote Postweg,"* once built by engineer Daendels, they walked in the direction of Tjimahi. After a while, it began to get dark. Jan became worried. He knew what it was like in this country. Darkness fell suddenly. And as night was beginning to fall already, even though they hadn't been walking for half an hour, it would soon be pitch dark. His courage sank.

"Why didn't we stay in Bandoeng? We'll never make it before dark!"

"If you walk a bit faster, we should make it."

Gerard agreed with Jan.

"I'm afraid we're not going to make it, boys, especially now that night is already falling. It is too risky, and we don't know if there are extremists in the *kampongs* along the way. Knocking on someone's door doesn't seem like a good choice either. Maybe we should go back."

He had barely finished saying this when a vehicle from Bandoeng came up behind them. Their hearts were pounding.

"What should we do? Hide?"

The vehicle stopped beside them. A Japanese officer got out and asked them in Malay what they were doing along this dangerous road at this hour of the night. They

241

explained to him where they were going. Displeased and disapproving, he shook his head and ordered them to get in. After they did so, he turned and drove back to Bandoeng. There, he dropped them off at the RAPWI school.

"Tomorrow, when it is light, you can head out again. Good night!" With those words, he left them.

"This is the second time today that we have miraculously escaped death and been rescued by someone from whom we would not have expected it," Jan said, nudging his oldest brother.

"It's all right," muttered Piet, vexed that he had put them in danger.

"We are anxious to see Father too," Gerard said, discerning Piet's chagrin. "An extra night won't hurt us."

Moreover, they were served a delicious meal and were given a place to sleep.

# Mother

*Tuesday, October 30, 1945*

This morning I woke up from a bad dream. We are swimming in the river, but I cannot make it to the other bank. The longer I swim, the farther the water's edge retreats. My head disappears under water; I panic and sink deeper and deeper.

We don't know where we're at. Little by little we fit the puzzle pieces together. Every now and then we catch a bit of information from the outside world. The Dutch governor-general Tjarda van Starkenborgh was brought from Formosa to Mansjoekwo, which has fallen into the hands of the Russians. Is that good news? Lord Mountbatten is constantly on the radio, letting us know what he wants to do. The Japanese are ordered to liquidate the republic proclaimed by Sukarno, but it is not clear whether anything is actually happening. There are riots everywhere. Trucks and passenger cars, full of armed natives, drive back and forth. There are gatherings. *Merdeka* is the key word: freedom.

Where is the occupying army? We are apprehensive of those menacing natives with their pointed bamboo sticks. It's really a vicious weapon, because if you are injured, small bamboo splinters remain in the wound, causing infection. So watch out.

The position of the Netherlands is unclear. Colonial Secretary Van Mook has arrived from Australia. We also hear that troops have arrived from Holland, but we don't see or notice anything here. It makes us bitter. We get the impression that the Allies are leaving our defense solely to the Japanese. When will the Japanese leave?

At any rate, our things are packed and ready to go.

Reports from Holland are not forthcoming. Is there still a parental home? What about my family? We have heard that the situation in Europe is far from rosy. Not all national borders have been established yet. There is a great shortage of coal, with winter approaching. It's chaos everywhere.

So we live from moment to moment. There is now enough of everything: soap, toothbrushes, eggs, sweets, cigarettes, and matches. Mail from the men's camps. Even spray cans to get rid of lice. We begin to feel clean again. Detangling, washing, hair short and fragrant.

We are bored. To dispel the boredom, we alter the clothing distributed to us, which never fits.

Perhaps the airplanes dropping their parcels could consider landing?

The future feels like a long, dark tunnel. It will never again be the way it was. At any moment, everything can change. That feeling.

The world has forgotten us.

# Jan

The next morning, a convoy would be leaving for Tjimahi. Fortunately, the boys could go along, and Jan was happy at the prospect of seeing his father again. He calculated that it had been more than three years since they had seen each other, and that it was a great miracle that they had survived the war and would meet again.

In the morning, they got the signal to board one of the trucks waiting in front of the school. Armed KNIL soldiers rode along. That was reassuring It was a ten-kilometer drive, but given the number of people in the trucks, they drove slowly.

Jan paid no attention to the scenery. He could think of nothing else than the approaching reunion with his father. When his father had been interned, he was forty-eight, and now he was fifty-one years old. In time, they reached Tjimahi. The trucks turned onto the grounds of Camp 4 and stopped on the square near the guardhouse. Around him, Jan saw white stone barracks. In comparison to Ambarawa, it looked neat and tidy here. They quickly got out of the truck and looked at the group of curious men surrounding the square. There was shouting and cheering, first signs of recognition by others. He had not yet seen his father.

Suddenly...he saw his father. On his wooden clogs, Jaan rushed over to the boys and shook Jan's hand.

"Ha, Jan, how are you doing? I am so happy to see you again!" after which he greeted Piet and Gerard as well.

245

Jan was disappointed at the cool reception by his father. Was that all after so much time? Despite that, he was happy to see him again.

"We are one step closer to reuniting; only Mother and the girls still. How are they? You have to tell me everything!"

Jan looked at him silently. There he was, his father, whom he had secretly adored and had missed so much. He represented strength, confidence, and security. Jan had somewhat anchored himself to these qualities all these years, and his father did not disappoint him. Jaan was skinny, but looked good in his khaki shorts and white undershirt.

He pulled them out of the hustle and bustle of the square to the room he shared with ten other men. Piet and Gerard had their sleeping place nearby, and indicated that Jan could join them. There were no high expectations of a place to sleep. They were together, and there was peace, but at night Jan preferred to sleep outside on the gallery, because there were lice inside, and he had had enough of that.

It didn't really sink in until that evening that Jan had been reunited with his brothers, his father, and his mother and sisters, even though the latter were still in Banjoe Biroe. They had all survived this terrible war. Now, back to the Netherlands to work on a new future there.

Safety in Tjimahi was relative. Jan quickly became part of the daily rhythm of the camp, and every day he and his father went to the Military Hospital outside the camp to clean vegetables. He had the opportunity to go to "school" where fathers taught. Classes consisted of teaching a few subjects, such as English and mathematics. They didn't consist of much, because the "teachers" had to rely on whatever they remembered. There was no specific planning. Piet worked at the bread bakery outside the camp, and Gerard did odd jobs here and there wherever help was needed. Everything had to do with providing assistance and killing time until departure for the Netherlands. Within the camp, everyone did what he could with what he had. A great potential of intellectual, cultural and educational ideas came to life in a creative way. There was enough food, so that the daily struggle no longer revolved around food. Men and women lived together, which resulted in relationships and even marriages. Then, the newlyweds got their own room, an unprecedented luxury, and, as Piet had said so beautifully, yet another reason to marry. However, none of the three young men was affected by the "infatuation virus." Jan discovered that a girl liked him and sometimes stared at him for a long time, but he was not interested. He had only one goal: back to the Netherlands, as soon as possible. He could meet someone there too, with whom he could start a family.

Inside the camp it was safe, but outside, tension increased. Extremists sowed death and destruction, not only among the Dutch, but also among that part of the native Javanese population that disapproved of their behavior and the struggle for independence. That is why the indigenous people sought safety within their camp, which in turn led to further growth of the camp. Jan did not leave the camp again after he was warned about snipers during a walk with his father. The warning had scarcely been uttered when bullets flew around their heads. After the departure of the Japanese, the guards consisted of British Indian soldiers who immediately fired back, allowing Jan and his father to run back to the camp. Machine gun nests with permanent surveillance had been built around the camp, from which shots were regularly fired at extremists and snipers. Fortunately, no one inside the camp was killed or injured.

Contact with their mother and the girls in Banjoe Biroe was done via letters. Because they were addressed to Jan's father, Jaan invariably told them that Mother and the girls were doing well, what was happening in their camp, and that they hoped to be reunited soon. But he did not share all the details. Jan did not want to believe that there was so little information in the many sheets of paper. Father also said that Mother and the girls were trying to come to their camp as soon as possible. From that message grew Jan's desire for the reunification of all. Whenever a group of women and girls appeared at the gate, they ran to it. Would they be there?

Since this led to repeated disappointment, they stopped going.

It wasn't until November 15, 1945, that a roommate came running in.

"Jan, Piet, Gerard, your mother and sisters are at the gate!"

# Mother

*November 15, 1945*

A group of men come running on rickety *tèklèks*. The tapping of the wooden sandals reminds me of the original skates made with animal bones. Eagerly, I try to find Jaan. Where is he?

"There is Father, I think." Hesitantly, I point at a tall figure in khaki shorts and undershirt. My eyes scan his body: that emaciated man, is that Jaan? I recognize his gait. Yes, it is, undeniably.

"Papa, Papa." Annie, caught up in the excitement of the moment, shouts out loud. She laughs and stretches her arms into the air. "Look, Papa, we're here."

I straighten my dress, tidy my hair. Not that it matters; I must look awful. Some women have saved special clothing for this moment, but not I. My threadbare clothes hang on my body. Will he still recognize me?

Jaan wrote back in early October. He had received my letter and was happy to be able to embrace me soon. I didn't have to worry; there would be ample time to listen to each other, even when it came to matters of the heart. That was an opening. Pleased with his answer, I wrote back and went a little further. That with the two forced moves, my love for him had been damaged. First to Bolsward, then to the Dutch East Indies. How I had been disappointed and hurt, and had finally withdrawn, responses had become perfunctory. I had even daringly mentioned that I was afraid—if we were given the opportunity—after all the horrors I had seen, whether we'd be able to once again live together as man and wife (you know what I mean).

In early November, the girls and I were suddenly high on the urgency list for family reunification. After that, things went quickly, although it wouldn't have taken much for things to go wrong. Gangs of insurgents were known to hide in the hills around Ambarawa with plans to drive women and children from the camp into the swamp.

That evening, the lights went out. The sound of stamping feet. A horde of people shouted something in unison. My God, we were defenseless. I broke out in a cold sweat. We made it here, I thought, to be slaughtered now. At any moment, we could expect the worst. The dread, the anxiety, weighed most heavily. We imagined all kinds of possibilities. Could we stop the first intruders? I got no further than to envisage throwing pepper (there was enough of it) in their faces. How many meters were there between the frenzied horde, bent on murder and revenge, on the other side of the fence, and us here? *Mata gelap*— crazy, blinded by rage.

We heard shots; we looked at each other. Was this the end? Cries, screaming, pandemonium, gunfire, explosions.

"They're firing from the gate!" Paula shouted, barely heard. "I believe that we've been saved."

Right after that, another shot. A heavily armed British Indian military column had arrived just in time. We laughed and cried at the same time. We have crawled through the eye of a needle. Thank You, Lord.

Under heavy guard, we were taken to Semarang by train. Protected by soldiers with guns at the ready, we traveled through a land that was hostile to us. From Semarang, the KPM ship "Van Heutsz" took us to Batavia.

Dismay at the recurring violence. Is this liberation?

Even though we knew that the Japanese had kindled the nationalist fire, I was only too happy to believe that not all Javanese hated us. I had the impression that most of the Javanese, staring at us with a blank look, had taken a wait-and-see attitude. Once on board the ship, the tension fell away. And for the first time in years, we ate white bread with butter, which tasted heavenly.

But the journey was not over yet. From Batavia, we flew to Bandoeng in a Catalina amphibious airplane. When I boarded, my eye fell on damage to the nose. I was not at ease. The engines started, and, fortunately, kept running. The girls enjoyed it, as could be heard from their "oohs" and "aahs." But that was certainly not the case for me. My jaws were so tightly clenched that I could barely separate them on landing in Bandoeng. Goodness gracious, was I relieved! We had taken another step. Now the last kilometers, by car—in a convoy—to Tjimahi.

And now we are standing here at the gate of the camp. Tired, excited, nervous, everything at once. Jaan and the boys are coming. As good as reunited. Nervously, I adjust my dress. I don't know what to do.

# Jan

*November 15, 1945*

The announcement that his mother and sisters were at the gate caused quite a stir. They ran to the gate, where they saw men, women, and children everywhere, crying, laughing, and hugging each other. Jan was embarrassed until he discovered his mother and sisters.

"Mother!" He ran to her and flung his arms around her neck. Then his sisters. Piet and Gerard too. His father, who also had heard the good news, came toward them, and stood before his wife and daughters, transfixed, and mumbled, "Johanna, Aafje, Willie, Annie?"

His mother nodded and stammered, "Yes, yes... it's us..."

They embraced each other, crying, laughing, and kissing. The boys formed a ring around them and took each other's hands.

They kept hugging and kissing. Emotions were given free expression.

"We're together again!" Mother looked at each one in disbelief. Father repeated several times, "God has answered our prayers."

And once again, kisses and hugs were shared.

Jan's father was the first to come to his senses a bit, and began to pray spontaneously: "Dear God, mighty Lord, we are together again, and unharmed. Thank you for so much grace and love. Prevent us from being torn apart from each other again; not our will be done, but Yours. Amen."

"Amen," the others joined in, and then it was time for each other's stories.

It seemed like old times.

# Jan

*November 22, 1945*

"Have you heard?" A question for Jan.

"No, what should I have heard?"

"The camp leadership is looking for young people to do work detail on the Indrapoera."

"For a trip to the Netherlands?"

"Yes, the trip back to the Netherlands!"

That was enough for Jan, and he ran to his father.

"Father, they are looking for young people to do work detail on the Indrapoera!"

"Who says that?"

"I heard it from someone."

"Who is looking?"

"The camp leadership. I want to sign up!"

"Go and talk to the camp leaders first, because I think there will be some conditions."

Jan was already gone, running to the camp leadership building, now managed by the Dutch.

Rushing inside, he asked, "Are you looking for someone who will do chores on the Indrapoera?"

They chuckled at his eagerness. "You want to come along?!"

"Yes!"

"There are requirements."

And they immediately told him that there were more enthusiasts than available places, but Jan didn't want to hear about that. Jan could be selected only if he could prove that he would attend a secondary school or a more advanced school in the Netherlands. Jan said that he wanted to go to the Hogere Burgerschool (former Dutch secondary school) and was added to the list of candidates. But first, his father had to confirm that this was the case. Once the application was complete, Jan ran back to his father and coerced him to come to the camp management to confirm his story.

His father saw that Jan was eager to go back to the Netherlands. He went with Jan and confirmed his story.

"We have a long list of interested parties, you know. So you may not be chosen."

It fell on deaf ears, because from that moment on, Jan could talk only about his return trip to the Netherlands. Almost every day, Jan went to the office of the camp management to ask if there were any more information, and each time he was told that no choice had been made yet, and that they would inform him immediately as soon as they knew.

His father and mother used the time to give him instructions in case it went ahead. For example, they gave him the address of his grandmother in Breukelen, where he'd have to go. His father had arranged that with her. He was given a list of names and addresses of people to visit when he arrived.

Unexpectedly, on Thursday, January 24, 1946, he was told that he had to be ready at seven o'clock the next morning at the gate for departure to the Indrapoera. Cheering and excited, he ran to his family's room in Camp 4, to share the good news. His mother began to cry.

"Then I'll have to say goodbye to you again!"

His father tried to reassure her.

"It is for only a short time, Jo. We will soon follow him and then we will be together in the Netherlands."

Jan paid no attention to his mother's tears. He was too busy with all the arrangements for his departure.

That night he barely slept. Well before seven o'clock, Jan was standing next to his bed to pack his meager belongings in his evacuation bag. After the family breakfast, for which there was barely enough time, the whole family walked with him to the trucks that were ready to drive in convoy to Bandoeng. Their goodbyes were excited and nervous. They trusted that they would meet again in the Netherlands. The past few years had taught them that anything could happen, and that thought briefly cropped up in his mother's head when she stood at the gate, waving farewell to Jan. She tried very hard not to cry. Jan climbed into one of the vehicles holding many unfamiliar boys. Heading up the convoy was an armored car, and in every truck there were a number of Gurkha soldiers to protect them on their journey. They rode through an area with many extremists. As the procession set in motion, Jan looked back one more time and waved to his family. He sat there with mixed feelings, excited and sad at the same time. For him it was a new adventure: on his way to freedom in the Netherlands, while again having to say goodbye to everyone who was dear to him.

The trip went smoothly and without problems. When they arrived at Andir airport in Bandoeng, the boys and the guards were housed in barracks. It was not clear when their flight to Batavia would depart. To kill time, they visited the military airfield control tower and some hangars to view aircraft. Jan took advantage of the opportunity, in one of the hangars, to climb into a

Mitsubishi bomber and take a seat in the cockpit. The airplane had the red circle of the Japanese flag on the fuselage, which was now something of a souvenir of a bygone war.

Three days later, they were informed that they would be flying to Batavia with Dakotas the next day. Finally the time had come, and with a pounding heart, Jan boarded an airplane for the first time. He remembered that before the war he had dreamed in the garden of their house in Djokja that he would fly one day, and now the moment had come.

After breakfast, they had to gather at a building on the airfield, where they were divided into groups of fifteen. Their names were called, and they were told to stay with their own group. They saw the Dakotas, like distant birds, approaching and landing on the airfield. The planes taxied in their direction, and, with engines roaring, came to a stop. The greenish-brown monsters with the British emblem of the Royal Air Force on the fuselage were bigger than Jan had ever thought. Each group was taken to an aircraft where it was prompted to board. Once in, they took a place on the narrow benches along the fuselage of the airplane and fastened themselves with the straps that lay there. After a final inspection to make sure everyone was seated, the hatch was closed and both engines started. There was a terrible noise, and Jan put his fingers in his ears. He was tense because recently a similar airplane had had to make an emergency landing and ended up in an area full of extremists. All the passengers had been brutally murdered. He shook off those thoughts and forced himself to think of the beckoning freedom. The plane taxied to the runway, where the engines roared louder until the racket was so complete that it was no longer a bother. The aircraft gained speed until it lifted off the ground. They were free.

"I'm flying, I'm flying!" Jan exulted silently, enveloped in the noise of the engines now humming sonorously. Jan looked around and saw that everyone was delighted. For all of them, this was the first time they were flying. After that first sensation, there was time to look outside; they were flying over the rice fields. In the camp, Jan had already written a letter to his family, and had promised to throw it out of the airplane above Tjimahi as a greeting. He had wrapped the envelope in a handkerchief. When he saw the camp barracks, he squeezed the package out through a hole. Would they hear the airplane? Maybe see it? For a moment, he looked back at Camp 4 where he had been for five months and realized that he would never go back there again.

After a calm flight over the heavily wooded hills, mountain slopes, and ravines, they approached Batavia after an hour and a half. Jan felt the pressure in his ears and realized that it had to do with the landing. He had to swallow a few times. The beautiful nature gave way to the messy suburbs of Batavia. The plane continued to descend and they were rapidly approaching the ground. Jan had the feeling that they were going to land in the middle of a shopping district, but it appeared to be next to the airport, because several minutes later, Jan felt the shock of the wheels hitting the runway. They bumped across the grassy field to the terminal building of Kemajoran airport. When the airplane had come to a complete stop, they were allowed to unfasten their seatbelts and disembark. Sweltering heat hit him in the face. Tjimahi, at a higher elevation, was considerably cooler than here, and soon sweat was streaming down his face. He saw the other Dakotas landing one by one. The boys were taken in trucks to the Tandjong Priok harbor of Batavia, where the Indrapoera, with its black slender chimneys, was already waiting. The harbor was full of ships, especially warships. The trucks turned onto the quay and stopped at the gangway next to the ship. Indigenous dock workers looked curiously at this transport. Somewhat farther away, Jan saw a group of Japanese prisoners-of-war at work.

Another roll call followed at the ship, after which the boys were allowed to go up the gangway. The Indrapoera made a big impression on Jan. He admired the colors of the ship that looked new. Someone told him that it had been recently painted, because it had been totally gray during the war and had served as a troop ship. He had no memories of his first voyage on this ship, but he knew that he had traveled from the Netherlands to the Dutch East Indies with this ship in 1930. The crew hung over the railing and watched the boys. Once they were on board, the space was allocated, with hammocks under the bow deck: their sleeping places for this voyage. There were lockers for their belongings. After Jan had settled in, he went to explore the ship with a number of other boys. Then they were informed of their duties during the trip. Jan had to clean, mop, and sweep a section designated for women and children. There were instructions regarding the schedule for eating and sleeping, and what to do in an emergency. First, they had to carry luggage and goods inside. The time of departure was not yet known, and the longer they had to wait, the more restless Jan became.

What if something were to disrupt things now, or extremists would attack?

Anxious thoughts still haunted him. It could still happen that the trip to Holland would not materialize. However, the hectic life in the harbor provided a distraction for his anxiety. There was so much to do and to see in the harbor that he hardly had time to think about other things. He wrote one last letter to his father and mother in Tjimahi, that he had just managed to mail, because the postal service was functioning normally again.

He wrote, "It won't be long now until the ship departs. Everything is on board, and today the last passengers arrived. We already have a lot of work to do, but it is not really hard. I hope you will be able to come to the Netherlands soon, and that there we can be together again."

It was not a long letter, because so much had to be done. The meals were good, and very tasty. He had not eaten so much or such delicious food in years. Even a plain bowl of porridge was so much more appetizing.

On Friday, February 1, 1946, they stood at the railing. The ship's engines had been started some time ago. At last the mooring lines were cast off and brought in, and the ship pulled away from the quay. Slowly the distance between those on the wharf and the ship grew. People cried, shouted and waved. Although Jan didn't know anyone standing there, he nevertheless waved furiously with the others. Away from the country where he had lived for so long, had known good times, but in recent years, had lived in hell. On the way to the Netherlands, the country that held promise, their homeland on the North Sea.

260

On March 1, 1946, the Indrapoera arrived in Amsterdam and moored at the quay of the Dutch Steamship Company. It was not until March 2 that Jan was allowed to disembark after undergoing all kinds of checks, processing instructions, and filling out loads of forms. On that day, after nine years, he finally set foot on Dutch soil again.

They were given refreshments and food for the road. Jan was in no hurry, fortunate as he was, finally, to be home in the Netherlands. He absorbed the Dutch atmosphere. The last time that he had experienced this was in 1936, when they had gone to the Netherlands for one year of furlough. Since then, his longing for this country had grown. He did not belong in the Dutch East Indies.

Now, his destination was Breukelen, and while he was wandering around, he got a signal that he could board the waiting bus. He said goodbye to the boys with whom he'd spent the last month, and they promised to write to each other. Glad to leave the noisy warehouse, he walked to the bus. He handed over his luggage, which had increased during the trip. In Ataka in Egypt the ship had lain for a few days, and Jan had bought extra clothing. It was cold in the Netherlands, something he hadn't counted on, but it didn't bother him. He saw that outside there was a thin layer of snow. Jan was the first to get off in Breukelen. He was nervous and tense. The bus driver had asked him where to stop, and when Jan recognized the Reformed Church, he could point the way to Korenpad. When he got out, he saw people peeking from behind the curtains. With his dark brown face and sun-bleached hair, he was a sight to behold in the wintry land. The door opened as the bus drove away, and Jan gave a quick wave to the others on the bus, who were on their way to a home in the Netherlands. In the doorway stood his grandmother, who was now eighty-one, and his Aunt Marie. Crying and thankful, they embraced him.

"Thank God! The first to come home. Now for the rest," whispered his aunt. During the war, they had not heard from those in Indonesia, and Jan was the first one they could embrace. He was taken to a tiny living room and given a cup of tea, while the old kitchen stove was refilled with peat. Jan was over seventeen years old, nine years older than the last time they had seen him.

During the days that followed, they told each other their stories. They knew nothing about the war in the Dutch East Indies, and Jan knew nothing about the war in the Netherlands. They, too, had suffered greatly under the occupation by the Germans. In particular, the "hunger winter" had been hell. Now you could get food with ration cards, and Jan gave them the ration cards he had received on arrival. That gave them the opportunity to buy extra food. For the time being, Jan would stay in their house.

In the afternoon, greeting him warmly, cousins from his father's side of the family came to visit. He didn't know that he had so many, and everyone talked a lot. They told him that he could walk freely on the street, and that he had nothing to fear.

"Are there no snipers or extremists here?"

Amused, they looked at him. "This is the Netherlands, Jan; the war is over and you don't have to be afraid of anything anymore. You can come and go wherever you like, whenever you like!"

It sounded strange to him. He didn't believe it.

"You're just teasing!"

After a while, he began to believe it.

On Sunday, they went to the small Reformed Church, and he sat next to his grandmother in the pew.

Tears came to his eyes as the pastor said his prayer:

"We thank you, God, Almighty Father. You have brought Jan Mobach back to his grandmother and family, from the distant and dangerous Dutch East Indies. That makes us grateful and happy, and we pray that You will bring his mother, father, brothers and sisters back to our country soon."

Jan's thoughts drifted off to his father, mother, Piet, Gerard, Aafje, Willie, and Annie. They should see him sitting here. He prayed his own prayer, that the Lord would reunite all of his family as soon as possible, and concluded with a silent "Amen."

During the following weeks, there were many things to do. A visit to the Ministry of Overseas Affairs in The Hague, in connection with money from his father. To the school to make arrangements, and to the dermatologist because he still had scabies. Fortunately, the white ointment that he received quickly put an end to this ailment. He wanted to visit his uncles and aunts here in the Netherlands, and everyone wanted to see and hug him too. He visited his maternal grandmother in Driebergen, and everywhere he went, he handed out cigarettes that he had bought cheaply aboard the Indrapoera. In the Netherlands, it was still a luxury item and hardly available.

After he had acclimatized, he was able to go to school, and ended up in the bridge-*Hogere Burgerschool* in Utrecht, where he saw several boys that he had met on the ship. It was a joyful reunion. In order to become accustomed to the Netherlands, and to build up his social contacts, he became a member of the youth association "Power through Belief" at the church. They met every Monday evening to discuss various topics. After the break, there was time for recreation.

Every week, he wrote a letter to Java, and he also received many letters in return. He told them what he was experiencing in the Netherlands. His mother invariably ended her letters with the sentence: "We will soon be back with you in the Netherlands. It won't take long anymore."
From other sources, he heard that the repatriation was coming along well, and all available space on ships was being used to bring all the thousands of people back to the Netherlands.

At the end of April 1946, his mother and the girls arrived with the Bloemfontein.

# Mother

*End of March 1946*

During the first days, we are almost always talking at the same time, chattering incessantly. The realization sinks in that we are alive, complete as a family. How special that is. In all the uncertainty, it is a precious mainstay. Below the surface, pressing questions arise. Will we be able to be self-sufficient? To what extent has our life been disrupted? What have we lost? What about our trust in people? I stay away from these questions. If they do have to be asked, it is undoubtedly too early yet.

We slowly regain a rhythm. The boys and girls go to the camp school; singing evenings are being organized. We take a dip in the swimming pool that is located just outside the camp. We realize that it is a false security, but we don't talk about it. Outside the camp, riots are increasing. The Javanese insurgents are targeting not only us, the *blandas*, the white people. Indonesian-Dutch, Chinese, and people living in Indonesian districts are also being hunted, and who knows what else. An attack could be launched at any time, so we are constantly on our guard.

In March 1946, our stay in camp Tjimahi becomes too risky. Bullets and grenades fly over our heads. From the camp, the dull boom of mortar fire is the answer. The camp leadership announces that women and children can go to Holland on a special ship. Do we want to do that? We are hesitant. It goes without saying that we want to leave—for almost all Dutch people, that is a foregone conclusion— but as far as we are concerned, with the whole family. Almost the whole family, because Jan already left for Holland in February, as a crew member on the Indrapoera. He is staying with Jaan's mother, who lives in a house with her daughter Marie. Every week, Jan writes us a letter, telling us whom he has been visiting: Aunt Nel, cousins, my father. Then I really long for home.

Saying farewell just seems to become more difficult. Our resilience is gone. We are being separated again, because only the girls and I can take the next ship to the Netherlands. We went to sign up; I registered with lead in my shoes. There was no other way. From the moment of registration, a lot had to be arranged. We receive an identity card from the Displaced Persons office. A medical examination is mandatory. We have to wait everywhere.

On March 21, 1946, the time has come, and we fly to Batavia to embark.

It becomes a long journey across endless water. The ship is filled with women and children, widows and orphans, and women whose husbands stayed in the Indies to save what can be saved. Most of them don't want to leave and cling to memories from before the war. I listen to their words full of nostalgia, to the way it was, their distress at what they had to leave behind: their possessions, friends, their dreams, the rice fields, the black magic (genie?), the coconut trees. They are afraid of the unknown, but happy because of the reunion with family. That's what their conversations are about. With melancholy they think back to their lost paradise; it is like phantom pain. Would they ever return? Hope, against all odds. I mainly listen. Again, I don't know what to say. Was it really so paradisiacal? I beg to differ. And for whom?

Right before the Gulf of Aden, things get tense. A storm is brewing. We have to get on deck with life jackets on. We're cold. Fortunately, the storm subsides. But it is not over yet. The ship has to circumnavigate the wrecks of blown-up or sunken ships. We hold our breath.

The ship makes a stopover in Ataka in Egypt. With small trains, we are taken through the desert to a warehouse complex, where German prisoners-of-war—former soldiers of Rommel—distribute winter clothing under the supervision of RAPWI—*Repatriation of Allied Prisoners of War and Internees*. It seems like one big dress-up party, which should make us Europeans again. Even more formalities. Registration, a medical examination, a line-up for distribution cards. In thick winter clothes, with an extra bag of clothing, shoes, hats, and scarves, we return to the ship for the last leg of the journey. The unaccustomed feeling of layers of clothing quickly disappears when we feel the cold on the top deck.

At the end of April 1946, we arrive in the port of Amsterdam.

In the bus to 7 Korenpad in Breukelen. We drive past meadows; see cows in the pasture. We are free. I can breathe again.

Jan opens the door, and I want to take him into my arms. In the hallway, he points at a parcel that arrived that morning. A welcome parcel from the Dutch Red Cross in collaboration with the "Dutch Committee Helping the Indies," with clothing and blankets. To keep us warm.

*Repatriation 1946*
They came to the Netherlands in five ships.

On March 1, 1946, Jan was the first to arrive on the Indrapoera.

Mother, Aafje, Willie, and Annie arrived at the end of April 1946, on the Bloemfontein.

Piet arrived at the beginning of May on the Klipfontein, which had left Tandong Priok on Monday, April 3, 1946.

Gerard arrived in the Netherlands on the Sibajak at the end of May.

As the last one, Father arrived in the Netherlands at the end of June 1946, on the Tegelberg.

The family was reunited and was able to pick up life again, although it wasn't until 1949 that it was finally assigned a single-family dwelling at 32 Eendrachtslaan in Breukelen. The many years in the camps had made them compliant and unpretentious. They felt as rich as a king in their new home. They had been lucky to survive!

# Mother

*Friday, December 30, 1949*

"In my time..." My neighbor lady and I are talking about the time before the Japanese occupation. The words pop out before I realize it. I am surprised to find that apparently something like "my time there" exists.

Tomorrow is New Year's Eve. I take the opportunity to reflect a little longer on recent times. Looking back to be able to have better insight into the future, let's say.

Proud of my first achievement—our new house at 32 Eendrachtslaan—dominates today. I had to move heaven and earth for it. We can still speak of luck, because the Minister of Reconstruction has repeatedly stated that the housing shortage is the number one enemy of the people. The war damage is great. There is scarcity and a lack of almost everything: materials, construction workers, money. Furthermore, the government gives priority to trade and the restoration of infrastructure. Our country depends on that.

Recently, we were able to move into social housing. I can't put into words how happy I am about it. Sheer bliss! Living together in the little house in Breukelen, billeted with Jaan's mother and Aunt Marie, worked out well, for which we are grateful. But it was time for my family to have its own home. More space, back to what we were used to. A fresh start.

In many situations, I suddenly seem to be the key figure; I take the lead, take care of things, take care of the necessary papers. I make sure that the rhythm returns;

structure is important, in my view. We have to learn again how to conduct ourselves as civilized people. I keep things together; I am the mother hen, the one with common sense.

Jaan has changed, has become more accommodating; I notice it in the way he asks me about things. But even more because he's actually asking me things.

"Should I…"

"What do you think, Johanna…" Every time, I'm surprised that my opinion matters. It strengthens me.

Jaan used to be more certain in matters of faith. He is now more irritated by the endless arguments among Christians on all kinds of religious topics. Very different from the way it was before.

"Jo," he said recently, "the intellectual exegesis and the hairsplitting causes only division. Isn't it about the power of simply witnessing?"

Jaan was the last of the family to arrive in the Netherlands at the end of June 1946.

Ten days after our departure from camp Tjimahi, the men and boys, also, were evacuated because of the danger. Jaan, Piet, and Gerard were escorted by armed Gurkha soldiers to Bandoeng, where they were housed in the convent of the Ursuline sisters, a transit house. From there, Piet was the first to leave, followed by Gerard. Finally word came that Jaan was on his way.

Once again, the journey had not been without risk. First, with a Dakota airplane to Andir, Batavia. Jaan was praying that an emergency landing would not be necessary. If so, they would almost certainly have faced violence by extremists. It went well, and Jaan could enjoy the unusually magnificent view, the sun lighting up the mountain peaks, the landscape of West Java in all its splendor, the endless winding rivers, the white sandy roads, the many shades of green and yellow. He had said goodbye frame by frame.

When he was transferring at Kemajoran Airport, it had been hallucinatingly hot. He had almost forgotten, he said, how hot it could be in the tropics. Once in Batavia, he had two days to wrap up his affairs in the department. Then there was the last trip, by open truck to Tandjong Priok —where the ship, the Tegelberg, lay ready. The end of his stay in the Dutch East Indies.

So, a reunited family, complete and unharmed. I feel energized. From time to time, I am haunted by the memory of what I was planning to give up, accompanied by a short-lived feeling of guilt. Would I really have wanted the Lord to take me away? Now I can't possibly imagine it anymore. My doubts have subsided. I want to move forward.

For deeper reasons, I feel rich, and less bound by my strict upbringing, which will remain a part of me, whether I like it or not. The commandments and prohibitions which were used to raise me, and by which I also govern myself. Jan, in particular, always confronts me with the facts in this respect. He does not conform easily. He doesn't just accept as truth whatever Father, the pastor, or the teachers say. Everything is followed by a rebuttal. If I understand it correctly, it began with the conversations with Mr. Gisius in Camp 11. They put him on a different path. Our values seem less and less resistant to his growing doubts. Jaan can't handle this very well. And although I find it very tiring myself, I do understand his search.

I have become gentler to myself. I am simply who I am and acted to the best of my ability. Period. With that, a burden has fallen from my shoulders, and I feel (which I am happy about) gratitude to my parents again. They, also, raised me with the best of intentions. I still become angry every time I think back to our departure to the Dutch East Indies, when they were not on the quay, but that anger lasts for a shorter and shorter time. There is always context. My punishing attitude towards others, toward myself, is no longer necessary; things can be different. How, exactly, I have no idea, but it will become evident. I trust that.

Uncertain—and difficult, to be more precise—is how I feel about living together as husband and wife, you know… It had to happen again (and it did), although I was unusually nervous. There is so much involved. The vicarious shame for everything I've seen. The harshness, the physical shock, that happened literally and figuratively. The images of the women and girls who were raped and returned as garbage, an empty look in their eyes. The goodwill that was not enough to prevent it. Women who let themselves be used, to spare their daughters, or for personal gain (not everyone is so particular). But what can I say about that? I understand. People want to survive.

Those images have influenced my own experience of "intimacy." I am not (yet) able to clarify what is happening in me in that respect. The mere presence of those thoughts is confusing and requires effort. Previously, this wasn't an issue for me; I just didn't think about it.

I make attempts. My confusion touches the desire, my dried-up desire, about which I never could or should speak earlier. I do my duty, I don't suffer, plain, straightforward. But can it also be done differently? I am looking for that sense of fulfillment, for the joy that suddenly strikes me in the Song of Solomon. I can't accept that we were reduced to such fearfulness.

I know one thing; it's too early to discuss this with Jaan. Even though I am in "normal" smooth water, I have to get used to myself first.

# Acknowledgements

This book is based on the reports of Jaan Willem Mobach and his son Jan. To keep it engaging, I've had to make choices about what to use and what not to use. The stories of Jaan Willem and Jan are very comprehensive and are a reflection of what happened in that phase of their lives.

The story of Johanna, written by the author Monique Melief, is partly factual and partly fictitious.

My purpose was to give you a portrait of a family that survived the Japanese camps. Of course, I wondered how their survival was possible and what gave them the strength to survive such misery.

All family members survived, each in his or her own way, everyone with his or her own struggle. Back in control of their own lives (at the end of the ride). It is remarkable that the whole family had the good fortune to survive.

Their story is laced with "coincidences," moments when death was closer than life. This applies to Jan three times, and to Jaan Willem and Johanna as well. Jan indicates that he "faced death," but that he was saved by the good fortune of having just the right people in his environment at those moments. In his case, they were Alfred van Sprang, his "roommates," and the engineer on the train who set the train in motion just in time, thereby preventing a bloodbath. Another train on the same route is known to have been raided, and many were murdered by the extremists. Those kinds of moments played a role for Jaan Willem as well, and at the moment Johanna wanted to die, she was "approached" by her son Jan, and she unexpectedly received medication.

When asked whether faith played a role, Jan replied that this was definitely the case with his father, and that, despite Jan's own doubts, it gave him moments of support. The Mobach family is no exception, although it is unique that the entire family survived. Many families were afflicted with the loss of family members.

For more information about the camps, I would like to refer you to Wikipedia. There you will find many details about the Japanese occupation of the Dutch East Indies and the internment camps, as well as the period after that which eventually led to the independence of the Dutch East Indies and the formation of the nation of Indonesia.

*– Daan Fousert*

# Chronological overview of the Mobach family

In 1930, Jaan Willem Mobach (1894), together with his wife Johanna (1896), and their three children Piet (1926), Gerard (1927), and Jan (1928), left for Djokdjakarta. There, the twins Aafke and Willie were born in 1931, and finally Annie in 1938.

Father Jaan Willem was interned in Fort Vredeburg in 1942. In 1944, he was transferred to Camp 4 in Tjimahi (9,400 prisoners), and in 1945 to the Tjitjalengka labor camp. In August 1945, he was sent back to Tjimahi.

Mother Johanna and the children were interned in December 1942, in Camp 11, Banjoe Biroe (11,000 prisoners).

In February 1943, Piet was transferred to Djoen Eng Salatiga. In 1944, he went to Tjimahi.

In February 1944, Gerard was transferred to Djoen Eng Salatiga. In 1944, he also went to Tjimahi.

Jan was transferred to Camp 8 in Ambarawa in 1944. In 1945, Jan was picked up by his brothers and taken to Tjimahi, where he was reunited with his father and his brothers.

Family picture of the Mobachs, in Holland, in 1946 or 1947. L to R: Jaan Willem, Gerard, Aafke, Piet, Annie, Wilhelmina, Johanna, and Jan.